THE SPRINTER

A Series of Worthy Young Ladies
Book Two

Kate Archer

ARE YOU SIGNED UP FOR DRAGONBLADE'S BLOG?

You'll get the latest news and information on exclusive giveaways, exclusive excerpts, coming releases, sales, free books, cover reveals and more.

Check out our complete list of authors, too!

No spam, no junk. That's a promise!

Sign Up Here

www.dragonbladepublishing.com

Dearest Reader;

Thank you for your support of a small press. At Dragonblade Publishing, we strive to bring you the highest quality Historical Romance from some of the best authors in the business. Without your support, there is no 'us', so we sincerely hope you adore these stories and find some new favorite authors along the way.

Happy Reading!

CEO, Dragonblade Publishing

PROLOGUE

50 Berkeley Square, 1812

PENELOPE PRESCOTT, MARCHIONESS of Heathway, had been listening to Louisa Stapleton rattle on about her marvelous new daughter-in-law Georgiana for the past quarter hour. In fact, they had *all* been listening to it. A Society of Sponsoring Ladies meeting had been convened in Penelope's drawing room and just now the duchess, Lady Easton, Lady Redfield, and Lady Featherstone leaned forward in rapt attention.

The society's raison d'être, its beating heart, its very lifeblood, was to make real the ladies dear-held wish to act as a mama to a charming daughter. There were those ladies elsewhere who fretted until a son and heir arrived. *These* ladies had never had such a concern, as sons had arrived with surprising regularity. Sadly, what had never arrived was a daughter they might dote on.

As none of them had born a daughter, daughters must be found. Each lady was determined to enter a season with a delightful girl in hand. Each lady dreamed of standing at the edge of a ballroom floor as their girl's card was filled, or trotting by the *ton* in their carriage and gathering admiring glances, or standing by a pianoforte of a musical evening and knowing their girl was far more skilled than the rest. It would be their moment in the sun, and it would be glorious.

How else could it be done except by stepping forward to

sponsor an honorable but disadvantaged girl?

Lady Mendleton had been the first out of the gate with the project and now, apparently, nobody was to equal this paragon of a girl who was now wife to Lord Langley. Of course, Penelope was delighted for Louisa, though she could not help wondering at the exceedingly odd circumstances. She would wonder silently, though, as the queen herself had made her approval of the match widely known.

In any case, she had far more interesting things to think about than the new Lady Langley. Unbeknownst to her friends, she was just now poised at the gate herself.

Hoping to bring Louisa's crowing to an end, she said, "We could not be more thrilled for you, Louisa."

Lady Mendleton nodded vigorously. "I should not be at all surprised to find a granddaughter in the house soon enough. Do you know they have no plans to strike out on their own? They shall stay with us and we've given over the west wing of the house for their use. Georgiana in particular wishes it. She really has become a daughter to me."

The other ladies appeared quite staggered by these ideas. A granddaughter to arrive at some blessed day, the couple staying on in the house, and most of all—the longed-for daughter had been made real *and* permanent. The duchess shook out the brocade of her skirt like a bird settling its feathers, Lady Easton chewed a biscuit with gusto, Lady Featherstone fanned herself, and Lady Redfield dabbed her eyes.

"My friends," Lady Heathway said, the note of determination in her voice apparent to all, "Louisa has found success and so must we all. We must drive this effort forward and I am prepared to do it."

Penelope paused dramatically so the ladies might take in her meaning.

"That is correct," she said. "I have found my girl. Miss Grace Yardley, daughter of the late Viscount Barlow. She has come highly recommended to me by my cousin Lady Gadden, who has

a neighbor who has a cousin in Miss Yardley's n[
turns out the estate was entailed, no son was pro[
new viscount has moved the girl and her mother .
house that has been described to me as...ramshackle.'

"Ramshackle!" Lady Easton cried.

"Goodness," Lady Featherstone said. "Ramshackle does not sound suitable for the daughter of a viscount."

"Ramshackle," the duchess said, "strikes me as detestable."

"It strikes us all as detestable because it *is* detestable, and not to be stood for," Lady Heathway said. "I have written Lady Barlow and enclosed a kind note for Miss Yardley too. I have indicated that I will send a carriage on Wednesday next."

"Do allow me to assist you with the dear girl, Penelope," Lady Mendleton said in a tone of gracious condescension. "I am now, of course, very experienced with daughters. It is more complicated than you might imagine."

Lady Heathway nodded at Louisa though she did not have the first intention of seeking out the lady's advice. She had been planning for a daughter for years and was well able to manage it without Louisa fluttering round her.

"We shall *all* assist in this very noble undertaking," the duchess said.

Lady Heathway gave the duchess an approving smile. She was generally of the opinion that the duchess threw round the word noble with rather careless abandon—but in this case, she had hit the mark. The girl had been thrust down to the brink of despair and would be lifted up again by her sponsor's generosity. There *was* something noble in it.

The door to the drawing room opened, though she had specifically instructed that the meeting of the society was not to be disturbed. Ranston hurried in carrying a letter on a silver tray.

"I am sorry for the intrusion, my lady," he said, "but you did request that any communications from Barlow House be brought to you immediately."

"Ah! Bring it here, Ranston. That will be from Lady Barlow,

₋ressing her appreciation for the scheme."

Lady Heathway tore the letter open, thinking how fortuitous it was that this missive of gratitude should have arrived with her friends present to witness it. She did not only expect Lady Barlow to express appreciation for the *scheme*, she expected the lady to express appreciation for *herself*. As the duchess had rightly pointed out, she acted rather noble.

As she perused the surprisingly short letter, her thoughts felt muddled. It was as if she were reading words that she could not in fact be reading. Was it a forgery of some kind? A joke, perhaps?

None of it made sense. She dropped it on the table.

Lady Redfield leaned over and peered at it. "Goodness," she said. "That is unexpected."

"Give it here," the duchess said imperiously. "It is too late in our history to have any mysteries between us."

Lady Redfield handed the duchess the note, though Penelope would have preferred to set it on fire. At this moment, her feelings were such that she would not have minded setting the whole house on fire.

The duchess read it aloud:

Dear Lady Heathway,

My mother and I cannot thank you enough for your courtesy in contacting us. It is rather wonderful to know that there is such a gracious individual living in the world. It is with a heavy heart that we must decline your generous offer.

My mother, Lady Barlow, does very poorly and has much need of me.

Again, thank you so much for the kindness.

Grace Yardley

"Well, that is unfortunate," Lady Easton said, "though she does sound like a dutiful daughter."

The butler looked almost faint at hearing the contents of the letter and staggered toward the door in a bid to escape the room.

Lady Heathway stood, feeling as if she did not move, she might explode into a thousand bits. "Unfortunate, you say? Unfortunate!" Her voice startled the company, as it was rather louder than most drawing rooms were accustomed to.

"Disappointing, then?" Lady Redfield said hopefully, never liking when somebody was out of spirits.

"Now Penelope," Lady Easton said, "she does say the mother does poorly."

"*Very* poorly," Lady Featherstone said, as if the addition of *very* must explain away all unpleasantness.

"Ranston!" Lady Heathway said imperiously, just as the poor butler had his hand on the door handle. "Pack a small trunk, tell the coachman I shall expect him at dawn tomorrow, and send word to my nephew that I have need of him forthwith! I will not be crossed by a lady who claims to do so poorly that she cannot gird herself to do what's right for a daughter. That sickly lady shall soon find she is to be overcome!"

The ladies round the table sat in stunned silence, having understood that Lady Heathway was prepared to run rampant through the countryside to retrieve Miss Yardley.

That they all thanked the heavens *they* were not the sickly lady who was about to be set upon was simply a matter of course.

One generally did duck when Lady Heathway aimed her cannon.

CHAPTER ONE

GRACE YARDLEY, DAUGHTER of the late Viscount Barlow, viewed her circumstances from the kitchen garden. It struck her once again that Barlow House had been named rather lofty for what it actually was. Though it was technically the dower house, Grace was not aware of any dowager ever having stayed there. Her grandmother certainly had not.

The cottage was only comprised of two bedchambers above stairs, and then a single room, kitchen, and small servants' quarters below. The primary room for living, having to wear many hats, was cramped with four chairs near the fire. On the other side stood a small dining table and a rickety bookshelf. Grace thought of it as the room of all things—the drawing room, the dining room, and the library, all rolled into one. Even had they been able to afford more than a cook and a maid, there would have been nowhere to put them.

The size of the place was one inconvenience, the condition of it was another. The roof leaked and there were buckets placed about strategically to catch the rain in her bedchamber. She must just remind herself to be gratified that her mother's own bedchamber remained dry. The lady was, at this moment in her history, too weak to stand up against the damp.

While he lived, the viscount had indulged Lady Barlow to a remarkable degree. When he had married the lady, he'd sworn he would care for her as a jewel in a velvet-lined case, and so he had.

Nothing had ever been required of her and nothing she liked had ever been denied her. She had slept late on fine sheets and eaten a leisurely breakfast near noon, and she had lived in a household that moved heaven and earth for her comfort. Had not one of the footmen been hired solely to see that fire screens were in endless motion to suit the lady? The summers were even more ridiculous, as large fans on pulleys were operated to keep her cool, as if she were an Indian maharajah. The housekeeper and butler together ran things with no need of Lady Barlow's involvement. It had been a life of indolence and coddling.

Nobody had ever begrudged the lady her comforts, though Grace was not unaware that this mode of going on had failed to prepare her mother to manage on her own with only her jointure at her disposal. Her father had always presumed that Grace would be long-married when he departed the world and his widow would be well cared for. But she was not yet married when he left them.

Upon her husband's death, the lady had some idea that she and her daughter were to go on living in Barlow Hall, despite not ever having met the heir. The place was enormous so why should they not? Why should she even be made to give up her current apartments? Surely, the new viscount might choose any number of rooms for himself. Grace had not been at all confident of any of these ideas, but to Lady Barlow, anything else had been unimaginable.

That gentleman, arriving from York and having a peculiar, direct way of communicating his ideas, had set her mother straight in the most shocking terms. They could live in the dower house, or go live with relatives, or live as vagabonds in the forest. They might explore the far east or set sail for the Caribbean if they liked, but where they would *not* be living was in Barlow Hall with him.

Grace supposed the new viscount had thought they would go off to live with relatives and he would be done with them. However, the only possible relative they might have imposed on was Lady Barlow's sister, and that was out of the question. Lady Barlow had long made her opinion known regarding her sister's choice of husband, she finding the baron a rough sort and not suitably elevated. This had caused a cooling between the sisters, with only yearly rather terse Christmas cards exchanged. All these years later, the baron had now made his own opinion known, and that opinion was that Lady Barlow was never to breach his doors.

And so, into the leaky dower house they went. Or rather, Grace went and Lady Barlow was carried. She'd taken to her bed immediately and claimed she'd never rise from it.

Through strong broth and encouraging words, Grace had convinced her mother to venture downstairs during the day. However, the lady generally only made it to the chair closest to the fire and had yet to be out of doors.

The running of the household, such as it was, had fallen to Grace. She was not unhappy to take on the role, as it at least gave her something to do. Doing something was far better than giving oneself time to contemplate the future. She saw nothing but gray skies ahead.

Then had come a flicker of hope. A flame, really. A certain Lady Heathway, who had heard of their predicament by some mechanism, had written inviting Grace to stay with her for a London season.

What a chance! She might marry and then her mother could be made comfortable.

Lady Barlow had seen the chance too, but she'd decided on a far bigger chance than what was currently on offer. They would regretfully decline Lady Heathway on account of Lady Barlow's ill health—she required Grace by her side. Lady Heathway would have no recourse but to invite Lady Barlow to London too.

They might both be made comfortable. Immediately.

Since then, her mother had been far more energetic than she'd been in months. She was full of plans and almost convinced the maid to pack her trunks before Grace put a stop to it. They had declined Lady Heathway and nothing further might come of it.

Lady Barlow took to pacing the drawing room and waiting for the post to be delivered. It could not be many days before the letter arrived that invited them both to London.

Grace was afraid that letter would not come. And, when her mother realized their hopes were dashed, that she had gambled a step too far, she really would take to her bed and never rise from it.

Grace Yardley would find herself entirely alone in the world.

PENELOPE PRESCOTT MIGHT be a marchioness now, but she had not always traveled in such a lofty sphere. She had begun only the daughter of a second son of a viscount. That uneasy circumstance had meant that her father had need of a living, and he had been given a living held by her titled uncle. She had spent her childhood as the daughter of the local vicar, all the while seething at her cousins' good luck to have been born to the eldest son.

Fortunately, her father had done well for himself and become a bishop. He had scraped together a passable dowry and rented a modest house in Town to allow her a season. Otherwise, she did not know where she might have ended up.

She had arrived to that first and only season with a vague feeling of not being up to snuff. Daughters of dukes and earls fanned about, wearing enough jewels to have paid for her entire wardrobe. A girl in her position might hope her looks would level the field, but she did not have that advantage either. She was not ugly, that she knew, but she was not the sort who would lay claim to a season as being *the* girl. It seemed everything in her life was to be middling, and she carried round a constant prickly feeling that made her want to cry and rage at the same time. She should have accepted her lot in life, but she could not.

Penelope had put her attention on how she might improve

her chances. Particularly, how successful ladies managed the *ton*. She'd noticed one thing especially—a lady who spoke her mind appeared rather striking, *if* it were done well.

She was determined to do it well. At her delicate age, she could not have spoken out like a Mary Wollstonecraft, it would have been regarded as vulgar. No, she instantly perceived that she must only have an original opinion on small, everyday things.

She had mastered the technique and it turned out she very much enjoyed having decisive opinions and sharing them out freely. She had since kept it as a lifelong habit.

Lord Heathway, only a viscount when she'd met him, had been charmed to discover that she did not think the park wonderful, though everybody sang its praises. Rather, with the amount of horse droppings and throngs of unwashed people milling about, it was an unkempt barnyard.

He had wished to know more of her opinions, and she had obliged. There were contrary opinions on books, and plays, and popular dishes. She'd even gone so far as to claim she thought white soup overrated. She actually did think that and thought it still—who ever thought to put almonds into a soup was a madman.

All went along splendidly between them until one evening when the viscount had taken a certain Miss Granger into supper, rather than herself. Penelope did her best to pretend she was not vexed, but fortunately, she was not entirely successful. The lord had divined her contrary feelings on the matter and was further charmed. He asked for her hand the very next day.

She had since reached the pinnacle of society. She was a marchioness, and her friends were all respected and powerful ladies. She could even go toe-to-toe with the duchess, and sometimes she did.

She was well aware that she was named Lady Naysay by those in society who thought themselves a wit. She supposed she ought to be offended by it, but she was not—the *ton* were a flighty set, and they often required a naysayer among them.

Now, she paced the drawing room. Her friends had long departed and she awaited the arrival of her nephew.

George, though he did not yet know it, would escort her to Lady Barlow's ramshackle dower house to retrieve Miss Yardley from the clutches of her ridiculous mother.

George would not need to know the precise details of the scheme, as she thought he might not be in full agreement. As it was, she had informed Lord Heathway of the plan to bring Miss Yardley to Berkeley Square in small drips, which he took in with good humor. Except when he was apprised of the dowry to be supplied, which he had taken in with less good humor. She had not bothered to warn him of the impending bills from dressmakers and such, feeling that particular sort of news was better arriving in small blows. In the end, he would not say much about it. He spent far too much gambling, which he did not seem to be very good at, and she was kind enough not to say much about *that.* Her nephew, on the other hand, could be more difficult to manage. The young man did insist on having his own opinions on things.

Ranston knocked softly and opened the door. "Lord Gresham to see you, my lady."

GEORGE WADE, VISCOUNT Gresham and heir to the Earl of Clayton, had received a message from his aunt while in the midst of a very interesting game of piquet. The lady should not have been able to divine where to find him, as he had not been at home, but he was well aware that she had her methods. One of her footmen had cornered one of his own and pried the address from him.

He'd stayed long enough to finish the game, and relieve Sir Matthew of a hundred pounds, and then he'd set off to Berkeley Square. He'd learned long ago that there was no point in ignoring a summons from Lady Heathway—another would come, and then another, and another—it would be as paper birds flying at him from all directions. Her notes delivered by breathless footmen had even become a joke at White's. He suspected there had even been bets laid on when the next would arrive, though he had not dared look in the bet book to find out.

As he was led into the drawing room, he hoped he would not find her out of sorts. She was very difficult to manage when she was out of sorts.

"Dear George," she said, looking not particularly out of sorts.

"Aunt," he said, kissing her on the cheek.

"How considerate of you to make haste to my side," she said.

"Was there a choice?" he asked with good humor.

"Perhaps not, but kind all the same," his aunt said. "Now, I must ask the smallest favor of you. You are so generous and kind that I know you will not mind."

George braced himself. His aunt's small favors were rarely small and he invariably did mind.

"You know all about our little society, I expect?"

He nodded. Of course he knew about it. Everybody knew about it. His aunt and her friends had looked about for a cause or project and somehow landed on the idea of dragging girls in from the countryside. Miss Wilcox had arrived first, to Lady Mendleton's house, and had married Langley before the last season had closed. They'd all heard the story of the lady rescuing Langley from a gang of footpads, which seemed an odd thing for a lady to do. For that matter, it seemed an odd thing for Langley to *allow* a lady to do. However, that was their own affair.

Good Lord. She did not propose that he somehow involve himself in her ridiculous club of managing matrons?

"Well," she went on, "you will be thrilled to know that a certain Miss Yardley comes to me on the morrow."

Thrilled would not be the description he was looking for. Filled with trepidation was closer to the mark.

"Aunt," he said slowly, "while I applaud your efforts, they

must remain *your* efforts, not mine."

"Of course, my dear nephew. However, my sons are still at their studies and so I must depend upon you from time to time. Family, you know."

"Depend upon me for what, though?" he asked, not very successfully hiding his suspicion and dread.

"Goodness, I only wish for you to escort me to Swanley to retrieve the girl. It is not twenty miles and if we change the horses strategically, we should be there and back in a day's travel. Of course, I'll allow you to map it out how you like. We could just as easily leave now and stay at an inn somewhere nearby Miss Yardley, and then return here on the morrow. I've had a trunk packed to be prepared for any eventuality."

Escorting his aunt to Swanley was not at all a task he would relish. On the other hand, it was not as difficult as some of the other favors his aunt had asked for. The last had been a request that he cut Henry Forgely on account of him accepting an invitation to her card party and then failing to make an appearance. News of his carriage overturned had not affected her in least—he'd walked away with no broken limbs and so she did not see why he could not have kept walking right into her party.

George had not cut Forgely, the fellow was a member of his club and well-liked. In the end, he supposed a fast trip to Kent to escort this project of a girl back to Town was not too big a burden.

"Very well," he said, careful to keep the sigh out of his voice. "I think setting off tomorrow will do." He was fond of his aunt— despite her somewhat abrasive exterior, there was a good heart under the bluster and she would do just about anything for him. Still, she could be very trying and it was likely to be a long day. No reason to stretch it into *two* days.

"Excellent," Lady Heathway said. "We leave at dawn."

Excellent. George only hoped the trip would be both the beginning and the end of his involvement with the Society of Sponsoring Ladies.

Hope was all he had, really.

THE POST HAD come and gone and still no letter had arrived from Lady Heathway. Grace supposed the lady had read the reply that had been sent, tossed it aside, and now thought of other things. Lady Barlow would not think of other things, she was becoming fretful and just now sat by the fire complaining that they might burn all the wood in England and still not dry out the damp of the place. Grace was afraid the lady's low spirits would very soon drive her back into her bed.

The situation was not cheered by the fact that the dower house sat hard by the lane that led to Barlow Hall—the grand house that had once been their own. Carriages, and wagons piled high with furniture, had trundled by in full view all morning—it appeared the new viscount and his lady were officially moving in. At each new sound of horses' hooves and carriage wheels approaching, Lady Barlow glared out the window.

Grace only hoped the new viscountess had not spied Lady Barlow's glare as she passed by in her carriage. It would be uncomfortable indeed to see such disapproval coming one's way every time one left or returned to one's house.

The only idea that soothed Lady Barlow at all was that the new viscount was on the verge of discovering that the butler and housekeeper who were to stay on and serve him had decamped. Manfred and Mrs. Bellevue had visited the cottage and had been outraged at Lady Barlow's current circumstances. That, combined with their opinion that the new viscount was a rather dull fellow, had prompted more than a few conversations between them. Their final conclusion, after perhaps a few too many glasses of sherry, was that the blowhard from York was not worthy of their service and that they quite enjoyed one another's company. They had since married, planned to open a shop in the village, and left notes of resignation on the great hall table for their would-be master. As far as anybody knew, the footmen who had stayed on were just now lounging in one of the drawing rooms, having helped themselves to the new viscount's wine cellar. It would not be the welcome the gentleman expected.

Grace just now stood by the door to the kitchen, consulting with Cook on what ought to be for dinner. There was not much to discuss, as the bones from the beef they'd had the evening before were being turned to a soup. Cook would bake a hearty loaf of bread, and perhaps there was still some cheese in the larder.

More carriage wheels rumbled. Lady Barlow glared out the window.

Then, the sound of carriage wheels ceased abruptly.

Grace froze, wondering if some person had decided to stop and ask Lady Barlow to quit her glaring.

"Heavens," Lady Barlow said. "It must be her. It must be Lady Heathway. How silly that we waited for a letter when the lady has come herself!"

Grace hurried over to peer round the curtains, having no such assurance that the mysterious arrival was Lady Heathway. She could not be certain who it was, but she could rule out some possibilities. It could not be the new viscountess, who would be young still. It could not be either of the viscount or viscountess' mothers, as Grace understood that one lived in Spain and the other was dead.

Whoever the lady was, she was middle-aged and looked rather imperious. She peered out her carriage window and surveyed the cottage with a disdainful eye.

A gentleman had dismounted his horse, opened the carriage door, and helped the lady down. He certainly was not the new viscount. Grace had met that fellow, and he was a rather dumpy individual.

There was nothing at all dumpy about this man. He was dark-haired, with sable-brown tints that caught the light, tall and slim, and wearing an exceedingly well-cut coat. There was something sophisticated, even urbane, about his manner. He seemed the sort of gentleman that had seen much of the world and for whom little could hold a surprise.

Grace pulled away from the window as the lady and the gentleman approached the house. "Maggie," she said to the rather startled maid, "you will answer the door when they knock, take their names, and then announce them."

Maggie appeared as if this string of directions was entirely too much. As well it would be—they had been used to a footman answering the door and then Manfred leading guests into one of the two drawing rooms. In this particular operation, the arrivals would step right into the room of all things—it was fraught with possibilities for appearing absurd.

Still, Grace did not know how else to proceed.

"You can do it, Maggie," Grace said encouragingly. "I know you can."

Maggie seemed to take heart from this assurance and courageously stepped to the door.

At the sharp rap from the other side, she opened it.

GEORGE HAD GONE on horseback on the trip to Swanley to avoid being trapped in the carriage all the day long. He held a firm affection for his aunt, but so long a time together might test that to alarming degrees. Further, there would be the return trip with the little miss to contend with. Blushings and stammerings for hours would make him wish to hang himself.

There was rarely anything worse than a girl just arrived from the countryside. Most of them had been raised in a cocoon of ignorance and seemed to find the discovery that there were men included in the species a highly shocking idea. Or at least, they pretended to, somehow coming upon the notion that the more they could appear shocked, the better.

No, ladies were far more sensible when they returned for a second season. Then, they found themselves able to put down their waving fans and have a rational conversation. Or as his friend Marksworth called it, *they were seasoned by last season.* There were always exceptions, of course. Langley had just married an exception. But, he could not imagine Miss Yardley would display the sort of composure of a Miss Wilcox. How many ladies were there in the world who could rescue a gentleman from a gang of footpads?

Still, he supposed his aunt would be charmed by whatever blushings and stammerings went on during the trip. He also could not help but feel some pity for the girl's circumstances as he now understood them.

Prospects dashed on account of an entail was an all-too-common tale. It was especially bad when it was the last generation subject to it. That was the case here, as it had already been in effect for four generations. The new heir could do what he liked with the estate, and it must have been devastating to Lady Barlow that it was not *she* who could inherit and do what she liked. It always seemed incredible to George that one infant or lack of one could upset so many lives.

It appeared the entailed heir was not prepared to do the decent thing and help the young lady on her way to a suitable marriage. She was the daughter of a viscount and had no doubt been raised with certain expectations. Expectations that she had every right to have.

Now, they'd arrived and he'd got a look at the dower house, which as far as he knew was the only arrangement the man had made for mother and daughter. It was a cottage more suited to a steward. Even a steward might think himself ill-used by the place. The heir had the good luck to inherit a title and a large and prosperous estate that nobody would think he really deserved, and yet he could not even bother to fix a very obvious hole in the roof?

If the new viscount thought to make his mark in Town, George would at least blackball him from White's. He would drop some hints to his friends who belonged to Brooks's and Boodle's too. He certainly would not acknowledge him anywhere. That, added to what was sure to be his aunt's condemnations, would result in Viscount Barlow being rather finished before he started. If he had any societal aspirations, then he had been very foolish, all to save a few pounds and pence.

"You see what I say?" his aunt said as they approached the house. "Positively ramshackle."

George nodded in agreement.

A moment before his aunt rapped on the door with her cane, she said, "Gird yourself, nephew. The mother may prove a problem."

George whipped his head around and stared at his aunt. "What do you mean by a *problem*?" he whispered.

Lady Heathway merely shrugged.

What did she mean? What problem?

George got a sinking feeling that he'd been told some of the particulars of this visit, but that he'd certainly not been told all of them. Why was there suddenly a problem? What on earth was he walking into?

CHAPTER TWO

G RACE WAS MIGHTILY relieved that Maggie had somehow got the lady and her escort into the house and seated without it seeming positively bizarre. The lady was in fact Lady Heathway, to Grace's great surprise. The gentleman was her nephew, Lord Gresham.

It seemed rather impossible that the lady would have come, and yet here she was. She was also far more terrifying than Grace had imagined she would be. She had somehow thought that a lady wishing to assist a girl in distressed circumstances would be a plump and comfortable type of matron full of good humor.

There did not appear to be much in the way of good humor about the marchioness.

As Maggie and the cook banged around in the kitchen, no doubt looking for enough decent china for a slapped together tea service, Lady Heathway regarded Lady Barlow with a discerning eye.

Grace's mother seemed not the least put off and rather looked exceedingly pleased. "You are welcome to our very humble house, Lady Heathway. I would have risen upon your entrance, but I do rather poorly these days."

"How poorly?" Lady Heathway asked. "What is the complaint, exactly?"

Grace was startled by the question. As far as she knew, nobody had ever asked her mother what was specifically wrong with her. It was…a general weakness? Whenever Doctor Gregory turned up, he made sympathetic noises, gave her a soothing draught, and confirmed her mother's opinion that she was not to overexert herself.

"How poorly am I?" Lady Barlow asked.

"I am sure my aunt does not mean to pry into such a personal matter as your health," Lord Gresham said.

"That is precisely what I mean to do," Lady Heathway said. "How poorly? What is wrong with you? You are upright, after all."

Lady Barlow glanced at the stairs, as if she wished she'd had the foresight to be abed upon the lady's arrival. "Well, you see," she said, "it is an imbalance of humors from the great shock of becoming a widow. It makes me exceedingly weak. I quite depend upon Grace to care for me and manage the household. Such as you see it. Naturally, it is not what I am used to, but we struggle on together."

Maggie came in with the tea. Grace was very afraid she might drop the tray, such were the girl's nerves upon serving the great lady currently occupying their modest room of all things.

Thankfully, she set it down with only a bit of a clatter. Grace poured the cups as Lady Heathway nodded her head vigorously at Lady Barlow, seeming delighted. Grace was not at all sure what had delighted the lady—it was certainly not their modest array of biscuits or their chipped teapot.

"As I suspected! Imbalanced humors," Lady Heathway said. "Excellent news."

"Excellent?" Lady Barlow asked.

"Naturally, it is excellent," Lady Heathway said. "The most common complaint in the world and easily rectified. I shall send my own doctor here to diagnose you, though I can see very well it is black bile that affects you. After a few good bleedings, cuppings, purgings, brisk exercise, and a bland diet, you will be set right."

"Bile? Well, I am not sure…of course, your concern is very

kind, Lady Heathway, but my physician thinks—"

"Do you say that my own London doctor, the esteemed Sir Henry Halford who counts among his patients the regent and now the king himself, is not up to the task of balancing *your* humors? Do you say so, Lady Barlow?"

"No indeed," Lady Barlow said, looking decidedly shaken at this verbal assault. "It is just, well I have been told that the Kent air is what has been most deleterious to my condition. I fear nobody can cure me while I remain in this neighborhood."

Grace blushed as she knew this was a rather bold gambit to convince Lady Heathway that her mother ought to be removed from the environs of Kent, preferably into the lady's comfortable house in Town.

"Country doctors," Lady Heathway said with a note of disdain. "They live in the past century. Another reason Sir Henry shall set you to rights. Air has not a thing to do with it and all of these people racing to the seaside for bracing salt air do themselves not a bit of good. Well!" she said, sipping her tea with obvious relish. "You shall be up and managing the household in a trice. All impediments have been whisked away."

Grace hardly knew where to look. All impediments had been whisked? Whisked where?

"Unfortunately, in my weakened condition," Lady Barlow said, "I cannot manage without Grace. If I am to stay in Kent."

"Nonsense," Lady Heathway said.

"No, I..." Lady Heathway seemed to have nothing further to say to Lady Barlow and instead turned her attention to Maggie. "What do you wait for, girl? A trunk must be packed! We will not wish to tarry and find ourselves on the road after sunset. Highwaymen, you know."

"But—" Lady Barlow stuttered.

Lady Heathway held up a hand at Lady Barlow's *but*. "Never fear, Lady Barlow," Lady Heathway said cheerfully. "I can read your thoughts. The maid cannot be relied upon to do the thing credibly. Miss Yardley, do go up and supervise. Bring whatever you have that's best, but do not fret over it! I have arranged for a modiste to attend us in Berkeley Square on the morrow."

Grace rose, as it sounded like an order rather than a suggestion. She curtsied to the lady and followed Maggie up the stairs.

She had not the first idea of what she should do when she got there. Should she actually pack her things? It did not seem likely that her mother would be willing to do without her. How would the lady manage?

On the other hand, it also did not seem likely that Lady Heathway had ever been defeated in any matter.

But it could not be right to leave her mother in her current state, no matter how determined Lady Heathway was about it.

Closing the door to the bedchamber, she said quietly, "I hardly know what to do."

Maggie looked at her strangely. "I reckon we'd best do as we're told. That lady down there is a regular hussar."

⋙⋘

GEORGE COULD NOT quite believe what he had just witnessed. They were meant to simply arrive, load the girl and her trunk, and be off. Now he was to understand that the girl's mother was sickly and had no intention of allowing her daughter to leave.

And it was abundantly clear that his aunt had known it all along.

As was her usual wartime strategy, Lady Heathway had plowed on and pretended she had not heard any challenges to her wishes whatsoever.

At the moment, Miss Yardley was above stairs, allegedly packing. Though, she might be hiding in a linen closet for all he knew. Lady Barlow had fanned herself and looked red in the face and had seemed to be ginning herself up to take another run at the field, but his aunt had been two steps ahead. She'd found a sheet of paper in the desk and directed Lady Barlow to write down all of her symptoms. The list would be handed forthwith to Sir Henry for his consideration.

My God, they were practically kidnapping the daughter. It was outrageous.

Despite the outrageousness, George could not be entirely sorry to see the girl removed from such a household. The mother was a malingerer, of that he had no doubt. Her complaints were vague and she had seemed quite animated when the mood suited her. She did poorly from the shock of being widowed, and yet it was the Kent air that affected her, and yet the Kent air had not affected her before she was widowed? She was likely loathe to part with her daughter because it would be an inconvenience.

For that matter, the blame landing decidedly on Kent air had been a hint, he thought, that his aunt ought to do something about it. Perhaps the lady was not loath to part with her daughter at all, but rather was loath to come out of it with nothing for herself. The lady had probably hoped that she might either come along with her daughter or else have a comfortable house in Brighton rented for her so she could take in that new and improved air.

Hopes like that could only spring up if one was not acquainted with Penelope Prescott, Marchioness of Heathway. Lady Barlow was on the verge of being left to her own devices and she could complain to the air all she liked about it.

As nearly a half hour had passed, and a rather uncomfortable half hour at that, Lady Heathway had begun to look at the stairs expectantly. Lady Barlow had hemmed and hawed over her list of symptoms and occasionally ventured that the air was exceedingly damp and then produced a dramatic cough to confirm it. None of this had made the slightest impression on his aunt.

Finally, Lady Heathway rose and stepped to the fireplace. She took up the fire poker and used the blunt end to bang on the rafters to move things along.

Miss Yardley hurried down the stairs at the summons.

His and his aunt's peculiar arrival to the house had hardly

given him time to really have a look at Miss Yardley—he'd been entirely too taken up by his aunt's outrageous directives and Lady Barlow's ineffective feints to try to hold her off.

Miss Yardley might be currently situated at a disadvantage, but even in a plain muslin she was striking looking—fairly tall, well-proportioned, raven-haired with large dark eyes and a generous mouth. She would do well in Town, assuming his aunt could get her out of the house.

George had presumed that Lady Barlow would be the only impediment. However, the girl was suddenly looking fiercely determined.

"Lady Heathway," she said in a measured tone, "while I do appreciate the trouble you have gone to, I find I cannot leave my mother to manage on her own. It is simply not right."

George thought it was rather noble of the girl to say so, though he had no doubt the mother was not at all failing. It was also far more courageous than he would have expected from a young miss. Lady Heathway was a rather frightening opponent and more experienced ladies had folded like a hand of cards rather than cross her.

He noted the maid crouching at the top of the stairs with one hand on the handle of a trunk. The girl looked as if she did not know whether to come down or throw herself out a window in a bid to escape.

He shuddered to think of what his aunt would say to Miss Yardley's daring refusal.

Lady Heathway, rather than turning on Miss Yardley, turned on her mother. "Madam," she said in a barely managed fury, "I presume you intend on residing in this ramshackle abode for the rest of your years, as that is precisely what will occur if your daughter does not have a proper season. Now, what do you say to that?"

"Well, I—"

"Furthermore," Lady Heathway said, not seeming to care what, if anything, Lady Barlow might say to that, "that awful fate rests on your shoulders alone. It is up to you and your misman-aged humors to assure the girl that she may go in good conscience. Do it!"

Lady Barlow appeared entirely overcome. George assumed the lady had not had experience doing battle and was prepared to wave a white flag.

Miss Yardley hurried to her mother and knelt by her chair. "Mama," she said soothingly, "I know you suffer. There is no need for me to leave your side while you are unwell."

Lady Barlow, much to George's amusement, did not look as comforted by that sentiment as one may have hoped. It seemed to him that she was far too busy considering his aunt's threats and making calculations in her mind as to the most profitable course.

"If only I could accompany you..." she said weakly.

George suppressed a smile. The lady was quite the actress and diabolically determined to impose upon his aunt. That nobody had ever successfully imposed upon Lady Heathway was not a fact yet known to her.

His aunt narrowed her eyes. "Lady Barlow, you will go no-where in *my* carriage," she said. "It will be as I planned it, or it will be no way at all. Now, I will make you one concession, since you seem determined to hint to your daughter that you have one shoe in a grave and the other shoe on a slippery street. I will hire a nurse who may occupy Miss Yardley's room. That good woman can wait upon you night and day and listen to all of your complaints until Sir Henry is able to cure you. That is my final offer and my carriage will depart this place in precisely three minutes."

Lady Barlow, faced with accomplishing precisely nothing if she carried on as she had been, appeared to have a remarkably speedy change of heart. She patted her daughter's hand and said, "I think I shall be all right with a nurse on hand. Yes, I really do think so. You ought to go, I am sure of it. If there are to be any different arrangements later on, then of course...well, we will see."

"Excellent!" Lady Heathway said, clapping her hands. "George, get the trunk. Miss Yardley, kiss your mother goodbye and let us be off."

George trudged up the stairs. Nothing could have been more ludicrous than the scenes that had played out in this house over the past hour.

He swore to himself that he would never again believe another of his aunt's small favors was truly small. From now on, he would brace himself for calamity no matter how simple the circumstance first appeared.

GRACE HAD BEEN at once delighted she would go to Town and terrified that she would go. She did feel that her mother would be well-cared for with a nurse living in the house. After all, that woman would be far more experienced at treating health complaints than she had ever been. As well, Maggie knew her job well enough and would not shirk too much of her work without supervision and Cook would manage very well on her own. Then, there was the idea that Sir Henry Halford himself would involve himself in her mother's care. And most importantly, this was her one chance for marriage, and marriage was the only way to get her mother out of the awful dower house. Lady Barlow would not survive many years in it, of that she was certain. She felt she left the house in good conscience, and she would not be so very far away that she could not return in all haste if her mother were to take a bad turn.

On the other hand, she'd thought it rather terrifying to put herself into the hands of Lady Heathway. Nobody had ever dared speak to Lady Barlow as she had. She wondered if anybody had ever dared speak to *anybody* in such a manner.

Much to her relief, Grace found Lady Heathway a remarkably changed woman once her point had been gained.

As the carriage rumbled off and Lady Barlow waved weakly from the window, Lady Heathway smiled kindly at Grace and said, "There now, my girl. It has been a trying time, but it has all come out right. There is not a thing wrong with your mother that Sir Henry cannot whip her out of. I expect he will diagnose her a hypochondriac and she will be well-pleased to know what's wrong with her."

Grace nodded, though she did not at all agree. The last thing her mother would be delighted to hear was that she imagined her complaints. Grace had sometimes wondered if Lady Barlow did not sometimes exaggerate, but she did not think the lady invented her general weak state. She thought that one so little used to exercise of any sort *would* weaken over time.

She glanced at Lord Gresham riding his horse alongside the carriage. He was devilishly handsome, and Grace was ashamed to reflect on all he had witnessed that day. She and her mother must seem quite mad. But then, she comforted herself that his aunt would have seemed just as mad. The lord himself had only looked perplexed, as one strange turn of events followed the next.

The carriage, which had been going down the middle of the lane Grace knew so well, abruptly angled to the side and Lord Langley dropped back behind them. Grace assumed another carriage came from the opposite direction.

As it was a private drive with only Barlow Hall and the dower house located on it, Grace was certain it was one of the endless carriages and wagons carrying the new viscount's belongings to his recently inherited estate.

She had not thought they would pause to find out, but a voice called from the other carriage just as they came abreast of it.

"Ho, there," a man said from his carriage window. "Had you been at the house to call? Are you a neighbor?"

It was the new viscount, dumpy as ever, and though he seemed surprised to see Grace in the carriage, he was not put off. His wife, the new viscountess, peered round his shoulder. Her hair was done in so many twists and turns it appeared to be a Medusa's maze one could never find the beginning of. It was piled high and had stiff ringlets on either side, all seemingly secured by a generous amount of pomade. Even more startling, Grace was certain the lady's cheeks were rouged. When the lady eventually passed by the dower house, she might expect *quite* the decided glare from Lady Barlow.

"I am Viscount Barlow," the man said, "and here is my wife, the viscountess."

Grace could feel Lady Heathway stiffen beside her. Tersely, she said, "I am the Marchioness of Heathway, come to collect Miss Yardley. I intend to do for her what you have seen fit to disregard. Do not bother coming to Town yourselves, as it would be a lonely place—I will ensure every door is barred against you and nobody will care to know you. There will be no club that will have you and you will be cut in the street. Such is the fate of *your* sort. While you are considering your mistakes, you might fix the roof of that ramshackle dower house. Further, madam, you appear rather flushed, but it is nothing a wet cloth and vigorous scrubbing cannot rectify."

Lady Heathway took a cane that had been laid by for the purpose and rapped on the roof. The carriage moved on and left the new viscount and his bride speechless on the lane.

Grace was certain she heard Lord Gresham laughing as they went.

Well, that was *one* way to welcome the new inhabitants of the hall. Lady Barlow would have been delighted to witness it. Grace found herself rather delighted too.

Grace was beginning to get the idea that Lady Heathway was perfectly agreeable when she was not crossed, but rather a Viking when she was.

She supposed she'd better make every effort not to cross the lady unless it was absolutely necessary.

⟫⟫⟩⟨⟨⟨

GEORGE WAS RELIEVED to be home again and gave his butler and footmen firm instructions that he was not to be found. Any footman of Lady Heathway's was to leave with no information regarding his whereabouts, even if he was at home. His aunt might chase him round the town with notes and messages, but he would do his best to confound her over precisely when he received and read them. As he did not live more than five houses down from her own house, he must just count on her not having the idea to sit herself at a window with opera glasses to catch him coming and going.

After they'd left Lady Barlow to her deleterious Kent air and he'd listened to his aunt deliver a rather satisfying dressing down to the new viscount, they had stopped at a nearby inn and changed the horses. George had thought that once they'd accomplished that necessity, he would be relieved of any further conversation on the journey.

How had he been wrong so many times in one day!

In between her conversations with Miss Yardley, which were pretty one-sided as far as he could tell, Lady Heathway would lean out the window and call to him on some matter.

Not wind nor dust nor what both of those things had done to her hair, appeared to put her off it.

What did he think of Mr. Roberts? Was the fellow as rich as everybody said? Should he be encouraged or ignored? It was necessary to know such things for Miss Yardley's sake. Might George make some inquiries?

Who ought to be hired regarding having a sidesaddle made for Miss Yardley? Might George see to it?

Which of her mares would suit Miss Yardley? Might George have a look at them and decide?

Miss Yardley was interested in books, might they all make a trip to Lackington and Allen one day soon?

Her notions seemed to get more whimsical as the journey went on. Should they pursue a voucher from Almack's? There was of course the difficulty of Lady Heathway not being on good terms with Lady Jersey on account of having named her *Lady Silence* as an ode to her never-ending chatter. But then, might not George convince her of the innocence of the joke? Or that it was amusing? Or that somebody else said it first?

As he rode forward, George ticked off the things he would do and the things he certainly would not do. He would arrange for a sidesaddle to be purchased and he would have a look at his aunt's stable of horses. He certainly would not approach Lady Jersey. That lady would delight in denying Miss Yardley a voucher—and then *Silence* herself would advertise it everywhere. He also had no plans to escort the ladies to Lackington and Allen, which they were well able to do on their own, nor would he make inquiries into Mr. Roberts.

When they finally entered the town and he was so close to making an escape, his aunt had used every bit of her determination to wrangle his promise to attend Lady Easton's ball on Thursday next. As a final dessert course to this harrowing day, she then suggested he take Miss Yardley into supper at the ball, as that would be the safest course until she understood who was who. The same had been done for Miss Wilcox and Lady Heathway did not wish to be outdone in any matter—especially not by Louisa Stapleton.

He could hardly refuse as Miss Yardley was within hearing of the bold request.

George could not say Miss Yardley herself was any more comfortable with his aunt's various directives. In fact, at one point she had looked at him with an expression that seemed to say she was sorry to be so much trouble.

She was not so much trouble, though. His *aunt* was so much trouble. Miss Yardley was rather lovely and seemed a sensible person with an admirable backbone. She would be no trouble at all if his aunt was not making her so.

He had not thought that his aunt deciding to sponsor a girl would have anything to do with him. Somehow, it was turning out that it *did* have to do with him, and Lady Heathway had devised a list of tasks before Miss Yardley had even stepped into the house.

He could not outright refuse to assist, it would cause a breach. He must just be very cagey about being caught. He would duck and weave like any Gentleman Jackson.

He could only hope that he won more matches than that pugilist ever had.

CHAPTER THREE

GRACE'S JOURNEY TO Berkeley Square might have been very pleasant. After all, she did not mind that Lady Heathway did so much talking and required so little talking from her in return. As she nodded, she also had the opportunity to admire the countryside. And perhaps admire a certain gentleman on horseback who was often in view.

It would all have gone very well, if the lady did not demand quite so much from her nephew. What a list of things she required from him! Grace could see well enough that he was not amused, though Lady Heathway did not pay the slightest heed to it.

The conversation about Almack's had been outlandish. Lady Heathway had said Lord Gresham ought to smooth things over with Lady Jersey and Lord Gresham had said Lady Jersey would sooner stab her own eye with a fork than smooth things over with Lady Heathway. Grace shuddered to think what had happened between the ladies, it was something to do with a bon mot that was found regrettable, as far as she could make out. All she could really be sure of was that she would *not* receive a voucher to that club.

Then, the lady had pushed Lord Gresham to take her into supper at a certain Lady Easton's ball. She would have been delighted if he had asked of his own free will. He was very attractive and she supposed no lady would mind being squired by him. However, it was embarrassing in the extreme to know that he'd been conscripted against his wishes while Lady Heathway acted as a single-handed press gang.

Of course, he had agreed, but he had not seemed particularly willing. That did prick her pride a bit, as it seemed to Grace that if he had been left to his own devices he would not have asked.

She only hoped he understood that she did not wish to be so much of a burden to him.

As for the rest of the carriage ride, that had been very informative. Grace had thought it was mere happenstance and luck that Lady Heathway had heard of her situation and been inspired to step in. That was not the case, precisely. Lady Heathway told her all about the society and named its various members. It seemed she was a project, of sorts. Though, she found herself not too proud to be one.

Lady Heathway had always planned to have a daughter of her own, and was still rather mystified that she had not, as fate rarely had the audacity to thwart her plans. Of those plans regarding a daughter, she'd had many. Her daughter was to be an unparalleled beauty, and absolutely astonishing in her accomplishments.

Grace was interrogated as to her skill on the pianoforte, her embroidery work, her seat on a horse, could she net an attractive purse and paint a fire screen, what was her understanding of literature, history, geography, horticulture, and philosophy, could she credibly manage a lady's maid, could she compose a menu, had she many people in the neighborhood who regularly called and was she accustomed to acting as hostess, and many more questions Grace had lost track of.

Interestingly, she was asked all those questions but was rarely required to answer. Most of the conversation went along in the following manner: "You are skilled on the pianoforte, I presume? Of course you must be. I never did hear Miss Wilcox play and have my suspicions about Louisa's pianoforte. I presume Miss Wilcox attacked it in some manner and *that's* why it has been broken all these months. Louisa is so evasive when I ask about it, as if she does not even want the instrument repaired."

Grace did not know Miss Wilcox nor what she'd done to a pianoforte and did not dare ask for the details. She was also certain she was not the unparalleled beauty Lady Heathway looked for and she did not deem her accomplishments quite as astonishing as Lady Heathway would wish.

For all that, she was fairly confident that she could meet at least most of Lady Heathway's requirements. She thought her looks quite passable and running in the middle of the pack. There were bound to be ladies who outshone her, but then there might also be ladies less fortunate.

As for Grace's accomplishments, her mother may have been indolent, but her father had not been. Especially not on her behalf. He'd had rather particular notions when it came to how Grace was to spend her time. A lady ought to be skilled at all the feminine arts, and then once the lady was married, if she chose to sink into a velvet chair and do nothing that was certainly her purview. One could put aside accomplishments only if one had acquired them in the first place.

Barlow Hall had been a parade of tutors all her life—she could play, draw, paint, and sew with what she believed was competence. She was fairly well-read, as she enjoyed it and had always been pleased to engage in lively debates with her father. She was not the paragon of Lady Heathway's imagination, but she supposed she was serviceable enough.

Finally, they had reached the outskirts of London. With every clip-clop of the horses' hooves, the activity around them increased. The town was so lively! Gone were the birdsong and crickets of the country. Here, people hurried everywhere as if they were exceedingly late to an important appointment. Lady Heathway's coachman made his way through the crowded streets slowly and with what seemed to be grim determination.

When they had finally arrived to Berkeley Square, it was apparent that Lady Heathway expected Grace to be overawed by the place. She supposed that was natural, as the lady had only ever seen her in the room of all things in the cramped dower house. However, she was not particularly overawed. It was a fine house, to be sure, but it did not equal Barlow Hall. That place, more like a castle than a house, had sat on that land for hundreds of years. It had been added to over the centuries and had taken on both an eccentric and imposing air.

It had begun as a large two-story house with two wings running east and west, built of local grey stone. A third wing had been added to the back and ran north. Nobody used the north wing now, but it had been added to by a viscount of old who had decided he required his own army and needed somewhere to house his soldiers. This need for an army had apparently sprung up over a long-running dispute with a neighbor. Grace did not know the details of the argument, other than it had to do with the rights to a well-stocked stream. It was said that when the viscount had raised an actual army, the neighbor threw up his hands in defeat.

Aside from the north wing, which was an endless and dreary collection of small apartments that had once housed soldiers, the rooms of the house were tall-ceilinged with heavy dark wood beams and roughhewn stone walls. The fireplaces were to scale, and one would have only had to slightly duck to walk into one. Corridors often ran to nowhere and alcoves appeared in surprising places. There had been times a guest had gone missing, having taken a wrong turn somewhere, and then found again entirely befuddled. There was a romance to the place and as a young girl Grace had often gone out to her bedchamber's balcony, pretending she bid adieu to her knights before they rode off to battle to save her kingdom. Now, the dumpy individual and his rouged wife had claimed its wonderful halls.

The house in Berkeley Square was far newer, which she thought did not have the same appeal. However, it was extremely large for a house in Town, exquisitely decorated, and without the cold drafts that blew through Barlow Hall. Further, she knew very well that she would never again live in such a place as her old home. Her current accommodations were a thousand times better than the dower house and it seemed the roof was in good order, as there was not a bucket in sight. She was determined to like it.

WILBERT RANSTON WAS all too aware that he led Lady Heathway's household staff like any battalion going forward into battle. He was in name the butler, but he *acted* as general.

He liked to consider that notion when he felt his nerves overcoming him. Most people assumed the war had caused his shattered nerves. The truth was he had always been a rather jittery person and came out of the war about as jittery as he'd gone into it. His mother always said he'd arrived wailing, and never really stopped. When he'd been seven, he cried for an entire day over losing a wooden toy soldier—half the day because he lost it, and then the other half of the day because he found it. Then of course there had been the incident at the Granville's Christmas party. He had been eighteen and a saucy maid had kissed him. He'd fainted dead away and awoke with a throng of people staring down at him. There had been many other incidents he chose not to recall, and it was hardly surprising—he was a cannon that only needed a match. As he got older, he got better at hiding such outbursts, but they were always there simmering under the surface and there were times they *would* make an appearance.

Unbeknownst to Lady Heathway, years ago he'd been fired as a butler to a Hertfordshire gentleman when he'd wept in front of forty guests attending a dinner because there was a skin on the gravy.

In his defense, there *had* been a skin on the gravy, and it had been purposefully allowed to form. The diabolical cook in that house had known how delicate his nerves were and was always trying to upset him. Just that very morning, he'd hid the coffee and pretended they'd run out. When Wilbert had sunk to his knees on the cold stone floor of the kitchens, the rogue had said, "Hah! No, we're not, I just hid it."

The skin on the gravy follow-up that evening had pushed him over the edge.

Mr. Gray had sympathized with his unfortunate tempera-ment and wrote him an excellent reference. While he sympathized, he was not sympathetic enough to keep him on. Somebody else could deal with a crying butler.

After that debacle and not finding his next employment, he'd been forced to become a soldier. It really was the last thing he was suited for and the fates had seemed to know it and enjoy toying with him. Of all the soldiers hanging about, why had *he* been chosen as one of the twenty-four to be the first to cross the Douro River? They were to venture in alone, into enemy territory. It was suicide! They would be cut down as soon as their feet hit the banks! He did not want to die!

As it happened, the crossing was rather uneventful, as it would later turn out that French General Soult had been asleep at the time. They landed at the base of a seminary, which they were welcomed into readily. More and more men began the crossing on two empty wine barges that had been commandeered.

It was all going rather smoothly and so he was surprised to find his feet pulling him away from the other men. He wandered down a long corridor of the seminary and poked his head into some of the rooms. He felt himself growing very calm.

Nobody had actually seen him slip into a closet and cover himself with piles of linen. He'd stayed there, and even slept awhile, as the battle for Porto raged out of doors. When it seemed that it might be safe to emerge, he'd hurried to find his fellow soldiers and claimed he'd been knocked out and lying in the street for the entirety of the battle. Some were skeptical, and one unpleasant fellow even felt around on his head for lumps. But in the end, nobody ever knew where he had spent the Battle of the Douro.

Now, he felt it his duty to force his staff to face the horrors of war head on, lest they venture into one. He told them terrible stories of all he had seen at Porto. Or at least, all he imagined he *would* have seen, had he come out of the seminary's linen closet.

At times, it all felt very real, and the memory of the closet and the smell of fresh-washed linen over his face faded as if it had never been. Had he in fact fought bravely, striking down the enemy left and right? Had the idea of a linen closet been only a dream? It was sometimes hard to tell.

If he *had* been in a closet, he had no wish to ever advertise that particular battle strategy. What he'd rather do was successfully lead the battle charge now. He had armed the servants with heavy wood clubs that stayed under their beds until the moment they were wanted. He waited with impatience for the day when thieves and rogues would attempt to breach the doors. Then, they would find out what Wilbert Ranston was really made of. There would be no linen closet then.

He did find though, that just now he felt himself more jittery than usual. Lady Heathway had installed a young miss in the house and she was forever smiling at him. Every time they crossed paths, she smiled. What was he to do? Smile back?

And then, there were rumblings that the girl's lady's maid was coming too. Another person at the servants' table. It was too much change! It caused too many things to do. Where on earth was he to find the right sort of hefty wooden club for under a new maid's bed on such short notice?

Just thinking of it all made his insides feel as if his blood was bubbling and he felt a bit woozy. He would go to his apartments and clean his fowling piece and then have a long lie-down. It was the only thing that would calm his nerves.

As GRACE SETTLED in, the following week's activities had been confined to indoors. The dresses she'd brought with her were found pleasant enough, but not to Lady Heathway's high standards—she felt it was vital that Grace's first showing in society be exceptional.

Her bedchamber was well-proportioned and bright and she often spent an early dawn at the window, watching the quiet activity on the street at that hour. There was, on occasion, a lord on a horse making his way home and certainly the worse for drink. But mostly, there were servants sweeping steps and having quiet chats among themselves as they did so.

Sometimes, she felt so confined in the house that she thought it would be amusing to join them. She could have done it if she had the nerve. A sturdy lead pipe used to funnel rain from the roof ran directly next to the window. Its various bracings to the house would provide easy foot and handholds. When she had been young, she often delighted in escaping a tutor by just such a method. Out a balcony and down a drainpipe she'd go. It often took them a good amount of time to discover how she'd escaped them and that she was then lounging in a hayloft in the stables. Of course, she was too old for that now and even if she were not, those servants would think her mad to join them.

She had been introduced to Lord Heathway, and he seemed a pleasant and good-humored older gentleman. She did not see him very often though, as he was so much at his club. Lady Heathway was of the opinion that the habit was what made him so pleasant. She never complained about the amount of time he spent there, and so he went on contentedly. If, on occasion, he began to forget how fortunate he was, Lady Heathway would mention that a lady of her acquaintance was most unhappy over her husband's too frequent absences. That would remind him of his own good luck.

The lady had been as good as her word about the modiste turning up to make a plan for the season's dresses. In fact, Grace had been rather touched by the meeting.

Lady Heathway had brought Madame LeGrange into the drawing room and said, "Now, I know you will be coming with your own ideas, of course that is why I called on you—you have done such excellent work for me in the past. However, I have planned for a daughter my entire life and so have taken the liberty of producing a few sketches."

Lady Heathway had then opened a case and took out her drawings. To call it a *few* sketches was not even close to the truth. There were scores of them. They had all been drawn in ink and then very prettily painted in watercolors. Grace thought it was very kind of Lady Heathway to invest so much time in the project. The sketches were also, both to her and Madame LaGrange's surprise, rather good.

The two ladies put their heads together and made little adjustments here and there and talked of suitable fabrics. There were to be all manner of gowns and day dresses in silks, satins, and fine muslins. A smart-looking riding habit in dark green was proposed. Pelisses were designed, though spencers were firmly off the table, as Lady Heathway deemed them ridiculous. She said the Earl of Spencer was an idiot for thinking up the idea. Elegant simplicity was to be the watchword in Lady Heathway's house.

As Grace poured the tea that Ranston had brought in to sustain the ladies, Lady Heathway said, "Madame LeGrange, I find we think alike. Grace's wardrobe is to be refined and not overdone."

"With what pleasure will I prepare these," Madame LeGrange said, waving her hand over the various sketches on the table. "You cannot know, my lady, how often I am forced to add more and more to a dress. More ribbon, more gold thread, more embroidery! I think, am I dressing peacocks or people? And now, the habit of adding military touches. On a young lady? My heart breaks over it."

Lady Heathway nodded sagely. "Those with no confidence cannot stop themselves when they ought."

"Just so," Madame LeGrange replied.

"Now, my good woman, we must develop a battle plan of sorts," Lady Heathway said cheerfully. "I know I cannot have everything at once, but an important ball is to be held Thursday next and we will need a dress by then. It will be Grace's first outing. The first time she will meet many important people. It must be perfect. Which do you think?"

Madame LeGrange looked critically over the sketches and pointed. "For a debut into society? It must be this one."

"As I thought too," Lady Heathway said. "If we both, as women of discernment, agree on the choice, it must be right."

"Naturellement," Madame LeGrange said, nodding.

Grace was rather pleased with the selection. As the weather was still quite cool, a gown had been chosen that she thought would do very well. The cut was to be as simple as a gown could possibly be, the silhouette softened and without the pinched-up bodice that suited nobody. The sleeves were simple and capped rather than puffed. There would be no added embellishments to it. It would only be elevated by its material, which would be a midnight blue velvet lined in a thin silk of the same color.

Since that happy meeting, Lady Heathway had shown Grace all the accoutrements she had purchased ahead of time, in full confidence that Madame LeGrange would approve of her sketches. There were gloves, bonnets, ribbons, stockings, parasols, and even a selection of reticules. Stacks of slippers had been made in various sizes as the lady had not been sure of the dimension of Grace's foot and they could often take so long to be made and delivered. The ones that did not fit were to be given to a charity school Lady Heathway patronized. Grace could not help but be grateful for how much effort the lady had put into things. It was rather extraordinary to know that one had been in another's thoughts and plans so often.

As the days passed and she became more acquainted with Lady Heathway, Grace was convinced that underneath what could be a terrifying exterior beat a rather generous heart. Her household certainly was not one that might be expected from a dragon-like lady. Grace had got to know it in both slow degrees and alarming lurches.

The butler, Ranston, seemed always a rather harried individual and Grace was soon apprised that he was prone to attacks of nerves. Another lady might have found the temperament inconvenient, but Lady Heathway appeared long accustomed to it.

On one particularly harried day, Ranston had been questioned over whether he'd put in an order for Lord Heathway's favored wines. Ranston had only got a faraway look in his eyes and stood like a statue in the middle of the drawing room. Lady Heathway had said, "Well, Ranston, you and I both know you'd better lie down for a while."

She'd told Grace later that there was no use in keeping up the questioning. If she'd done so, Ranston would have had a crying jag right in the drawing room and be abed for days to recover. As it was, he would rest, and then he would put in the order.

Grace could not imagine what Lord and Lady Barlow would have done if their own butler, Manfred, had a crying jag in the drawing room. But then, Lady Heathway had told her, "Ranston, like others, had a bad time in the war and so I find it is patriotic to look the other way when one's butler is on the verge of a breakdown."

The footmen, all young and tall and of an age where boys were wont to mock any hint of weakness were surprisingly respectful of Ranston. Grace could not imagine what horrors the butler had faced in the war, but she suspected the footmen knew the particulars and were chastened by it.

The housekeeper, Mrs. Redwiggin, appeared to understand her mistress very well. Lady Heathway liked to view her standards as the highest, and the housekeeper happily complied. Mrs. Redwiggin was forever coming to Lady Heathway to report that this or that business that supplied the house was now found to be falling in their standards, but that Mrs. Redwiggin had contracted with another business that was so exclusive that they regularly turned away less lofty customers. Or some such nonsense. The queen's name was often bandied about and Lady Heathway was gratified by her housekeeper's various gambits on the subject. For all Mrs. Redwiggin's officiousness, she too was very considerate to Mr. Ranston.

It was all exceedingly odd, but then Grace had been delighted to discover that she was to get back her lady's maid. Lady Heathway was perfectly amenable to rehiring Betsy, who had been let go when Grace had moved to the dower house. Dear Betsy had stayed on in Kent with an aunt who did not live very far away from Barlow Hall and she had at once been sent for. It was not three days before Betsy was very happily back in employment.

Grace was comforted to have her back. It seemed as if part of her old life had joined her in Berkeley Square. And in any case, she supposed it was always helpful to have at least one friend below stairs. One might learn a great deal that way and it was how Grace knew that Manfred had always had a soft spot for her father's hunting dogs. Apparently, the butler had made it a habit of saving choice bits of meat for them. Grace supposed Betsy would have a lot to say about Mr. Ranston's shattered nerves.

Grace was surprised at how often she saw Lord Gresham at the house. She'd thought he'd been quite aggravated when his aunt had pressed him to take her into supper at the upcoming ball, but that had not seemed to put him off arriving nearly every day. It seemed no matter was too small for him to inform his aunt about. He would come to apprise Lady Heathway that Lackington and Allen had expanded their hours for the season, or that Lord and Lady Penmar had arrived to Town, or that Lord Nankin had a mare for sale that she might like for her own stables. One day, he even forgot what he came for.

Interestingly, he seemed to know the household schedule very well, and invariably turned up for tea or dinner.

What a well put together man he was! His dress was always perfection, his valet clearly knowing his work. And he was no fop either. There was nothing of fussiness in his appearance, rather it had a rather careless and unstudied air that could only be arrived at by thoughtful composition. Though he always looked so well, she did not think he was one of those gentlemen who spent all their time on appearance as he was proving himself very well read. She could also not help but to notice that he sat a horse very finely.

She found she very much enjoyed conversing with him, and of course Lady Heathway was always delighted to see her nephew.

Everything went along exceedingly pleasantly in Grace's new circumstances. Until one occurrence brought the Viking that Lady Heathway was capable of being back out on view.

A letter from Lady Barlow arrived.

CHAPTER FOUR

T HE LETTER LADY Barlow had sent had, unfortunately, revealed that the lady was still of a mind to be removed from Kent. She wrote that she was certain the London air would do her more good than the country air ever had. Further unfortunate, Grace had shown it to Lady Heathway thinking she might relent and allow her mother to come. The lady had been incensed and directed Grace that she was not to answer such a ridiculous salvo. A nurse had been secured and was even now installed in the house and they would trust the reports from that lady and Sir Henry only.

Grace had not been entirely comfortable ignoring a letter from her mother and had slipped a note into the outgoing post regardless. Her words had been kind, but firm, and she had apprised her mother of the real case of things. There would be no point in hinting she ought to come, as Lady Heathway would not be moved. It would be far better to allow the nurse and Sir Henry to treat her illness, and Grace promised she would do her best to see that her mother did not remain in the dower house forever.

Now, it was the evening of Lady Easton's ball. She was finally to leave the house! And, to leave it in such a gown. It was positively glorious, the cut fit perfectly to her figure and the velvet of the highest quality. The silk lining allowed the skirt to move freely and gave it a wonderful drape. There had been a matching pelisse made too, trimmed in beaver and lined with dark blue satin. It had two clever inside pockets, as Lady Heathway was of the opinion that clothes should be both elegant and useful. A rather perfect pair of white gloves, and pretty satin slippers completed the arrangement. Lady Heathway had lent Grace one of her own necklaces—a delicate silver setting holding a brilliant aquamarine surrounded by smaller sapphires.

Betsy worked on her hair and went through the servants one by one, giving her expert assessment. Cook was a grumpy old man who believed in tradition, except for white soup, which he appeared to nurse a deep hatred for in solidarity with his mistress. The kitchen maid, Jenny, was rather sly and Betsy did not like her or trust her. She'd not been in the house a day before Jenny was trying to engage her in gossip, which of course, she did not like. Betsy was also sure Jenny stole things out of the larder and sold them as she'd seen her pocket a handful of tea before Mrs. Redwiggin remembered to lock the chest. The housemaids, Meggy and Anne, steered well clear of Jenny and Betsy would too—somebody else would have to take Jenny to task. The footmen, Benny and Gregory, were just as you would expect—young men who could not decide if they were adults or children. Mrs. Redwiggin had standards, at least one would assume so—she rarely talked of anything else. Mr. Ranston was a conundrum, a nervous creature and yet a warlike creature. One never knew if he would weep or wax on about the war.

Grace supposed Betsy had sized them all up quick enough. As for Jenny stealing tea, it was on one hand something Lady Heathway should know, and on the other hand, it was not the role of a visiting lady's maid to unmask a thief in the household. Grace thought Betsy was right to simply steer clear. If Betsy knew it, then Mr. Ranston and Mrs. Redwiggin must know it and it would be their purview to determine what to do about it.

"The Viscount would be right proud of you, and Lady Barlow too," Betsy said. "Look at you, getting ready to march into that ballroom and slay all of London."

"I hardly think I will march," Grace said, laughing, "and a ball is not a battlefield."

Betsy sighed. "I expect you're right. I been listening to Mr. Ranston too much at my meals. He does tell the most terrible stories! It turns my stomach sometimes, if I imagine the battle scenes too closely."

"Dear me," Grace said, rather surprised to hear the butler was telling war stories at table within hearing of the female servants.

"Dear *me*, and double," Betsy said. "He scares the wits from me on occasion. Do you know we all have a wood club under our beds in case the house is breached? He says if we hear any unusual sound in the night, we're to creep silent down the halls with our clubs raised and prepare to fight. We're to fight as hard as we can until he can get there with his fowling piece and then he'll blow the intruder to bits. He keeps the gun loaded and cleans it every Sunday."

"Now, I think you are teasing me, Betsy," Grace said.

"I wish I was," Betsy said, arranging the last curl. "We're to be specially on our guard tonight, as robbers like to pounce on a house when the family's gone out. I might very well sleep *under* my bed as on it."

"I cannot imagine Lady Heathway knows any of this," Grace said, a bit alarmed to discover that Betsy had not been teasing. "It seems a very odd way of going on and I'm not sure I like you being frightened so."

"Never you mind me, miss," Betsy said, stepping back to admire her handiwork. "I'd rather be havin' nightmares here than trapped in my aunt's stuffy little sitting room with no prospects on the horizon. Anyway, you go out and take the place by storm, just like how Mr. Ranston would prefer it."

As THEY MADE their way to Lady Easton's house in the carriage, Lady Heathway told Grace more about her friends that had formed the Society of Sponsoring Ladies. Prior to this, Grace had been told their names, but had thought of them rather vaguely.

Now she was to know that Lady Mendleton was an agreeable

creature, but would no doubt boast of her new daughter-in-law, née Miss Wilcox, for an unconscionable length of time. Grace presumed this was the same Miss Wilcox who had mysteriously broken a pianoforte.

The duchess was nearest to being Lady Heathway's equal, though the lady often made the mistake of thinking she was somehow superior because of her title. The duchess was also in the habit of naming things noble far too often and Lady Heathway was convinced it was a ploy to align herself more closely with royalty though there was not a royal bone in her body.

Lady Redfield was exceedingly soft, so much so that she did not seem to hold any authority over her servants. She could not bear to see anybody unhappy and so the easiest way to win an argument with her was to look decidedly unhappy.

Lady Featherstone was a pleasant woman, though the lady had a rather macabre interest in Lord Ryland's criminal society. It was faintly ridiculous, as the society had not a need of her to go about solving crimes and she did not seem to have much of a head for it.

Lady Easton was a sensible woman, and almost as rigorous in her standards as Lady Heathway herself. She did, however, sometimes cling to rather old-fashioned ideas about how society was to comport itself. There would no doubt be a white soup at her ball, because it was tradition, though Lady Heathway had pointed out many times that almonds had never meant to be sipped.

Grace was rather astonished and thought the ladies sounded entirely eccentric. But then, it might just be Lady Heathway's own eccentricity. After all, it was beginning to look as if Lady Heathway ran an extremely eccentric household by way of her at once warlike and weeping butler.

Either way, she would face these friends of her sponsor in not too long a time.

As their carriage doors were opened, Lady Heathway concluded with, "Well, you do look stunning, if I may congratulate myself. I have certainly topped anything Louisa was able to do for Miss Wilcox."

Grace smiled, though she was getting the distinct feeling that this group of ladies were rather competitive.

GRACE HAD BEEN quite surprised by Portland Place, the width of the street was striking and seemed at least over one hundred feet. She had never seen such an avenue. She had mentioned her admiration of it to Lady Heathway as they made their way into the house but was counseled not to comment on it to Lady Easton. Apparently, their hostess took a great amount of pride in the width of her street, as if she'd built it with her own two hands.

"Clara," Lady Heathway said as they approached Lady Easton.

"Penelope," Lady Easton said. She was a formidable-looking matron with an air about her that said she knew what was right and dearly hoped you knew it too.

"May I present to you Miss Yardley," Lady Heathway said.

Grace curtsied. When she rose, Lady Easton said, "Charmed, Miss Yardley. Here is my nephew, Lord Bertridge. He lives on the other side of the street. We favor Portland Place for the street's generous proportions."

As Grace curtsied, she forced herself not to laugh. She could practically feel Lady Heathway sigh at the mention of the width of the road.

"Miss Yardley," Lord Bertridge said, looking every bit as if he entirely agreed with his aunt's assessment of Portland Place.

As they moved off, Lady Heathway muttered, "Generous proportions indeed."

Their cloaks were taken and Grace was given her card. She felt a sense of nerves come over her, which was a surprise. She had not thought she would be nervous; it was just a ball after all. She'd had a dancing master for years and her father had regularly hosted mock balls for a few nearby families with girls of their own.

This was different, though. There were so many people, and so many of them looked...how did they look? At once sophisticated and world-weary. As if the ball almost bored them. Certainly, it was a mask put on for show. Was it the thing in Town to look a bit bored? If it were, she doubted she would be much good at the attitude. She'd end up laughing if she attempted to put on such a play.

A gentleman approached Grace, looking fairly determined. Grace could not say she minded, he was rather handsome—his hair a dark blond that she guessed would lighten in summer, and a rather strapping physique.

"Lady Heathway," he said, bowing, and giving a quick smile to Grace.

"Mr. Vance," Lady Heathway said, sounding just the slightest bit disapproving. "I imagine you have flown to my side for an introduction."

"Precisely," Mr. Vance said.

"This is Miss Grace Yardley," Lady Heathway said. "I will allow it, but not the first or supper. Supper is in fact already taken and as to the first..."

Mr. Vance was already writing his name down for the second. "Oh, I know, Lady Heathway. Gunmaker grandfather."

He bowed and strolled away, not seeming the least put off by Lady Heathway's...well, it was bordering on rudeness.

Grace looked at her inquiringly. "Gunmaker grandfather? What does it mean?"

"Mr. Vance's grandfather was in trade you see," Lady Heathway said. "He will be a baron someday but of course he carries that strike against him. Most gentleman would distance themselves from the fact, but Mr. Vance appears to delight in owning it."

Grace did her best to match Lady Heathway's serious expression, though she was rather delighted with Mr. Vance.

Any feeling of a smile coming on was soon chased away by what Grace saw heading toward her next. Four matrons bore down on them like ships under a strong wind. Their leader was an austere-looking woman clad in yards of heavy brocade.

Grace glanced at Lady Heathway. Lady Heathway said softly, "There they are."

"Penelope," the lead lady said, her brocade skirt swishing round her as she came to a stop.

"Theodosia," Lady Heathway said, "You will wish to know Miss Yardley. Grace, this is the Duchess of Stanbury."

Grace curtsied low, low enough for the queen. After all, she had been told that the duchess liked to think of herself as noble. She would not care to challenge that notion.

"Your Grace," she said.

The duchess nodded and smiled with lofty condescension.

Before she knew it, Grace was introduced to the rest of the ladies. Lady Featherstone of the ill-advised criminal society. Lady Redfield of the mismanaged servants. Lady Mendleton of the oft-mentioned Miss Wilcox. She was surrounded by them and, as eccentric as Lady Heathway had painted them, they were very kind.

She was congratulated on her care of her mother, though it was also hinted that she must have been misguided. Her hair was found to be lovely, her eyes striking, and her curtsy very pretty. Lady Mendleton did not wonder a moment but that she would become fast friends with her daughter-in-law Georgiana. Grace had not the first idea which of these attributes would be found interesting to Lady Mendleton's daughter-in-law.

Lady Featherstone examined Grace's gown and said, "Penelope, this dress is a triumph."

The other ladies nodded their agreement, though the duchess nodded as if she were giving up a point. Reluctantly acknowledged or not, Lady Heathway beamed. "The design of it is from my own sketches; Madame LeGrange took on my every idea."

"Lady Heathway has been most kind in her attentions to me," Grace said.

"Sketches, goodness," Lady Redfield said. "Very industrious,

Penelope."

Lady Heathway nodded. "Ah, here comes George. Now, Louisa, I remember how you very sensibly had Lord Langley take Miss Wilcox into supper at her first outing and I was determined to do just the same."

"Excellent notion," Lady Redfield said.

"Well considered, in my opinion," the duchess said as if she were handing down a pronouncement from a judge's bench.

Grace had felt a general case of nerves since entering the house. The approach of the ladies had heightened the feeling somewhat. But, on viewing Lord Gresham she found them rise three-fold. He could not possibly appear more dashing. Nobody could.

He wore a close-cut coat of a blue so dark it seemed almost black, with wonderful gold buttons. His shirt was a blazing white and his cravat was such that she suspected his valet considered it a victory—it was intricate, and yet not finicky.

She did so wish he came to her of his own accord, and not because he had been directed to by his aunt.

It appeared Lord Gresham knew all of the ladies very well—their greetings spoke of long acquaintance and they were very obviously fond of him. As they fussed over him, which Lady Heathway seemed to very much approve of, he put his name down on her card. As he handed it back to her, his gloved hand grazed hers.

The touch felt both familiar and foreign. It was as if she had felt such before, though she could only liken it to a still summer evening when the night sky almost hummed and lightning was soon to strike. Grace hoped she was not blushing; she was not prone to it and would not appreciate such a thing making an appearance just now.

She must not look stupid. The poor man had been *forced* to put his name down for her supper and she could not bear to seem as if she did not know it. To blush would signal that she was flattered, and she must not be flattered. No particular attention had been paid.

Grace was at once gratified and unhappy that Lord Gresham moved off with alacrity. She did not want him to stay lest he perceive her feelings, but then she did not wish him to go so quickly as that certainly showed his own.

She was not given much time to dwell on it, though, as various gentlemen approached. Lord Bertridge was to take her first. As he was nephew to the hostess, the ladies flanking her like birds on the verge of flying south were well-pleased that their society had been honored in some way.

The duchess even mentioned that it might be considered a *noble gesture*. Grace did not know if that were true or not, but she was well-prepared to compliment the size of Portland Place's avenue when it came to it.

GEORGE STOOD ON the far side of the ballroom, surreptitiously glancing at Miss Yardley as she was surrounded by his aunt's cabal of matrons.

He had vowed to himself that he would steer well clear of his aunt and her current project, but somehow, he had encountered Miss Yardley far more often than he'd thought he would. Of course, it could not be helped. He felt a duty to inform his aunt that Lackington and Allen had expanded their hours for the season. And then on another day, that Lord and Lady Penmar had arrived to Town. The very next day he discovered that Lord Nankin had a mare for sale that his aunt might like for her own stables and that could obviously not be put off. Then there had been the day he forgot what he came for and he was still trying to remember what it was.

As long as he was going to her house to tell Lady Heathway something she needed to know, he'd thought he might as well go when food was on the horizon. He'd grown very tired of the food at his club and his aunt always did have a very good cook. Dinner was preferred, but he'd come for tea twice too.

He'd found Miss Yardley an interesting lady. She appeared well-educated and could speak creditably on a variety of subjects. She spoke French elegantly, and a smattering of German too. She had the delicate manners of one who had been raised in a refined household. He supposed most of all, he did not at all mind looking at that face and all its many expressions. She was downright adorable when something went wrong with her embroidery and she bit her lower lip while she pulled out the stitches.

But now...my God, she was stunning. Her color was high, and her hair perfectly composed, and that dress. She was...

She was rather magnificent.

As he gazed round the room, so as not to make it obvious that he kept looking in one particular direction, he spotted Langley escorting the new Lady Langley. They looked well-pleased with each other and it was his understanding that they were always to be found together, coming and going from Buckingham Palace.

Lady Annabelle looked equally well-pleased with her escort, and George had heard she'd recently married a baron from her own neighborhood. He seemed a red-haired beast of a fellow and towered over her, but large though he was, he clearly took his direction from his diminutive wife. Lady Annabelle was just now shaking a finger at him as he laughed. She was a silly creature, George had always thought, but his governess used to always say there was saucer for every cup. It seemed this particular saucer and cup had found one another.

It had not escaped his notice that Miss Yardley's card was filling rapidly. He knew Vance was on it, and Bertridge too. Now the duchess' son, Lord Blackwood, had muscled in, with Lord Ryland close behind.

Well, he supposed they would. Any gentleman coming in late would find himself mightily disappointed. Miss Yardley was going to be very popular this season. She really did stand out as exceptional. Tall, slim, wonderful dark hair and those large expressive eyes. And then she was dressed so simple and yet elegant, which was especially striking amongst the other ladies who worked so hard to decorate themselves with endless amounts of trimmings.

He found he could not like it. After all, she was just arrived from the countryside. What did she know? She might easily be taken advantage of—he'd already seen evidence of her gullibility. After all, had she not fallen for her mother's ridiculous ruses? Had she not believed the lady was desperately ill when all with eyes could see that she was only pretending at it? Did that not speak of a certain innocence and naivete?

He'd have to find some way of putting her on her guard.

It would be a duty. A duty to his aunt. At the very least.

Bertridge approached and said, "Your aunt's project, Miss Yardley, is very pretty. I've taken her first—got to pay proper homage to the old gals' society, you know. I suppose my own aunt will jump into the thing at some point."

George nodded, though he was not in the least convinced that Bertridge had taken Miss Yardley's first set for any such reason. As for Lady Easton *jumping into the thing*, he found he did not care one way or the other what the lady jumped into.

He felt himself vaguely dissatisfied with the whole situation. He'd sworn he would not have anything to do with his aunt's society. But now, he felt he really must step in. He must guard Miss Yardley from...

From all of *them*.

Just until a suitable choice of marriage partner had been made, of course. Then, she would be off his hands. He would be able to dust himself off from his involvement in this project and his aunt could bask in her success. All would have been satisfactorily concluded.

As for the moment, though, he must warn Miss Yardley about *them*. It would be duty, or family honor, or something along those lines…

HAD GRACE BEEN in a more usual situation and been brought to the ball by her mother, she would not have felt she was treading the boards as an actor on a stage. Had Lady Barlow been her chaperone, that chaperone would have retreated to the card room long ago.

Her mother had never seen the point of close supervision. It would have seemed a lot of effort to no purpose. Lady Barlow was not one to put out a lot of effort, even if there *were* a purpose.

Some of these ladies, though, took a different view. Lady Heathway, Lady Featherstone, the duchess, and Lady Redfield stayed in the ballroom and examined every step she made. It was only Lady Easton taken up by her duties as a hostess, and Lady Mendleton too engrossed in admiring her new daughter-in-law, that did not keep her in view every moment.

She'd been led through the first by Lord Bertridge and it had been very formal, as they were in a set with Lady Easton and the Duke of Stanbury. Lady Easton had established the tone, and Lady Easton's tone was decidedly reserved. Grace had found a very willing audience in Lord Bertridge, however, when it came to the size of his avenue.

Mr. Vance had led her next and he was quite the opposite. He made her laugh several times, though each time she did she could almost feel the frowns coming from Lady Heathway.

The duchess' son, Lord Blackwood, was a genial enough gentleman, though he was one of those who thought his horses were the most interesting thing in Town.

Lord Ryland was an eccentric gentleman who wished to talk about crime, most especially murder or forgery. Grace thought it the oddest thing in the world, but apparently, he had his own club on the subject and told her she was welcome to attend the public evenings when they discussed a real case. She smiled and while she did not say so, she rather thought *not*.

All along, as she stepped and spoke, she thought of Lord Gresham. She did not wish to have her thoughts kidnapped in such a manner, but she could not seem to stop their direction.

She saw him sometimes, leading another lady round the floor.

He was so elegant!

He was also so uninterested in Grace Yardley. All those ladies he led around had been chosen by him. *She* had been chosen by his aunt.

Would anybody know it? Would they sense it? Would they see in his demeanor that he'd been pressganged by his aunt? Her embarrassment would be tenfold if that were the case.

Well, she would just get on with it. He did his aunt a favor and she would express her appreciation for it and make him know he need not feel obligated to do so in future.

Yes. That would be best. Just face the thing head on and be certain that *he* understood that *she* understood the real case of things. She was not flattered, only thankful of the favor and not requiring another.

If he wished to approach her at some other ball, well that would certainly be fine, but not expected. In truth, it would be more than fine, but she would not let him know it.

"Miss Yardley," Lord Gresham said, holding out his arm.

CHAPTER FIVE

G EORGE HAD SPENT the preceding sets half listening to what was said to him and half rehearsing what he would say to Miss Yardley to put her on her guard.

Apparently, Langley and his wife had no plans to set up a house of their own and would stay on with his parents. George thought it was deuced odd, but then they were an odd pair to begin. Seemingly happy with each other, but odd.

Lady Annabelle, who he'd really had no intention of approaching, had somehow practically handed him her card. Much to his relief, she had seemed to have given up her relentless fishing for compliments and only spoke of Mr. Pottsgrove, her new husband. It appeared that Mr. Pottsgrove provided plenty on the flattery side of things and George was also to know that he regularly assisted her upon her horse with one hand. George was not sure where the charm in that was, but equally sure Lady Annabelle was suitably satisfied by the habit.

Now he led Miss Yardley to their place on the ballroom floor and he could not avoid noticing the looks of envy from various gentlemen. He was particularly irritated to see Jacobs and his callow friends eyeing the lady. Jacobs was well-known as a hopeless flirt who had led more than one lady into that embarrassing state called disappointed hopes. He was also an inveterate gossip worse than anybody's spinster aunt. He was an irritating and immature person who had likely never done a kindness to anybody in his life, but he was rich and so mamas were always pushing their daughters forward. At least his aunt would have more sense.

Perhaps more worrying than Jacobs, Skeffington seemed to have his eye on Miss Yardley. That man was more subtle in his stares, and far more dangerous. It was well-known that Skeffington was currently hosting an actress in his very house and there had been some talk a few years back that he'd meddled with a government clerk's daughter. It was said he had charge of a ward somewhere that he paid shockingly little attention to. George thought that was very good news for the ward, whoever he or she was, as nothing suitable would ever be learned from that gentleman.

The quadrille commenced and he stood next to Miss Yardley awaiting their turn. Determined to do his duty, he said, "Miss Yardley, I hope you do not think me too direct, but I would wish you to understand that in London, a gentleman's attentions may signify nothing."

She turned sharply toward him and seemed shocked to hear it. Clearly, she had not considered the idea.

He nodded knowingly and was glad to have warned her. He'd gone back and forth on the idea of informing her of this fact, but now he felt confident he'd chosen correctly. It was well that she was now apprised of the dangers lurking round her.

GRACE HAD REHEARSED a speech in her mind that she would say at her first opportunity. She would allow Lord Gresham to understand that she knew her situation and did not read more into his attentions than were really there. He had done his aunt, and her, a kindness in agreeing to escort her into supper at her first ball. And a favor was all it had been taken for.

It must be said carefully and delicately to be able to get her exact point across. She was thankful, and yet not deluded. If she said it well, he would feel her appreciation of his courtesy without feeling as if she attempted to put it in a false light.

Now, she practically recoiled from him. How stupid she had been! She had taken him for a gentleman. Instead of waiting one blasted minute to be thanked for his courtesy, he'd rushed in to tell her that he assumed she *had* misread his attentions for actual interest and that she must give up the idea.

I would wish you to understand that in London, a gentleman's attentions may signify nothing. Indeed! And then he wondered if she would think him too direct!

She was insulted. She may have admired his person, but she had not given herself away. Of that, she was sure. It was not her actions that prompted him to warn her off, it was his own self-importance.

If she might say or do what she liked, she would have quite a lot to say to the gentleman now. She would disabuse him of his self-congratulations and help him to understand that not all the world adored him.

As it was, she could not say what she liked. She had been well-trained by her father. His counsel had always been to retain one's self-control and exact payment through composure. Composure, more than anything else, was a silent slap. It told the other party that one was so little affected by their opinion or action that one could not be bothered to react.

She would require every ounce of her composure at this moment. She would be calm and unruffled.

"Now that you've had a moment to parse my warning, you do see what I say?" Lord Gresham asked.

Good Lord! Now he was wondering if she had the mental acuity to understand words!

Grace felt her composure leaving her like a bird taking flight.

"Lord Gresham, I may have lived a life in the countryside, but I am not a dolt. Further, I would wish *you* to understand that, in the country and no doubt here, a *gentleman* may also delude himself into seeing admiration where there is none."

Lord Gresham seemed entirely confused and Grace was very tempted to inquire if he, himself, was having trouble understanding words. She did not, though. Her father had also taught her that sometimes it was just as satisfying to think a thing, as to say it.

"I am sure there might be cases of a gentleman misreading a lady's inclinations. I only think ladies are more...likely to be deceived, or to deceive themselves. I only say, you must be on your guard."

"Or what?" Grace said tersely.

Lord Gresham looked decidedly uncomfortable. Finally, he said, "Well, you might find yourself a victim of disappointed hopes, for instance."

This man's opinion of himself reached new heights with every sentence he uttered. Now, she risked disappointed hopes?

Grace worked to keep her expression a mask of serenity. "Consider me on my guard, Lord Gresham. Though, I find I have never been less disappointed in my life."

While Grace had aimed her arrow, it did not seem to pierce its target. Lord Gresham appeared oblivious to her meaning and only nodded.

Their time for the steps had arrived and he led her with confidence. Of course, he would do. A gentleman with such a favorable opinion of himself would hardly be put off by the quadrille.

"Excellent. Then I think that's all that need be said on the subject," Lord Gresham said.

She should rather think so. Far more had been said than had ever been needed.

Grace felt a fool for her prior admiration. She could, in part, excuse herself. He was devilishly handsome and that had not changed. She supposed she was not the first lady who had come to a conclusion based on a handsome face.

Perhaps there was a lesson in it going forward. She was not to allow her initial impressions of a gentleman to inform her opinion. She must wait and see what his real nature was, as it emerged. Of course, that was right. Many a fool or rogue had hidden themselves behind a handsome face and a well-cut coat.

As the dance went on, Lord Gresham's real nature continued to emerge before her eyes. He spoke of general pleasantries as if he'd not just told a lady that he was convinced she had set her cap on him and to try not to be disappointed to find it was unrequited.

Perhaps he had such conversations often. He did not seem to find anything unusual in it.

Grace was careful in her answers, lest she give the lord another reason to think she was besotted with him. When she did not speak, she silently repeated the word, *composure*.

>>><<<

LADY HEATHWAY FOUND herself both thrilled and worried. It was thrilling that her girl could not be denied. Grace was the loveliest girl in the room and the dress she had designed for her was, as Lady Featherstone had so aptly named it, a triumph. She'd seen it all in her mind's eye and now here it was, made real.

As her hearing was rather good, and as she was always interested in what other people were saying, she heard no end of snippets about Miss Yardley. A beauty, and very elegant, were most often heard. Sometimes a question—who was she? And then the delight of listening to the other party explain the Society of Sponsoring Ladies and that this was Lady Heathway's girl.

As her eyesight was as good as her hearing, she did not miss the occasional scowl of an unhappy mama. They had thought their daughter would be the most celebrated at the ball, but then they had been faced with the elegant Miss Yardley. Bits and bobs and fripperies had been defeated by lovely simplicity.

It was all rather heavenly.

However, not all her thoughts were to run to heaven. As she *was* so perceptive of what went on around her, she did not miss that there was some unwanted attention on Grace.

That scallywag Mr. Jacobs and his rude friends, for one. She really did not understand why Clara had even issued them invitations. She supposed Lady Easton had been pressured by some mama who had her eye on Mr. Jacobs's deep pockets for a daughter. That mama was a fool, as everybody knew Mr. Jacobs was perfectly happy to toy with affections and then joke about it in his club the next day. No lady he flirted with was safe, as the fellow had flapping lips and made a jest out of everything. He considered himself a wit, though he had not the style of Brummel nor the connections of Alvanley.

Thankfully, that young fool was not on Grace's card. Nor was the more serious worry—Lord Skeffington. How that man was allowed in any decent house was a mystery. He had ruined at least one young miss of the gentry and it was said there was currently an actress coming and going from his house. He had enough power to face it all down and she wondered if he would dare attempt to meddle with the daughter of a viscount. Even being seen in his company would not do Grace any favors.

Lady Heathway stared at Lord Skeffington as he watched Grace dance. Finally, she caught his attention and kept her stare, unflinching.

He quickly looked away, and she was sure she had embarrassed him. He had been warned. If he needed a firmer warning, he would get it. As it had ever been, men strolled forward, deluding themselves into thinking they held all the power. Anybody who crossed Penelope Prescott found out the truth of it, though. Anybody who dared upset her plans for Miss Yardley would find themselves dueling with a well-armed, deadly, and determined opponent.

As for Mr. Jacobs, she supposed there was no point in a staring contest. He would only make a joke out of it. She was near certain that it had been he who had first named her Lady Naysay.

On the other hand, as he *was* such a flighty fool, she doubted very much that Grace would have any use for him.

Perhaps he might make a joke about *that*.

>>>×<<<

RANSTON'S NERVES HAD been teetering on the edge of a cliff all evening. When the lord and lady were out at some entertainment, he was always on the watch for a break-in. He knew very well that thieves were everywhere and that they kept their eyes on various houses, waiting for their opportunity.

That there had not been an attempt to break in so far only meant the clock was ticking. Their luck could not hold forever.

Lady Heathway's carriage had not departed the house an hour before someone had banged on the door. He nearly fell over in apoplexy, until it occurred to him that a thief would probably not knock. It had been a fast messenger with a letter for Miss Yardley. No doubt from her mother, who he understood to be a malingerer of the highest order. He'd had a great wish to beat the fellow about the head for alarming him on such a night, but he'd instead taken the missive and put it on the silver salver in the hall and had a glass of brandy to steady his nerves.

Then, he heard a noise! It came from the back garden and was the distinct whine of the gate. For just a moment, he had a great urge to find a linen closet and repair there until the danger had passed.

He did not do it, though. He picked up his fowling piece and ran out into the night like any hardened soldier. All the while, his footmen chased after him, saying things like, "It was just that cat who comes over the gate every single night."

Innocent fools! They could not even perceive when danger was upon them!

He had planted himself next to the bank of rose bushes and cried out to the intruders. "I am armed and prepared to blow you to bits!"

There was no sound after that and he was satisfied he'd terrorized them and chased them off.

He spent a pleasant half hour considering his bold actions, until another idea began to form. Yes, the rogues had run away in abject terror in the face of his bravery. But didn't every gang of thieves have a leader? When those criminals returned to their den or hidey-hole or wherever criminals lived, would not their leader be enraged?

He'd send them back to finish the job.

Of course, he would. He wouldn't be the leader if he didn't.

The night was to be a long siege and Wilbert Ranston would be at the ready.

GEORGE SUPPOSED HE should have known there was no telling a young miss anything. He had helpfully spoken to Miss Yardley regarding the dangers of men like Jacobs and Skeffington. He had made her understand that not all attention from a gentleman was to mean anything. He had very sensibly put her on her guard.

One might have imagined that she'd be grateful for the hint. Instead, she'd become very cool.

He could not outright fault her words or behavior. She did not say anything he could point to. But it was there all the same. He supposed she thought she was not like other girls. That if the likes of Jacobs and Skeffington paid her marked attention it would certainly be sincere.

She was naïve if she thought so.

As Miss Yardley's dinner partner to her left had turned, she was forced to turn back to him. And, *forced* she did look.

"I can see perfectly well that you are unhappy with my hints," he said. "I am sorry for that, but I did consider it a duty to my aunt. I would have been remiss if I did not point it out."

Miss Yardley narrowed her eyes just the slightest bit and said, "There was nothing to point out, though. I think that is what you fail to comprehend."

Ah. So she did think herself special and worldly. It was too ridiculous.

"Perhaps not," he said, in an attempt to mollify. "But, a warning given and not needed is far preferable to a warning needed and not given. My aunt would be made deeply unhappy if there was any sort of talk."

"Then perhaps we ought to stop talking," she said, her smile not matching the coldness of her tone.

He really did not know what was to be done with such a girl. From afar, she was everything a lady should be. More, even. He did not think there was lady in the room who surpassed her looks. But now it was beginning to seem that...

Well...she was rather impossible.

⟫⟫⟩✕⟨⟨⟨

GRACE HAD NEVER had the experience of being insulted. And then insulted again. And then again. It had verged on the bizarre.

Lord Gresham sought to warn her off him and then continued on with it as if she had declared she would not give him up.

Somehow, he had convinced himself that she was unhappy that he could not return her affections, rather than being unhappy at his various insults.

What an outsized opinion of himself he did have.

Though she had counseled herself toward composure and had kept pretty well to it, she had allowed herself to say they ought to stop talking. She'd meant it, they really ought to stop talking.

And so they had, though she heard the occasional huff from that side. Not speaking gave her the opportunity to gaze round the room and she rather wished she had not. There was a gentleman seated some way down the table and across that persistently attempted to catch her eye. He was older, perhaps late thirties, and there was something in his manner she did not like. Then, there was the boisterous young gentleman who she was certain had winked at her in an off-puttingly sly manner.

She'd had such different ideas of what London would be like. She supposed she'd thought it would be like her own neighborhood, those friendly and kind people just transplanted into the town. But it was not like that. There was a harder edge to these people.

Now, she was in the carriage as Lady Heathway rattled off various people at the ball. Apparently, the boisterous young man was Mr. Jacobs and to be avoided. He was a flirt and a gossip. The gentleman who stared at her at dinner was Lord Skeffington and to be avoided. He was…just to be avoided. There was no particular harm in Mr. Vance, other than his grandfather was in trade, so not necessarily to be completely avoided but avoid an attachment.

Grace had a great urge to add one more to the list of those to be avoided. Lord Gresham was to be avoided. But then, he was her nephew and, in any case, there was no pause in Lady Heathway's diatribe to have said anything anyway.

She could not wait to be alone in her bedchamber, where she might finally put aside her composure and stamp her foot over the lord's effrontery.

The carriage had come to a stop in front of the house and much to Grace's surprise, Ranston came hurrying down the steps carrying a gun.

As he helped Lady Heathway down, and then Grace herself, he said, "My lady, I came to escort you into the house armed, as there has been a prowler in the back garden this night."

"A prowler!" Lady Heathway cried.

They were hurried into the house as Ranston told of the diabolical whine of the gate and his daring charge into the garden. This harrowing tale was occasionally peppered with comments from the footmen, who were convinced a stray cat had made the noise.

Grace was inclined to believe the footmen, as she'd been already apprised of Ranston's peculiar belief that the house would be robbed at any moment. Any sort of sound might have confirmed to him that it was in the offing.

She could not divine what Lady Heathway made of it, but while Ranston was outlining his plan to patrol the house until dawn, Grace spotted a letter lying on a silver tray. The handwriting was distinct. It was from her mother.

Grace casually walked over and slipped it into the inside pocket of her pelisse. Lady Heathway would not be pleased to see it there and might perhaps even confiscate it. But it *was* her letter.

"My lady," Ranston said, "rest assured I will guard this house to my last breath. My piece is loaded, I will standby for Lord Heathway arriving home from his club, and I will protect the house until the safety of the glorious sun has risen once more."

Lady Heathway nodded. "Well, it *is* England, Ranston, so don't pin all your hopes on the sun making an appearance. Now, it's nearly three already. If you find yourself feeling a bit on edge, do have a lie-down."

GRACE HAD REACHED her room. Betsy had come in and helped her out of her dress while recounting what had gone on in the house while they had been at the ball. Mr. Ranston had been ready to fire in any and all directions. No sound was too small to be ignored.

At Barlow Hall, when the family went out it was a lovely evening of chatting and cards and an extra glass of wine from Manfred. *Here*, they'd been forced to get their clubs from under their beds and wait silently for the assault on the house while the butler strode through the rooms like a madman.

Grace thought it was very gracious of Lady Heathway to indulge such a fellow, but not exactly comfortable for anybody below stairs.

She had removed her mother's letter from the pocket of her pelisse and laid it on the dressing table. Betsy had noted it and shook her head. "I hope Lady Barlow does less poorly than when I saw her last. The poor dove always did have a delicate constitution. She took to her bed for a month every winter, if I recollect, with a weakness complaint."

Grace had nodded, as Betsy's recollection was entirely accurate. After the holidays, Lady Barlow would inevitably retreat to her bed for at least a month to regain her strength. Grace had always thought the activities of the season, which she quite enjoyed, wore her person down. Then, the subsequent absence of parties wore her spirit down.

Betsy left the room, closing the door behind her. Finally, Grace was alone with her thoughts.

She did throw over her composure and stamp her foot once or twice, but found she did not get much satisfaction from it. The ball had not been as she'd thought it would be. There had been some pleasant moments, to be sure. Mr. Vance had been entertaining, and Grace sensed in him a fine gentleman, despite the concerns over his gunmaker grandfather. Lord Bertridge and Lord Blackwood too, were gentlemen she was pleased to know.

However, there had been not so pleasant moments. The awkwardness of being stared at by Lord Skeffington at dinner. One might take it a compliment to be so singled out, but it had not felt like a compliment. Then, Mr. Jacobs and…was it a wink? She thought so. Whatever it was, it had somehow seemed underhanded.

But most of all, Lord Gresham.

She had so looked forward to dancing with him. She had spent so much time rehearsing what she would say about Lady Heathway forcing him into it. She would make him understand that *she* understood. Then, they could start again on equal footing. Then, he could ask her at some other ball of his own volition. Or not ask her, as the case might be.

If she were honest with herself, she'd hoped he would ask.

Instead, she had been told in no uncertain terms that her interest was not welcome. If her cheeks had not flamed a thousand shades of red over the course of the dance and supper, she would be very much surprised.

She must stop thinking about it. About him, in particular. It had been her first experience of thinking well of someone, and perhaps hoping for more, and finding herself rebuffed. It stung. It stung deeply. But she must not be so arrogant as to think it was the last time it might happen to her. She would just be better prepared next time.

In any event, there was no possibility that another uninterested gentleman could possibly convey his feelings in as rude a manner as he had done.

She was determined to put the whole matter aside. Her mother had written a letter and she must discover what it said. She dearly hoped it was not another bid to come to Town as she well knew Lady Heathway would not agree to it.

Grace tore open the paper.

My dear daughter,

Sir Henry has been to see me, and nearly drained all the blood from me. Or so it feels. I fear he has little to offer in the way of help as these walls continue to oppress me and I am weaker than ever. The nurse Lady Heathway has sent is an uncaring beast of a woman. I am not to eat what I want or when I want, she insists on waking me at dawn and dragging me on long walks. My dear darling, you know how walking tires me! She even opens the windows in my bedchamber to let in the "fresh air" though I have told her repeatedly that it is the air that is the very problem.

I pray you are finding amusement in Town and that we will someday be together again. I miss you terribly.

Your mother

Grace dropped the letter and it fluttered to the floor. She felt a seething anger growing in her. It was outrageous that her mother should be treated so! Not allowed to eat what she wished? Woken at dawn? Force-marched like a common soldier?

She must rectify the situation at once.

CHAPTER SIX

G RACE REREAD THE letter, and the rereading did nothing to comfort her. Lady Barlow was being treated abominably. She could easily see how it had unfolded—the nurse had at once perceived the delicate nature of her mother and rode roughshod over her.

Grace fully understood that her mother was not as strong as might be wished. Not in body, and not in mind. One might even lay the blame for her ills at her own door. Her mother might have made more effort over the years. Or at least more effort when they'd been forced into the dower house. But, the fact was that she was weak, she was not in good health, and nobody had the right to treat her like a prisoner! It was too unkind.

Grace snatched the letter from the floor and tied her robe. She was certain Lady Heathway would still be awake and she must make arrangements to leave first thing in the morning. She would go to Kent and remedy this ghastly situation. She would hire a trustworthy nurse. None of it should take above a week, but she *would* see that her mother was made comfortable.

She softly knocked on Lady Heathway's door. When she was admitted, she found the lady in curl papers and already in bed.

"I am sorry to disturb you, my lady, I know you must be very tired," Grace said.

"What is it, my dear?" Lady Heathway said, sounding alarmed. "You have not heard a sound down below? I was certain it was only Ranston's nerves provoking him, but then one never knows—he's bound to be right one of these days."

"No, it has nothing to do with Ranston's fears of a break in. It is my mother—"

"Your mother is well taken care of, your mind may be at ease on that point."

"But indeed, she is not," Grace said, handing over the letter. "This was on the tray in the hall when we arrived home. She does very poorly."

Lady Heathway perused the letter and let out a long sigh. "Your mother's complaints are all nonsense," she said. "The best is being done for her—you must trust in my judgment in this matter. Now, you are overtired. Go to bed and things will seem far less dire in the morning. Depend upon it. Off you go."

With that, she was dismissed.

As Grace walked back to her room, she felt herself bristle. It was all very highhanded! Who were these people, that they could dictate how her mother was to be treated? Lady Heathway even hinted, and not for the first time, that there was nothing at all wrong with Lady Barlow. Whatever her mother's situation, or whether it was self-inflicted or not, the lady did not flourish.

Something must be done. *She* must do something. Who else did her mother have to depend on but her daughter?

As she closed her bedchamber door behind her, an idea came to her. She drifted to the window and peered out at the drainpipe that led to the pavement. The sun would rise in two hours, maybe sooner.

She might dress herself, go down the pipe and to the end of the street to the stables. It would, of course, be far more sensible to go out the door, but Ranston was still downstairs, pacing the front hall and prepared to fight off thieves. She had just heard him explaining to the arriving Lord Heathway that he had fended off an unseen attacker in the garden. The Lord did not seem too concerned to hear it, but was perfectly agreeable if the butler wished to keep watch. Ranston would tell Lady Heathway of her departure before she was halfway down the street.

If she left by way of drainpipe, however, she could rouse the stables and tell them she required both a horse and a groom. She would be safe enough in daylight and accompanied. The route was straightforward, and it was not so very far. She could decide what to do once she arrived to the dower house. The nurse would be dismissed, and she would send a note back to Lady Heathway with the groom.

Yes, that was what she should do. She was tired of being managed and she would not allow any of these people to turn her from what she knew to be right. Her mother was mistreated by a bully of a nurse and had called for help to her only daughter. She would not ignore it. She would not betray her mother in such a fashion.

>>><<<

GEORGE HAD STOPPED at his club on the way back from Lady Easton's ball. He had never sat through such an uncomfortable and interminable supper in his life. He found, at the blessed end of it, that he required a stronger drink than Lady Easton provided.

He had not been alone in the idea, as he'd seen Jacobs and his friends there too. He'd avoided them by going into the pool room, but then when he was set to leave, it seemed they were too. He'd dallied to avoid accompanying them as he was sure they went in the same direction. Jacobs's house was nearby Berkeley Square and seemed to be where they all convened until they were too exhausted to carry on further.

After letting them have a good head start, he set off for his own house.

The more he mulled over his conversations with Miss Yardley, the more muddled they seemed. Why had she been so prickly? He'd only been trying to give her a hint because...well because she *was* very lovely and would attract both the right sort of men and the wrong sort of men.

Jacobs and Skeffington were most definitely the wrong sort.

Bertridge seemed rather taken with her, and he of course would be the *right* sort of gentleman. Bertridge never put a foot out of place. Whoever had dreamed up the word *sensible* had been thinking of Bertridge. And yet, George thought he would not be quite right for Miss Yardley. Not the wrong sort, exactly, just not the definitely right sort.

And she was, after all, very lovely.

But why should any of it be his concern? The lady was very fortunate, having been rescued from poverty by his aunt. If she chose to squander the chance on some feckless individual, why should that concern him?

He could not say, he could only notice that he *was* concerned.

George turned the corner and reined in his horse at the sight of the activity ahead of him.

He squinted his eyes, certain his first glance was mistaken.

Was he drunk? Or was Miss Yardley just now sliding down a drainpipe while Jacobs and his friends watched, and his aunt's butler waved a gun?

GRACE HAD POKED her head out the window to be certain she would not be spotted. The street had been quiet in the early dawn.

She had donned her riding habit and had almost hesitated. It was a mad plan, she knew well enough. Was she being too hasty? Too dramatic? Too foolish?

Perhaps all of those things. But foolish or not, she had a duty to her mother and she could not very well ignore a cry for help. She had done the sensible thing first—she had gone to Lady Heathway. Getting nowhere with that, though, forced her to do the not very sensible thing.

Firm in her resolve, she'd hitched her skirt and climbed out.

As she made her way down the side of the house, the sudden sound of horses' hooves trotting on the cobbles pierced the silence of early dawn. A group of gentlemen on horseback had rounded the corner and were making their way down the street. Grace stayed still, pressed against the stone of the house and hoping they would not notice her.

The trotting slowed, and then ceased. They had reined in their horses. As there seemed to be a deal of laughing, it became clear enough that they *had* noticed her and had no intention of moving on. So be it, they could not stop her, and in any case were probably so drunk that when they sobered up they would not be sure what they'd actually seen. It was not as if she could change her mind and go back up—down was the only direction she had strength for.

She continued her descent, ignoring the idea that she now had an audience. Reaching her foot down to the next brace, she put her weight on it and it gave way with a very loud scraping sound.

She reached her now dangling foot for the next below, praying it was sturdier. As she did so, the doors below slammed open and she heard a very loud shout. "Ah hah! I knew it, you rogue!"

A moment later, a bullet whizzed by her head.

Did Ranston just try to shoot her?

Heavens above, he had. The butler was completely mad. And she was in danger of another bullet coming her way if he could reload fast enough.

"Mr. Ranston," she called to him, "it is only me. Grace Yardley."

She let go of her handhold and reached for the next. She missed it and felt herself flying through the air. She landed with a thud into the shrubbery.

Grace was stunned for a moment. Her head slowly began to clear as she assessed the damage. She did not seem to have broken anything, but it began to dawn on her that perhaps broken bones would have been the least of her problems anyway.

The men on horseback were roaring with laughter. Ranston was loudly weeping in despair. A window opened above her and Grace could just make out Lady Heathway in her curl papers. Worse, Lord Gresham's face suddenly appeared above her own. "Miss Yardley?"

This had not been one of her better executed plans.

GEORGE HAD PULLED Miss Yardley from the shrubbery, chased off Jacobs and his drunken friends, walked Ranston into the house and given him a large brandy, met his aunt flying down the stairs, and waved to his uncle who peered over the banister. He had, he hoped, managed to get the doors shut before curious neighbors poked their heads out of their windows at the sound of a gunshot.

Now, they were all in the library. Ranston stared into his now empty glass and muttered, "I thought it was an intruder, how could I know it was Miss Yardley? How could I have foreseen that she would be hanging from the side of the house? Nobody told me she might be hanging from the side of the house!"

"Ranston," Lady Heathway said, "you must calm yourself. Take comfort in the knowledge that your aim is not very good and calamity has been avoided."

Ranston did not look particularly comforted by that idea and only held out his glass for more brandy. George refilled it and hoped a second dose would steady the fellow.

Much to his amazement, Miss Yardley looked neither shaken by the experience, nor abashed to have been caught hanging onto a drainpipe, nor concerned that the skirt of her riding habit was ripped in several places. Rather, she said, "I am sorry to have inconvenienced everyone, but it is necessary that I go to my mother immediately. It is true I took an unusual route out of the house, but I did not see another option."

Lord Heathway said, "But what were you planning to do, my dear? You did not intend to ride there alone?"

"Oh no," Grace said, "I would take a groom."

How sensible! She would take a groom. She had climbed down the side of the house like a housebreaker, but never fear! She would take a groom. Really, the girl was incomprehensible.

"Grace," Lady Heathway said, "I know your mother complains of her treatment, but she *is* being treated. Sir Henry says that walking, hearty bland food, and fresh, cool air are necessary for her recovery. And in fact, Lady Barlow has increased in strength despite all of her complaining." Lady Heathway paused for a moment, then said, "I ought to have told you that when you came to me tonight with her letter. I take some responsibility for this; I should have seen how her letter had upset you and informed you of the real case of things."

Miss Yardley seemed to consider this. She said, "Sir Henry really believes she is getting stronger?"

"He does," Lady Heathway said. "I will show you his letter when we retire above stairs. She is able to walk much further than when the nurse started with her, her appetite has increased on account of it, and her complaints have gotten louder, which Sir Henry does not consider a bad sign."

"I wish I had known," Miss Yardley said quietly. "I do know that sometimes my mother may be prone to exaggerate, but her letter did sound so dire, she did sound so mistreated, as if she were being held as a prisoner. She has nobody else."

"I sought to protect you from unpleasant matters," Lady Heathway said, "and perhaps that has turned out to be a mistake. But really, Grace, I cannot think what possessed you to climb out a window. I must insist nothing like it ever occur again."

Miss Yardley nodded, though George did not take this to be the hearty agreement they all might have hoped for.

Lady Heathway waved her hands and said, "Then we'll say no more about it."

George had listened, rather fascinated, to this conversation.

One never knew how Lady Heathway would choose to view a thing. Let Lady Easton serve white soup and he would hear about it for days in consequence of her violent opinions about almonds. But let Miss Yardley climb down the side of the house and she'd *say no more about it?*

She might think there was nothing more to be said, but he had a few things to add. "*We* may say no more about it, but Jacobs witnessed the entire episode—you can be sure he will say plenty about it. We could very well be on the precipice of a scandal."

Miss Yardley looked curiously at him. "But I don't think he would—"

"You don't think he would...what? Tell all and sundry what he viewed? Devise a few bon mots to go along with it? Add and embellish for his own amusement?" George said heatedly. "He will do all of those things."

Miss Yardley flinched, as if she had been stung. He hadn't meant to have such an effect, but she was so naïve! Of course it would be talked of. What else did people like Jacobs do but be always looking about to find something to laugh at?

For the first time since this ghastly adventure began, Lady Heathway looked exceedingly shaken. "I hadn't considered...what will the ladies say..."

Lord Heathway, unwilling that his butler drink absolutely all of his brandy, had poured himself a glass. "Well now, Penelope, you know your friends—they have something to say about everything. However, as it is their precious society involved, I suggest you close ranks and face it down. That Jacobs fellow, rich as he is, is only the son of a baron. You are a marchioness and Theodosia is a duchess—that ought to do it."

"Yes," Lady Heathway murmured, "close ranks. Theodosia will be the most helpful. The rest are not particularly fit for battle, but Theodosia *is* and her duke will do whatever she asks. And you, my dear nephew, you will join us in the fight?"

George did not know precisely what his aunt was proposing,

but felt both his aunt's and Miss Yardley's stares keenly.

"You might get him blackballed from White's?" Lady Heathway asked hopefully.

"That would be the last thing we should do," George said. "At the moment, he is feeling jolly with a jolly story to tell. A blackball would turn him from amused to enraged. My advice is, simply deny. He and his friends did not see what they saw. Some will believe you, some won't, but it will give them all a way to side with you. And my uncle is right, you are a marchioness—most will not wish to cause you too much trouble."

"That is right," Lady Heathway said. "I am a marchioness. I must remember that I am more powerful than that little bug of a mister. If he goes too far, I will crush him under my heel."

"That's the spirit," Lord Heathway said.

"It's nearly daybreak," Lady Heathway said. "We'd all best retire. Ranston, stay abed tomorrow—do not allow your nerves to get ahead of you."

George thought that might be good advice for everybody as he saw rough waters coming toward them all. He was, as he always seemed to be, rather confused by Miss Yardley. What lady even thought to climb down a drainpipe? Had she really been intending to ride to Kent with only a groom? It was madness. And not at all what a blushing and stammering miss would dare to attempt. When he had accompanied his aunt to Kent, he'd been certain they would bring back a blushing and stammering miss. What *had* they brought back?

Whether he understood her or not, one thing was clear: he could not predict what she would do next. He had a mind to put a watch on the house to ensure that no further bizarre escapes were attempted. They were to be a laughingstock for the foreseeable future, but there was no need to add further fuel to the fire.

GRACE RETURNED TO her room exhausted, but with Sir Henry's letter in hand. She struggled out of her ripped riding habit and into her nightdress, and then curled up in bed to read it.

My dearest Lady Heathway,

I am writing to update you on the treatments ongoing of Lady Barlow in Kent. As is so often the case, the lady in question has been opposed to every single remedy. How else do they suppose they got themselves as weak as a baby but by following their own inclinations? However, Nurse Maddington is made of stern stuff and drives the lady forward to good effect. At the beginning, Lady Barlow was barely able to walk twenty steps, now she is capable of above two hundred yards. Nurse Maddington reports that while the diet is complained of, most certainly Lady Barlow has gained in weight. As for the windows being opened, while the lady claims the air is somehow deadly to her, in fact she has regained a rosiness in her cheeks. Those windows are promptly opened at the reasonable hour of ten in the morning, which of course the lady claims is still the middle of the night. As for all the complaining she does, which the nurse says is at any moment that she is awake, it may be tedious but I do not perceive it a bad sign. Those who are too far gone generally don't have the strength to complain very much. You were right to put me on the case, as her country doctor is terrified of her and allows her to direct what his opinions are.

I currently categorize this case as: positive outlook.

Sir Henry

Grace let go of the paper and it fluttered to the coverlet. Both her mother and Sir Henry confirmed one another, they just had vastly different opinions of the facts. On the one hand, she did not like that her mother was made unhappy. But on the other hand, it did sound as if she was improving. Grace had carried so little hope that her mother would get stronger and now it seemed she was. Perhaps this was a case of she did not like it, but it was for her own good?

It must be so; Sir Henry was unlikely to fabricate to Lady Heathway.

Perhaps she ought to write her mother an encouraging letter to continue on with what she was being asked to do, even though it was not entirely comfortable.

After the facts of the letter sank in, Grace began to reflect on what else had occurred this night. She had, at first, only been disappointed that she had not gotten away, and a bit terrified that Ranston had taken a shot at her. She'd gone out the window to avoid his prowling downstairs but had never imagined he would come outside and shoot at her.

And then there was the fact that Mr. Jacobs and his friends had witnessed it all.

And Lord Gresham, for that matter.

Oh, how she wished it had not been him staring down at her while she lay sprawled in the shrubbery! And then he had been so sharp with her when she'd suggested that Mr. Jacobs would not tell the tale far and wide. No, in fact she'd not even got that far. He'd cut her off and informed her of precisely what Mr. Jacobs would do.

On top of the lord imagining she had somehow set her cap on him and must be dissuaded, she now appeared entirely ridiculous! A fool who was set on embarrassing Lady Heathway.

Oh, and poor Lady Heathway. What had she brought upon that lady? She must be grateful that the dear woman had been kind about it, though it would strike her deeply to be laughed at.

Grace quietly groaned. She'd meant to slip out of the house and be off, but instead she had made a spectacle of herself. And a spectacle of Lord and Lady Heathway too. And even Lord Gresham, she supposed.

There was a soft knock on the door and then it swung slowly open. Betsy poked her head in, and seeing she was awake, entered the room.

"I had to come and see with my own two eyes that you were still alive," Betsy said.

"Very much alive," Grace said. "I have only been busy humiliating myself."

Betsy let out a long and slow breath. "Things is topsy-turvy in the servants' quarters. We was all woken by Mr. Ranston wailing in the men's quarters. Mrs. Redwiggin went to investigate and now she swears that Mr. Ranston tried to shoot you off the side of the house and he's so undone over it that he'll stay abed for days."

Grace only nodded.

Betsy said, "Gracious. He *did* shoot at you. I thought it might just be his fevered imagination. But what was you doing on the side of the house? You never did think to elope with some fella?"

Grace sat up straight at even the hint of such a thing. "Goodness, no! Please correct anyone below stairs who says so." She got a sinking feeling that theory might be thought by more than Betsy. It might take hold in society, an idea that Lady Heathway had likely not even considered.

Betsy's eye traveled to Grace's ripped riding habit and whispered, "What was you doing?"

Grace sighed and said, "Lady Barlow wrote me a letter and appeared to need me, so…"

Betsy nodded knowingly. "You was going to run to her."

Grace nodded.

"Aye, Lady Barlow never did well on her own. She's the kind of lady, if you don't mind me sayin,' that my ma used to call a flower on the wilt what needs a lot of watering. Well, I suppose all's well that ends well."

"I do hope it ends well," Grace said, "but I am not convinced of it."

Betsy picked up the skirt of the riding habit. "I'll see if this can be cleaned and mended. Meanwhile, I'll slip downstairs and pour you a nip of sherry to put things right."

Grace did not answer. She was not certain there was enough sherry in the world to put things right.

CHAPTER SEVEN

T HOUGH GRACE HAD remained abed until noon, Lady Heathway had been up and planning before the clock struck eight. She had sent emergency missives to all the ladies of the society—she required their attendance in her drawing room at four o'clock sharp.

When Grace had come into the drawing room, looking very down in the mouth unfortunately, Penelope had set her on some sewing. Then, at half past three, she'd packed her into a carriage with her maid so the air might lift her spirits. The coachman was directed to drive round the park until at least five.

In truth, she wished the girl well away from the house during her meeting with the other ladies. She could not know what would be said and would not wish for Grace to overhear anything less than complimentary. In a disaster such as this, spirit would be everything. She would need Grace to be chin up and confident. Or, as confident as one *could* be after sliding down a drainpipe and being shot at.

Now that the appointed hour approached, she found her resolve firm. Penelope Prescott would overcome this minor setback. She was not a marchioness in name only, she was a marchioness in resolution and perseverance too.

She had removed herself from the drawing room and went above stairs to her bedchamber to peer out the window. She would not see her friends until they were all gathered, as she had no wish to repeat the story five separate times. In truth, she had no wish to repeat it ever, though it must be done at least once.

A footman had been directed to set up the tea, as Ranston was still weeping in his room over almost murdering his mistresses' houseguest. Theodosia had already arrived, and Penelope was all confidence that she would manage the serving, as the duchess felt her title empowered her to take over anybody's drawing room but for the queen's own. Nobody understood where she'd got such a notion, but it would be convenient at this very moment.

The last carriage finally pulled up. There was Lady Redfield, looking around as if she were about to be set upon by footpads. For some reason, Penelope's unanticipated summons always had the effect of discomposing the lady—she looked as nervous as a cat who wondered where the dog was hiding.

Penelope pulled in a breath, rose, shook out her skirts, and prepared to run the gauntlet otherwise known as her friends.

BEFORE LADY HEATHWAY had even got to the drawing room door, the voices reached her in the hall.

Lady Easton said, "Apparently, it is the talk of every club! My nephew says Miss Yardley was absolutely clinging to the side of the house in a riding habit at five o'clock in the morning."

"But did Lord Bertridge say anything about the shot?" the duchess said. "My son claims Ranston was out firing his gun at her like a madman. Why should he wish to kill Miss Yardley?"

"Why should she be clinging to the outside of the house?" Lady Easton asked.

"I think we may be getting ahead of ourselves," Lady Featherstone said. "We must examine all the clues. I conferred with Lord Ryland on the street just now. Gresham himself claims none of it even happened, though Lord Ryland claims that mysterious. He says stories may be embellished but are not likely to appear out of thin air."

"Lord Ryland thinks everything is a mystery," the duchess

said, with some asperity.

"If you mean to hint that you do not approve of my membership in Lord Ryland's criminal society, I am quite immune to it, Theodosia," Lady Featherstone said with a huff.

"I never hint, my dear," the duchess said, in a tone that really said, *And I have won the point.*

Lady Heathway girded herself and strode in. "Ladies, thank you for coming on such short notice. I will apprise you of the real facts, and then we will decide what to do about it."

As Lady Heathway did lay out the facts, the expressions on her friends' faces were not encouraging. Nor were their rather breathless comments.

Precisely how often did Lady Redfield intend to clutch at her neck and whisper, "Goodness!"

Was not one, "She did what?" quite enough from Lady Easton?

Did Lady Mendleton really have the nerve to just say, "I am only glad Georgiana never thought to climb out a window."

At least the duchess did not seem to be overcome by the tale. She set down her teacup and said, "There is no point in us fanning ourselves over this...escapade. We must stand together and protect the reputation of the society, and therefore the reputation of Miss Yardley, and therefore ourselves. We are the most powerful women of the *ton*. Oh, I know the Almack's patronesses like to think they lead in some way, but what a collection! Most of their relations cannot bear close scrutiny and everybody knows it. Further, they are forever squabbling amongst one another. We present a united front and so Lady Jersey can spout off all she likes, Lady Castlereagh can buy another tiger over it, Lady Cowper can pretend she is not having a dalliance with Lord Palmerston, and the rest are not even worth mentioning."

Penelope nodded encouragingly. The duchess always became enraged when she thought of the patronesses and their airs.

"Precisely my thoughts," Lady Heathway said. "We act as one force, as we always have done. Now, I believe I am to understand the gossip flies already?"

The ladies nodded reluctantly.

"I gather that what we know so far," Lady Heathway said, "is it is talked of that Miss Yardley climbed down a drainpipe in her riding habit and Ranston shot at her. It is imperative we know everything that is being said in order to combat it. Has anybody heard anything else? Anything at all?"

As Lady Heathway gazed round the table, her eyes stopped and settled on Lady Redfield. That lady twisted her handkerchief into knots and stared out the window as if she saw something frightening out there.

"Out with it, Cecilia," the duchess commanded, deducing just as quickly that Lady Redfield *had* heard something else.

"Oh dear," Lady Redfield said quietly. "I so little like to upset anybody. Well, I did hear, how shall I say it, what I mean is, how shall I put it..."

The duchess stared her down and said, "For the love of heaven, put it any way you like, but put it some way."

Lady Redfield took in a deep breath, as if she would need extra air on account of upsetting people. "All right. I heard that perhaps Miss Yardley was attempting to elope?"

Lady Redfield gripped the sides of her chair to brace herself against the stunned silence that surrounded her. Pressing on, she said, "And, that awful Jacobs fellow has named her..."

"Named her?" Lady Heathway said, the dread settling over her like a shroud. Once a person was named, it was near impossible to shake it loose. She, herself, would be *Lady Naysay* forevermore, Lady Jersey would be *Silence*, Lord Melrose would be *Lord Short Pockets*. People even sometimes remembered that all those many years ago, Lord Mendleton had been named *Break-A-Leg-Benjamin*. Penelope was certain *that* one had only faded because it was attached to an event—Lady Brathwaite had broken her leg on his too-polished stairs. But, let a name be a personal adjective and it seemed to stick.

"Yes, well," Lady Redfield hurried on, "it is not so very terrible a name, I do not think."

"But what is it," Lady Easton asked. "You must tell us what it is."

"Oh, yes, that," Lady Redfield said, her cheeks flaming. *"The Sprinter,* is what I was told."

The Sprinter? Good Lord, what did it mean? Did it hint at an elopement? If people thought Grace was attempting to elope, the story would have wings. The speculation would go on and on over who the gentleman was. There was nothing the *ton* liked so much as to speculate on a hidden romance.

"A disaster," Lady Easton said.

"A fiasco," the duchess said.

"A debacle," Lady Featherstone said.

"A calamity, I was thinking?" Lady Redfield said hopefully.

"I am only glad my Georgiana did not think to climb out a window," Lady Mendleton said, shaking her head sadly.

Lady Heathway drew in a breath. She must keep her mind on the task at hand and not on her wish to beat Louisa about the head if she mentioned her unimpeachable new daughter-in-law one more time.

"This may be a steeper hill to climb than I had first imagined," Lady Heathway said. "But nothing is impossible, not for *us.* Our reputations are unsurpassed. We have founded a society that must be defended. What we need, at this moment, is a plan."

Most in the room looked fairly lost, leading ladies of London though they might be. But the duchess nodded in agreement. "A very forceful plan," she said. "And I believe I know just what we must do."

Lady Heathway breathed a sigh of relief that *somebody* knew what was to be done, as she had not the first idea.

GRACE HAD NOT particularly wished to go out in the carriage, but

Lady Heathway was determined about it. She insisted the fresh air would do Grace good.

She'd woken up in the morning embarrassed and had lingered in her bedchamber until she thought she could not any longer. Embarrassment was a feeling she was not very accustomed to. She had been foolish and then gone ahead and done something remarkably foolish. She'd had her reasons, of course, but it did not appear those reasons had held up under further scrutiny. She had been bristling over Lord Gresham and then bristling over Lady Heathway's dismissiveness and certain her mother was being held as a prisoner.

However, a person hearing the tale would not know the first thing about her reasons. What would she, herself, think, if she heard the tale told of some other lady?

By the by, did you hear that Miss So-and-So was recently hanging like a vine on the outside of her house in the early dawn? Yes, it appears she then evaded a bullet coming her way and promptly collapsed into a stand of bushes. I suppose she had her reasons...

As the carriage meandered through the park, Betsy had tried to cheer her by commenting that she could not be the first lady who'd climbed out a window and been shot at.

She wished that were true, but she rather thought she might be.

Lady Heathway had sent them out in the barouche with the top down as the day was particularly warm. Grace sometimes got the feeling, as they passed people by, that she was being stared at. Certainly, it was her imagination. She had not the first idea of what would be said of her adventure the night before, but whatever it was, it could not possibly have been said so soon.

Nevertheless, she kept her eyes straight ahead and avoided making eye contact.

"Is that Lord Gresham?" Betsy said. "Aye, it's him, neckcloth as smart as ever. Mrs. Redwiggin says his valet is very famous. In valet circles."

At the mention of Lord Gresham, Grace felt her heart pick up its beat. She had been doing her absolute best to avoid thinking of the scolding she'd heard from him the night before. It had said so much about his opinion of her—she was foolish and naïve. She was further stung by the suspicion that he was right.

She followed Betsy's glance, though she had not intended to. She had for a moment thought they might pass each other by and pretend they did not see one another. He would probably prefer it. But, her eyes had drifted of their own accord.

He was mounted on a large bay who had rather wild eyes, as if he was anticipating the signal to gallop. Betsy had told no tales regarding his person. His jacket was a dark green wool, and he wore buckskins and marvelously polished hessians. His valet would be well-able to retain his position at the top of the valet circles—his neckcloth was done meticulously.

She really did wish he was not quite as handsome as he was. He was very hard not to admire! Even if he *were* constantly insulting her.

Grace had a wistful feeling steal over her when she thought of when he had stepped into the room of all things at Barlow House, entirely unknown to her. She, at that moment, was equally unknown to him. When she had come down the stairs after Lady Heathway had sent her up to pack, she had flattered herself that he'd given her an admiring glance. She admitted to herself that she had not been at all opposed to it.

But now, all of that unknowingness, that newness that might have gone in any direction, had gone in quite the bad direction. Some of it was his fault and some her own, but regardless of who lay at fault, it was a shame. And if she were to look at things in a cold, hard light, her performance of last night must surpass anything rude he'd said. He had only offended *her*; she may have offended all of society.

Lord Gresham reined in his horse. "Miss Yardley," he said, "I trust you do well today?"

Grace nodded. "Lord Gresham. I ought to thank you for your assistance last night."

He seemed to brush off the idea and said, "I have given the matter more thought."

Why? Why must he think more about it? Certainly it would be better if he did not think any further than he already had done.

"I find I cannot entirely condemn a daughter's wish to answer the call of a distressed mother, even if the notion was misguided. And the means...unfortunate."

"I did not know what else to do," Grace said. "It seemed an emergency, I felt I must act quickly."

"So I understand. I just pray there is not to be a repeat of the escapade."

Grace could feel the heat on her cheeks. He always managed to go a step too far. He had begun so pleasant and now they were back to scolding.

"May I speak freely in front of your maid?"

Betsy, to Grace's amusement, appeared entirely affronted. As if there could never be any secrets kept from her.

"Betsy has been with me for years and is well-acquainted with the events of last evening."

Betsy nodded vigorously. "If I may say so, my lord, you shouldn't harry Miss Yardley 'bout climbing out the window. Mr. Ranston was downstairs creepin' round with a gun and her ma is a wilting flower that needs lots of water. Everybody knows it."

"That is perhaps enough for now, Betsy," Grace said.

"I cannot say if *everybody* knows it," Lord Gresham said, staring at Betsy as if she were a unique specimen, "but now I know it." He patted his horse's neck and said to Grace, "There is, unfortunately, already talk of what occurred."

Already? Why would people be so interested in what she was doing last night? Whether that be reading quietly or slipping down a drainpipe? Did they not have other things to think about?

As soon as Grace thought those things, she realized how foolish were those hopeful ideas. In her neighborhood at home, news of the smallest occurrence traveled from one drawing room to the next like a flock of birds settling on a recently-harvested grain field. Last Christmas season, at a moment when nothing else in particular was in the offing, Mr. Stanfield's new horse had been discussed for a month.

"What-ho!" a voice nearly shouted from behind the carriage. Lord Gresham's expression instantly darkened.

Grace turned her head to see Mr. Jacobs trotting up.

She turned back just as quick and hoped he had been calling to somebody else.

"Miss Yardley," he said, trotting alongside the carriage and tipping his hat. "Gresham."

Lord Gresham did not answer, and nor did Grace. Why was the gentleman stopped to speak to them? Had he not already caused her enough difficulty? Certainly, it was he who had spread the tale so quickly. He had been one of the gentlemen so amused by the sight of her coming down the drainpipe and she already understood he was an inveterate gossip.

"We were not formally introduced last evening, but I pray it was sufficient under the unusual circumstances. I trust you have recovered from your daring descent?" Mr. Jacobs said, with an unpleasant curl to his lip.

"We have no idea of what you speak, Jacobs," Lord Gresham said sternly. "Perhaps you were the worse for drink and have begun imagining things."

Mr. Jacobs raised a brow. "So that's the game, eh?"

"There is no game, and as for your *own* games, careful you do not go too far one day or you may find yourself on a green at dawn. You have not been introduced to the lady, nor will you be. The marchioness finds you distasteful, as do I, and there will be no cause to approach Miss Yardley again. Now move off, if you please." Lord Gresham said.

Grace felt near-paralyzed. Lord Gresham's expression was enraged and his voice was low and deadly.

Mr. Jacobs only shrugged. He turned his horse and said over his shoulder, "A green at dawn? You are far too serious, Gresham. Good day to you, Miss Sprinter."

"I apologize, on his behalf," Lord Gresham said, watching Mr. Jacobs' departure. "He is a coward who thinks a great deal of himself until he is challenged on the idea."

"Miss Sprinter," Grace said softly.

"Unfortunately, yes," Lord Gresham said. "But all you can do is face it down. My aunt will no doubt be an effective ally."

"As you have been. I thank you for defending me," Grace said softly. "He seems a very unpleasant person."

"Unpleasant!" Betsy cried. "I'd knock him off his horse as soon as look at him!"

Grace suppressed a sigh and laid her hand on her maid's hand. "That is perhaps enough for now, Betsy," Grace said.

⫸⫷

GEORGE LEFT THE park seething. Jacobs was no gentleman and if he thought it would not make things worse for Miss Yardley, he would have been happy to take his aunt's suggestion and get him blackballed from White's.

He had denied the whole circumstance though he wondered if that were really the right course. It had seemed so the night before, but he had given a deal more thought to the circumstances and it had changed his opinion of Miss Yardley's actions.

Yes, what she'd done was outrageous. Not to mention reckless and dangerous, had she been shot by Ranston, or cracked her head when she fell, or had she been able to get away unseen. Anything might have happened to her on the road, accompanied by a groom or not.

For all that, though, he could not help but admire her sense of duty to her family, which now only consisted of her mother. Lady Barlow was a malingerer extraordinaire, but her daughter did not perceive it. As far as Miss Yardley was concerned, her mother was being mistreated. She had gone to his aunt about it and been turned away. Her next step, climbing out the window, had not been at all rational. It had been loyal, though. As unpredictable as she was, it did seem she possessed finer feelings than were to be found in most.

And then her expression when Jacobs had accosted her in the park, and on her discovery that she was named *The Sprinter*.

He'd wanted to protect her, to assure her that nobody would get by him to hurt her.

Of course, he could not say such things. He was a little shocked he even *felt* such things.

He had been so angry with her the night before. Now, he was angry at everybody else.

Well, he could not be sure if denying what occurred was the right path forward, but that was the path they had chosen and there was no turning back now.

And, as a practical matter, he'd set a watch on the house. He could not guess if Lady Barlow would send off another ridiculous list of complaints or whether Miss Yardley's finer feelings would drive her to make another run from the house.

⟫⟩⟩✕⟨⟨⟪

PENELOPE PRESCOTT, MARCHIONESS of Heathway, and Theodosia Whitby, Her Grace the Duchess of Stanbury, had put their heads together to compose two things. One, a list of people that must be contacted. And two, the outlines of a letter that would be sent to each person on the list.

They would bring the power they had between them to bear on the *ton*, and rescue Miss Yardley from her very large misstep. Or, *mis-descent*, as the duchess took to calling it, somehow considering herself amusing.

Each letter had been personalized to its receiver, but most followed along very similar lines. Penelope's letter to Lady Tredwell had been typical.

My dear Lady Tredwell,

As you must be aware, myself, the Duchess of Stanbury, Lady Mendleton, Lady Easton, Lady Redfield, Lady Featherstone, and all the various lords and ladies of our extended families are always delighted to receive an invitation to your annual masque ball. Of all the events we are pleased to attend, we always consider your ball one of the standouts of the season.

However, there is one little matter I must bring to your attention. A certain Mr. Robert Jacobs, who is a renowned gossip rivaling somebody's spinster aunt who has been left alone in the countryside for too long, has recently taken to outright lies. Gossip may be tedious, we do not engage in the habit ourselves, but fabrications will not be tolerated by us.

We find we cannot condone placing ourselves in the same house with Mr. Jacobs.

Of course, my dear Lady Tredwell, we would not be so bold as to meddle with your guest list. We only wish to be apprised if Mr. Jacobs will attend the masque, so that we may act accordingly.

My very warmest regards,
Penelope Heathway

Letters had gone flying out the door, with every footman in the house doing the rounds of London's various addresses.

Let it be seen whether the likes of Lady Tredwell would be willing to lose six powerful matrons and their sisters, brothers, sons, nephews, and nieces on account of the gossipy and irritating son of a baron.

Penelope thought not. She doubted many, outside of a handful of equally juvenile gentlemen, even *liked* Mr. Jacobs.

As for Mr. Jacobs himself, he was on the verge of finding invitations dried up and receiving various excuses as to why he should not arrive to balls and parties that had already been accepted. The size of the room having been miscalculated or finding there was an imbalance of ladies to gentlemen were two of the most likely. There would be red-faced ladies all over Town, as it was a ghastly thing to do.

But then, Mr. Jacobs was rather ghastly.

What would be the feelings of ladies receiving their letters? Penelope supposed they would vary—some would shrug, some would feel aggravation, some would fret.

But what all of them would conclude was, *Lady Heathway and Her Grace have spoken.*

CHAPTER EIGHT

G RACE HAD BEEN shaken by her encounter with Mr. Jacobs in the park and had hurried into the drawing room to see Lady Heathway and apprise her of the meeting.

After recounting the ghastly details, Lady Heathway said, "George was quite right to give him a firm set down. Finely done, I expect."

"But," Grace said, "what Mr. Jacobs said. That I am named *Miss Sprinter*."

"I had heard it was *The Sprinter*, but either way it is unfortunate," Lady Heathway conceded. "However, I believe the duchess and I have thrown a wet cloth over Mr. Jacobs' merriment. And perhaps a wet cloth on anybody who chooses to indulge him. We have let society know that if they want *us*, they'd better dump *him*."

"Can you do that?" Grace asked, not at all certain that she could.

"Of course we can do that," Lady Heathway said, "Between our extended families, we have more than twenty-five high-placed people, including a duke. What hostess will face that sort of united front, all to accommodate one fellow with a lowly title? Mr. Jacobs may have money, but that is *all* he has."

Grace was at once frightened and relieved. She was under the protection of powerful ladies and that carried with it a soothing sense of safety. But on the other hand, how angry would Mr.

Jacobs be if he saw that he was being excluded and discovered she was to blame?

Ranston came in with the tea and Grace was surprised to see him risen from his bed so soon. When he caught sight of her, he had almost a look of terror.

Grace smiled encouragingly.

"Now Ranston," Lady Heathway said kindly, "you're not to look at Miss Yardley as if you've just seen a ghost because, fortunately, she has not been made a ghost."

"No, my lady," he said, setting the tea tray down. "Miss Yardley, accept my humble apologies for...firing off my gun precipitously."

"Please do not apologize, Mr. Ranston," Grace said. "There was no reason you should have known it was me up there. The fault was my own."

"I did rather think that!" Ranston said. "Mrs. Redwiggin tried to blame it on my imagination getting away from me, but as I told her, a figure was on the house! Where is the imagination in that?"

"You are quite right," Grace said.

Mr. Ranston, rather than seeming satisfied that he was proved right, got a faraway look in his eyes. He stood motionless in the middle of the drawing room.

"You'd better go have a lie-down now, Ranston," Lady Heathway said.

As if his mistress could call to him in the deepest reaches of his mind, Ranston came back to the present. He nodded and wandered out of the room.

Lady Heathway poured the tea and shook her head. "It was the war, you see. One shudders to think what that poor man witnessed. I have heard from my maid that he sometimes has terrible nightmares and can be heard shouting, *"I'm in the linen closet."* None of them dare ask him about it, lest they bring a horrific memory to the fore."

Grace nodded. Betsy had yet to hear it for herself, but she had been told of the circumstance by Mrs. Redwiggin. The house-keeper thought it wise to prepare the lady's maid, lest she awake some night and think someone really was in the linen closet. There were a few other frightening things Mr. Ranston shouted from his nightmares, none of which anybody could make heads or tails of. He sometimes yelled *skin*, which seemed almost gruesome if he were dreaming of the war, but then sometimes it came out, *the skin is on the gravy*.

"I suggest you wear the white muslin with the embroidered lily trim to Lady Redfield's musical evening. Lilies signal purity and will send just the right message."

Grace was taken aback. Somehow, she'd thought she would hide in the house until the story about her died down. "We go, then? This evening? So soon?"

"We do," Lady Heathway said. "You are not to fret about it. Neither Mr. Jacobs nor any of his friends had been invited and so do not need to be disinvited. It will be a smallish party with dinner and then all the young ladies will be invited to play."

Lady Heathway paused, suddenly looking alarmed. "You do play? I have come to the conclusion that Louisa only pretended that Miss Wilcox could play. You do play, though?"

"Yes, indeed I do," Grace said, smiling despite herself.

"In front of people? What I mean is, you play well?" Lady Heathway asked, peering at her intently.

"Well enough, I believe," Grace said.

"You believe…I see…hmmm," Lady Heathway mumbled.

"Perhaps I ought to play now? To put your mind at ease?"

"Excellent notion!" Lady Heathway said, likely unaware that she was clutching the gold pendant she wore round her neck.

Lady Heathway watched with obvious trepidation as Grace made her way to the pianoforte and sat down on the bench. She chose a Haydn sonata that was a favorite and that she could play without needing the sheet music.

As the sonata unfolded, its formal structure of notes wafting through the drawing room, Grace could almost feel Lady

Heathway's relief floating along with it.

She could not say she looked forward to venturing out on this night, but she reminded herself of a few salient facts. First, *she* was the one who had caused the trouble, and second, Lady Heathway had spent a significant amount of time and money on the hopes that she could one day sit in a music room with her contemporaries and bask in the admiring glances directed at her protégé.

As her fingers flew across the keys, Grace was determined that she would not let the lady down.

MR. ROBERT JACOBS, eldest son of a baron named Lord Grimsbury, paced his library as he awaited his friends. Something was happening, but he was not certain what it was.

Three years ago, he had first arrived to London, determined to take the town by storm. He knew he did not arrive with as lofty a title as some others, but he did have a title. Or would have one of these days. He would be a baron. He would also have a lot of money.

His father, the current baron, had droned on and on about how he was to comport himself through the season. He was to be circumspect and give all due respect and deference to those who outranked him.

It had been absurd. Nearly everybody outranked him. What was he to do? Bow and scrape at every turn?

No, he'd had a better idea. He'd always been known as the jokester amongst his friends, and so he would become a noted wit. How else to rise to the top without a lofty title to carry you there? Now, on his third season, he'd accomplished it. So many of his bon mots were repeated widely. So many of his nicknames stuck. *Lady Naysay, Lord Short Pockets, Miss Woebegone.* Only Alvanley and Brummel could claim a similar success and Brummel was sure to disappear into oblivion sometime soon for having quarreled with the regent.

His latest triumph had fallen into his lap—*The Sprinter*. The name was already being circulated.

Step one of his long-term plan had unfolded flawlessly. Step two, which he had not been all that eager to get to, was to make a brilliant match. Easily enough done, now that he had made a name for himself. He was invited everywhere and need only choose.

But today, something odd happened. First, a note from Lady Cadmium apologizing profusely but her nephew had unexpectedly arrived from the continent and must take his place at dinner on the morrow. Then, a note from Lady Tredwell explaining that she'd overestimated the size of her ballroom and had been forced to cut her list for the masque.

The first note had only produced irritation. After all, there was only one eligible lady set to attend, a certain Lady Mary, and he supposed he would not be so lucky as to be placed beside her at dinner. He'd probably only escaped being bored by Lady Featherstone and her blathering on about Ryland's criminal society or Lady Jersey yakking on like a parrot. Or worse, Lady Easton and her pronouncements about what was right and what was not—that lady had the sense of humor of a rock.

The second note he'd received, though, had produced more than irritation. It had produced incredulity. What lady overestimated the size of her own ballroom? What ball was not overcrowded as a general thing? Lady Tredwell hosted a masque every single year—now suddenly she did not know how many people she was in the habit of inviting?

It could not be true!

His butler opened the door and led in his friends, Grubbs and Lester.

"What's this?" Grubbs said. "Why am I dragged out of bed at two o'clock in the afternoon?"

"I asked the very same thing," Lester said. "I wasn't abed, but I would have wondered over it if I had been. Deuced early, old fellow."

Jacobs ignored their complaints, as did his butler. The man ever so slightly raised his brows and departed the room. Jacobs well understood that Mr. Crumley viewed himself far superior to Grubbs and Lester. He was sometimes afraid that Crumley viewed himself superior to *him*.

After the door closed, he said, "Have either of you been dis-invited to Lady Tredwell's masque?"

Grubbs and Lester looked at one another and shrugged. "Not that I know of," Grubbs said.

"I'd remember if I had, and I don't remember, so I haven't," Lester said, seeming satisfied with his thread of logic.

"Well, I have," Jacobs said, throwing the note on his desk.

"Good God, what did you do to the old matron?" Grubbs asked.

"Nothing," Jacobs said. "That's the problem, I did nothing to Lady Tredwell. Something is afoot."

Grubbs rubbed his chin as if there were an answer there. Lester bent over and looked at his feet, presumably at the mention of *afoot*.

Jacobs thought, and not for the first time, if he'd been able to find more intelligent friends, he would have done so long ago. But here he was. He'd have to unravel this mystery by himself.

"I'm going to pretend I never got the note," Jacobs said, the idea just coming to him. "I'll wear a very good mask so she won't recognize me, but if she does, I'll pretend I don't know what she's talking about."

"There you go, problem solved," Grubb said.

"Oh, it's solved, is it?" Lester said, tearing his eyes away from his feet. "Excellent news."

Jacobs' butler came back into the room with a note on a silver salver. "This just arrived, sir."

Jacobs tore it open, his fingers trembling and trepidation filling him over what it might contain. It was Ryland's mark and if it was another *Sorry old man, do not come* missive he would know he was on his way to ruin.

As he scanned its contents, Jacobs felt as if his heart was slow-ly dropping in his chest. Lord Ryland was sorry to say that it turned out the mystery he offered this year would be better solved in a smaller crowd. Ryland was terribly sorry to rescind, but was certain Jacobs had plenty of other diversions on his calendar and would not miss it.

"Somebody has got to these people! Somebody is setting out to destroy me!" Jacobs cried.

"Who is it?" Lester asked breathlessly.

"How should I know?" Jacobs said, attempting to control his irritation. Lester was all well and good for a few laughs over brandy, but he was absolutely useless for anything else.

"Well," Grubbs said, "it's probably somebody you mocked. I don't know where you would start with *that* list, old boy."

WHILE GRACE DID feel some little trepidation about attending Lady Redfield's musical evening, she reminded herself that it would be small and she would be among friends. She was also not at all opposed to the dress that Lady Heathway had suggested, as it was lovely. Made of the finest India muslin with embroidered lilies at the hem and around the bodice and sleeves, it had a soft and elegant drape. As was true with all of Lady Heathway's designs, the lily pattern was subtle and in the same white as the dress. The whole effect was fresh as springtime and unencum-bered. It was to be topped with a marvelous cloak of white velvet with the tiniest lilies in silver thread running round the trim. Her only jewelry would be a delicate gold cross. Lady Heathway's taste really was unsurpassed.

She wondered if Lord Gresham would attend, and she won-dered if he were a friend or no. It was becoming difficult to land on one side or the other. He had done a terrific job of insulting her. But then, he had not condemned her as harshly as she probably deserved the night before *and* he'd proved himself a powerful ally in the park with Mr. Jacobs.

She had thought, on the night of Lady Easton's ball, that she had taken his measure. Now, he seemed inscrutable. What he did not seem, though, was any less handsome. Even in his quiet fury in the park he'd been the best-looking man she'd ever seen. As she must get herself married though, he was turning into a bit of an impediment. Even gentlemen she thought pleasant and attractive were somehow measured against him and found wanting.

She really must get past admiring his person. She'd probably limited herself as to a choice of husband quite seriously, as any gentleman would have to account for the actions of *The Sprinter* to his friends and family. Not many would like to be associated with such a story. She must consider herself lucky if anybody asked at all. She must also be prepared to like him, whoever he may be.

It was the most pointless idea in the world to wish it might be Lord Gresham. She did not even like him! Or he, her. And yet, did she like him? It seemed very strange that she would. Yet, her thoughts did seem to continually drift in his direction.

As she had time before Betsy would arrive to help her into the dress, she wandered to the window to observe the doings on the street. Though she had climbed out of that window the night before, it was a far more usual habit to sit on the wide sill and watch the activity below her.

It was that time of day, the sun nearly set, when the street grew quiet. Residents of the neighborhood had returned from their outings and now prepared themselves to go out again in the evening.

She had thought there would not be much to see, and indeed there was not. Only a lone gentleman across the street. He was tall and remarkably lean and dressed in a somber black suit that hung on him like a rack. She would have presumed he was somebody's physician, but he did not seem to hurry in any particular direction.

As she watched him, she thought his behavior very odd. Rather than going in one direction or the other, he paced back and forth.

Perhaps he was waiting for someone to arrive?

The man stopped and peered at her window. Grace looked back at him, wondering why he did so.

He looked almost shocked to see her there and promptly jumped behind a lamp post.

What on earth was he doing? His behavior was almost comical. He might be thin, but he was not thin enough to be concealed by a lamp post.

The man slowly peered round the post, looking up at her again. Finding her still looking back at him, his head snapped back and disappeared again.

An idea began to dawn on Grace. And, the more she thought about it, the more sure she was right.

This man, whoever he was, had been hired to watch the house. He'd been hired to watch her window. He'd been hired to ensure she did not attempt a second descent.

Why would Lady Heathway do such a thing?

No. It was not Lady Heathway. She thought she understood the lady well enough to know that if she *had* done such a thing, she'd come right out and say so. She'd say something like, "Now Grace, you won't mind that I've hired a fellow to watch out of doors. I really cannot have you climbing down the drainpipe again—it shatters Ranston's nerves."

Lady Heathway was opinionated and could be prickly, but she was not secretive.

No. This circumstance smacked of Lord Gresham, who was highhanded enough to do such a thing and who thought he always knew best.

Of course, it *would* be best that she never reenact the ridiculous drainpipe descent and she had no intention of doing so. But to put her under guard! Did he think her such a dunderhead that she might try again at any moment? It was outrageous.

Further, if she ever did decide to exit the house in some unusual manner, that fellow would hardly be able to stop her. He had no more weight on him than a grasshopper.

Lord Gresham thought he was so very clever, and yet he'd managed to hire the most incompetent watchman in England.

Grace leaned her face close to the window, knowing the fool was attempting to watch her surreptitiously. She laid her forefinger on the outside of her eye and then she pointed at him. That would let him know that she knew what he was there for.

Clearly, he understood her signal, as the absurd fellow had just thrown himself into some shrubbery.

Betsy came in to dress her and Grace apprised her of the development. Fortunately, she could always count on her maid to be firmly in her camp. Betsy went to the window from time to time and opened it, then left it for a few minutes before closing it again. Let the fellow be certain she was making an escape, and then not, and then doing it again.

That ought to keep him awake at his post.

Between those amusements, Betsy regaled her with the doings below stairs. It seemed Mr. Ranston had taken her words and embellished them somewhat. It was now understood among the servants that Miss Yardley had declared that Ranston would have been derelict in his duty if he *hadn't* taken a shot at her.

Betsy was prepared to challenge him on it, but Grace thought not. If that idea gave the butler any kind of peace of mind, let him have it.

WHEN LADY HEATHWAY was not looking, Grace had waved to the watchman as they left in the carriage. He had taken to concealing himself in the shrubbery and now, in the darkness, he looked like just another lump of greenery. She knew he was there, though.

They were not in the carriage long, as Lady Redfield's house was in Grosvenor Square. It was the sort of distance that Grace might have easily walked in the countryside, but of course in London one arriving on foot to a party would appear exceedingly odd.

The house itself, while looking quite usual on the outside, was rather interesting on the inside. As Lady Heathway had explained, the now deceased baron had been an avid collector of Indian art and furniture. He felt the English mode of decorating was too staid and that India knew how to style a house with color, liveliness, and exuberance.

Lady Redfield, herself, did not prefer the liveliness and exuberance. However, she was of such a nature that she could not bear to make the baron unhappy, even though he was dead. So, it all remained, just as he'd liked it when he lived.

In the drawing room, ebony wood chairs upholstered in bold colors and patterns fought one another for attention. What might have begun a simple table had been embellished with inlaid metals and its legs carved as peacocks. Intricately carved statues of gods seemed to be everywhere and in every size, including an alarmingly large statue of Ganesh. Even the bookcases had ornate carved edges. All of this sat upon a carpet of orange and red gone positively dizzy with geometric patterns. It was only the pianoforte that appeared usual and it looked like a dowager sat in the corner, frowning at boisterous high spirits.

The whole effect of the room was wonderfully lively and Grace was delighted with it.

The guests were not to be above forty and were rather a conglomeration of people—mamas and their daughters, single gentlemen, and older couples who were no doubt long-standing friends of the baroness. Of course, the ladies of the society were there—Lady Easton, Lady Mendleton, Lady Featherstone, and the duchess.

Lord and Lady Langley had come in, looking a dashing couple, and Lady Mendleton had hurried Lady Langley across the room to Grace.

"Miss Yardley," Lady Mendleton said, "I finally have the

opportunity of introducing you to my daughter, Georgiana, Lady Langley, she is married to my son and so is my daughter-in-law. That is, technically she is my daughter-in-law, but really my own daughter."

Grace curtsied. Lady Langley said, "Dear Louisa has quite taken me into the family. Now, shall we take a turn round the room, Miss Yardley? There is a rather wonderful statue of Ganesh at the far end."

Grace nodded and Lady Langley held out her arm. As they strolled away, Lady Mendleton called after them, "I knew you should be friends, of course I knew it. I understand Georgiana as I do my own mind."

Lady Langley smiled over her shoulder at Lady Mendleton. "She is such a dear, is she not? I was the first project of the society, and here you are the second," she said. "I had hoped things might go smoother for you than they did me."

Grace was taken aback by the lady's directness. But she found she also welcomed it.

"I did not realize that things did *not* go smooth for you," Grace said. "Well, except for some idea of being attacked by footpads? And perhaps an unfortunate encounter with a pianoforte? But I see you have heard of my own embarrassment."

"I have," Lady Langley said. "And your own pales in comparison to mine, though mine remained…more shrouded in mystery, I suppose. Among other things, if anybody at all suggests I play tonight you might fully expect my mother-in-law to throw herself over the pianoforte and claim it broken, such is my alarming lack of skill. And *that* was really the least of it. Do not lose heart over this little bump in the lane. I understand Mr. Jacobs has been sent packing and I am certain nobody will miss him. But I must know—did you *really* attempt to leave the house via window and *where* were you going?"

They had reached the statue of Ganesh, which Grace could not decide was either frightening or friendly-looking. She said quietly, "I thought to make my way to Kent as I was under the impression that my mother did very poorly, and I knew I would not be given leave to go and see her."

Lady Langley seemed very approving of this idea. "It was not Gretna Green, so that is excellent."

"No, certainly, there is not anybody…and even if there were I would hardly…"

They had turned to face the room, preparing to make their way back to the party. Grace's heart skipped a beat as she saw Lord Gresham enter.

Lady Langley glanced at her and whispered, "Are you certain there is not *anybody?*"

CHAPTER NINE

GEORGE WOULD LIKELY have to find a new watchman for Lady Heathway's house, as Melberry appeared on the verge of collapse.

Ryland had referred him, believing he needed a watchman for his own house after George had invented a story of a break-in. The fellow had seemed competent when he'd interviewed him. He claimed he did such work all the time. He'd been recommended by Ryland. How hard could the task be?

Watch the house and if he saw Miss Yardley coming out a window, quietly raise the alarm and make sure the butler didn't shoot her. That was all.

On his way to Lady Redfield's musical evening, he'd stopped outside his aunt's house to see how things were going.

At first, he could not even find the fellow and wondered if he'd just up and quit.

Then, Melberry had rolled out of the bushes and blathered on for a quarter-hour.

Miss Yardley threatened him with some sort of pointing to her eyes and then pointing at him. If that weren't enough, the lady kept opening the window as if she would make her move and then just when he was set to race into the house to raise the alarm, she'd shut it again. Then, she'd actually *waved* to him as she left in the carriage.

He ended the tale with, "My lord, she is taunting me, as anybody can see!"

George had suppressed a wish to inquire of him if he were by any chance related to Mr. Ranston. Instead, he'd just spurred his horse and went on his way.

He didn't know what to do with the fellow.

For that matter, he did not know what to do with Miss Yardley. The lady had been under surveillance for all of a quarter-hour before figuring it out. Further, she had not taken the information quietly. What was she doing, pointing at her eyes and waving at his watchman?

On the other hand, jolly clever of her to surmise the situation so quickly. And, if he were honest, it was rather funny that she was taunting Melberry. She was a very daring sort of girl.

George reminded himself to be serious. She *was* a daring sort of girl—that was the problem. She'd already made herself the talk of the town. If she tried another run for Kent, she would find herself labeled *The Sprinter* forevermore.

She was set to appear at Lady Redfield's party to face the thing down and his aunt had asked…no…*required*, that he attend to shore up the defenses. They were all to say it never happened, Jacobs had made the whole thing up. Their story was weak on its face, but would absolutely crumble if Miss Yardley were to try something like it again.

GRACE HAD BEEN discomposed by Lady Langley's hint when she had noticed her staring at Lord Gresham as he entered the room. How embarrassing to be caught out in such a manner. And even more embarrassing if Lady Langley were to understand the real circumstance.

The real circumstance, such as it was beginning to seem, was that no matter how she tried, she could not fail to be struck by him. *That*, she had already admitted to herself. Now she was to know she did not even do a credible job masking it.

The other real circumstance was that Lord Gresham had not wasted a moment warning her off him. She had been so insulted that he'd presumed her interest, but had it been the truth all along? Had he seen what she had not yet seen in herself?

She had since rejoined Lady Heathway who was just now conversing with Lady Redfield.

Fortunately, she was not required to speak, as Lady Heathway had gone in-depth in describing how she'd thought of the particular design of Grace's dress.

"These are the things you must think of, Cecilia, when you have your own girl and are on the verge of adding a flower pattern to her dress. What does the flower say? I seem to remember a lady a few seasons ago that had a marigold trim and I thought, what on earth is she sad about? These details must be considered!"

"Goodness," Lady Redfield said breathlessly, "I have been in the habit of leaving those things to my modiste. It is all is rather complicated."

"Now," Lady Heathway said, lowering her voice and leaning toward Lady Redfield, "send in Grace with my nephew and if you could put Sir Richard on her other side that would suit. I'll direct George, you steer Sir Richard. I do not want Grace to be peppered with questions regarding...recent events. Sir Richard only likes to talk about his dogs, which will do very well. This night is for appearances, not explanations."

Lady Redfield nodded, her brows knit as if she must commit these various directions to memory.

Grace searched her mind for a reasonable way to change the scheme. She did not want to be seated next to Lord Gresham. But then, she did want to. Neither yes nor no, nor here nor there seemed to suit.

She was an unconscionable ninny and not a thing presented itself to her mind. It was as if her thoughts were worn out and decided to retire for the night. She would be taken in by Lord

Gresham and she was both pleased and displeased. He was the man who had insulted and scolded and yet, also defended her when they'd encountered Jacobs in the park.

He was the man who fairly took her breath away.

He was also the man who had hired a watchman because he took her for an imbecile.

He was probably right. She was an imbecile.

WHILE GRACE NODDED at Sir Richard as he did most of the talking, she was keenly aware of the person on her other side. She wondered if Lord Gresham was annoyed at his aunt's and Lady Redfield's maneuvering to place him as one of her dinner partners. He must be growing exceedingly tired of it.

As for Sir Richard, Lady Heathway appeared to understand him very well. Grace almost felt she knew his two beloved spaniels personally at this point.

"It's the eyes, you see," Sir Richard said. "They're soulful, as if they think more deeply than other dogs. There is really nothing so nice as a cozy night in, brandy in hand and fire going, and Edgar and Jack staring up at me with those soulful eyes. Do you know, I recently hired a butler named Mr. Edgar and I made him change his name to Mr. Edmund. I could not very well go about shouting for Edgar and have them both come running." Sir Richard paused and then murmured, "I wonder what he's doing just now."

Grace presumed he wondered what Edgar the spaniel was doing just now, rather than his butler.

As other couples were turning and Sir Richard seemed to notice, he nodded to her and said, "Remind me to tell you what direction they prefer for a walk. It is very amusing!"

He then turned to his other partner and Grace heard him say, "Lady Easton, you'll want to know how Edgar got on with your suggestion about his diet. You are to be congratulated, madam..."

She had turned and Lord Gresham had turned, and there they were, seeming to have nothing to say among the chattering all round them.

They sat rather more close together than would be usual, as Lady Redfield's table was not oversized and it seemed to be better suited for thirty-four, rather than the forty that just now crowded round it. The room was sizable enough to accommodate a far larger table, but Grace could guess that it had been another of the deceased baron's Indian purchases that Lady Redfield could not bear to give up.

Grace could practically feel the heat of him coming through his coat and he had a scent that smelled...what was it? It reminded her of early morning walks through her father's forest—fresh and clean and of the woods. It was a scent to fall into and Grace scolded herself that it was only a soap his clever valet had secured from France or some such place.

She resisted the urge to lean closer to it.

Finally, Lord Gresham said, "How do you get on, Miss Yardley?"

"Well enough, Lord Gresham. "And you?"

It was a bland enough reply, but for some reason Lord Gresham seemed dissatisfied with it.

"I know that you know about the watch on the house," he said quietly.

"He is not a watch on the house, he is a watch on me. And of course I know," Grace said, almost finding some amusement in the idea that the man in the black suit had run to his master to report on their silent exchanges. "You could not have discovered a less subtle fellow had it been your primary purpose and it took me not a moment to discover *him*."

Lord Gresham sighed. "He is rather ridiculous, I'm afraid. He feels you are taunting him."

"Then he is not as dull-witted as he looks."

"You are angry that I did it," Lord Gresham said, "but I only wished to ensure..."

"That I would not make another attempt."

"Yes," Lord Gresham said. "As it stands now, you can face

this down. You are here, everyone can see you do not hide, they've been told it's not even true, and when you encounter Jacobs you will not acknowledge him. But if it were to occur again, there would be no way to save the situation."

"It will not occur again," Grace said, "if only for the reason that I discovered the braces holding the drainpipe to the wall are not particularly secure. As for Mr. Jacobs, I do not imagine I will ever encounter him again."

Lord Gresham's brow wrinkled. "Of course you will, the fellow is everywhere. He's bound to be at Lord Ryland's mystery ball the day after next and my aunt said she had plans to take you to it."

Grace felt a bit flustered upon hearing of encountering Mr. Jacobs. She had thought she understood from Lady Heathway that would not happen.

"But," she said, "Lady Heathway assured me that the letters she and the duchess have sent off everywhere would prevent it."

"What letters?" Lord Gresham asked, his expression at once appearing to darken.

"The letters they sent round to say Mr. Jacobs ought not be invited anywhere we were expected to attend. Lady Heathway said that he would be told not to come to whatever he'd already accepted that we had accepted too. Some excuse would be made." Grace paused, then said, "I did worry that he might become very angry over it, but your aunt assured me it was the right course."

Grace watched in some alarm as Lord Gresham's hand tightened on his fork. "That is the worst thing they could have done! It was only a joke to Jacobs, now it is to be his obsession. What man who finds himself thrown out of his society does not become enraged?"

Grace felt herself go very pale. She did not answer, as she did not have an answer.

"It's not your fault," Lord Gresham said grudgingly. "You couldn't have stopped those two if you tried. They can be so intemperate—especially when they are together."

People were beginning to turn to their opposite dinner partner. Lady Redfield was a jittery hostess and it seemed the moment she ran out of things to say to the duke, she turned to Lord Heathway, and vice versa. It had been like a tennis match so far and Grace wished she'd had more time to continue the conversation with Lord Gresham.

She felt a sense of foreboding over what he'd said. And also a feeling of shame, as if she were responsible for the letters being sent. It had not been her idea, but she *was* responsible. She had climbed out a window and now Mr. Jacobs was to be enraged. It felt frightening.

Grace turned to Sir Richard and forced a smile.

Sir Richard said, "Now, you will be interested to hear that as soon as we walk out of doors of an afternoon, Edgar insists on going left. He is the leader, you see, and where he goes Jack follows. This turning left is *very* scandalous, as he is fond of stopping near the gate to Carlton House and leaving a memento. What do you think of that? Does he hold political opinions? I really do not know! I like to think about it, though."

GEORGE'S CONVERSATION WITH Miss Yardley had been in bits and pieces, as Lady Redfield was a veritable sparrow hopping between her two dinner partners. Miss Yardley had seemed deeply alarmed over his reaction to the letters that had been sent out. *He* was deeply alarmed. Though, he had attempted to put her at her ease, as there was nothing she could do to remedy the situation. He did not know what could be done, but he was concerned about what a vengeful Jacobs might do.

Now, he settled himself into what was certain to be two hours of excruciating tedium. Mothers would put forward their daughters, daughters would demur and pretend they'd never seen a pianoforte in their lives, then they'd inch up to it reluctantly, then with a secret smile they'd put forth all that their music tutor had managed to bang into their heads, and then with a flourish of an ending, appear shocked at the applause and compliments that had been wrung from their listeners. It was like a recipe everybody had agreed on.

They would all be competent. No sensible lady would allow a daughter to sit down and play for a party if she were not. If an unfortunate lady possessed a daughter with a tin ear, the invitation would not have even been accepted, as the danger of exposure would be too great. Let some fellow discover his music room was to be the scene of a racket *after* the wedding.

Competence would reign, but what seemed always absent was any feel for the music they played. They marched through the notes with grim determination, never giving a thought to what the composer had meant by it.

George allowed his mind to drift as Miss Mellydon strode confidently through a Scotch air.

What had his aunt and the duchess been thinking to send out letters condemning Jacobs? It was as if they did not understand human nature at all.

What had Jacobs surmised at this point? He would have received a few withdrawals already, but did he know why?

He probably did not know why definitively. There were so many he had insulted over the seasons. But he might well guess it was a more recent happenstance.

Well, perhaps he'd take it as a lesson—spend your life fanning flames and at some point, you would set yourself afire.

As for himself, if Jacobs approached him at the club he would feign ignorance. If Jacobs wanted an answer, he could go straight to Lady Heathway and the duchess. And heaven help him if he did.

George glanced at his aunt, wondering if he should have a word with her about the letters. He could not decide. It was so misguided! But then, what was done was done.

If he did decide to speak to her about it, it would not be this night. An attempt at the moment would be entirely fruitless. Just now, the lady was seated next to her protégé, looking as proud as a hen with a hatched chick. Lady Heathway would count on Miss Yardley to do her credit, so that she could happily *take* the credit.

SO FAR, IT had been a very long hour and a half. One young lady after the next had risen to advertise her wares. George was always confounded by these gatherings. Somehow he'd forgotten that along with the nodding and applause he must give at the end of each performance, there were the constant glances of proud mamas. Their daughter was at the instrument and what did he think of that? It was very hard to feign a constant expression of interest and delight when he felt neither. He sometimes wondered if any of these daughters were just as bored as he was. It was amusing to think about—perhaps the only enjoyment being had was by the matrons, and even then probably only when it was their own daughter in the spotlight.

Still, he'd so far got through the interminable time creditably. At least, he hoped so. Even when Miss Crawden had made a great show of claiming she usually played the harp and so must be forgiven in advance for her clumsiness on a pianoforte, he thought he'd kept a neutral expression. He'd not believed her for a second, and he was right as she was quite good, but he did not think his skepticism showed.

As there were only two young ladies yet to play and one of them was Miss Yardley, George thought his aunt looked ready to explode into bits with anticipation.

Finally, Miss Yardley was urged to the instrument.

To her credit, she did not look shocked to be asked to play or provide any hint of reluctance. She simply rose and went to it, as if she very sensibly had come knowing she would play and now she would play and there was no particular mystery in it.

George hoped, for his aunt's sake, that Miss Yardley could play well and distinguish herself in some manner his aunt could hold onto. He did not understand why Lady Heathway and her friends put so much stock into such things, but he *did* understand that they did. There would be much discussion of the evening in the days to come—the highs, the lows, the surprises, and the disappointments. It would be important to his aunt to be on the winning end of those conversations.

Miss Yardley began to play at once. George was surprised she did not require a piece of sheet music, as the other misses had made a great show of thumbing through them for some tedious minutes before settling on something. At least, most of them had. As always, Miss Jenners had announced she would play a haunting and poignant Irish air. George was fairly convinced it was the only song she actually knew. Still, he could not denigrate her strategy, she was a rather jolly soul and it was always entertaining to hear her explain to the party that the air was, indeed, haunting and poignant.

As Miss Yardley's fingers raced along the keys, George sat up a little straighter than he had been.

Not only did she not require sheet music, she'd chosen a rather difficult Beethoven sonata. Further, she played it as it was meant to be played—not quite big and grand enough for a concert hall, but very grand indeed for a private house. There was no hesitation or shyness in approaching its determined tone.

She really was quite extraordinary.

As he watched her, her head slightly bent toward the keys and a charming curl escaping her lady's maid's best efforts, he could not help but reflect on the first time he had really seen her. When she had walked downstairs in the cottage in Kent. He had thought her marvelous then, and he supposed he still did. He began to wonder what might grow between them if she were not so…not so what? So much trouble?

No, that was not it. She *was* so much trouble, but that would hardly stop him.

He suspected he'd gone faintly red as the real problem bubbled up in his consciousness. It seemed he had been avoiding the truth of it. She did not like him. She thought him very high-handed. Which he supposed he was. She did not appreciate all his hints and advice.

He was further embarrassed to realize that he'd got quite in the habit of expecting to be liked. He was a viscount, to be an earl eventually. There was no end of marriageable-aged ladies prepared to like him. Of course not him, particularly, but the comfort and status that he could provide. He'd known that, and yet somehow he'd at the same time allowed himself to believe that he was universally liked for himself. His valet had even convinced him that he was handsome, though all along he suspected that the fellow thought his handiwork was handsome, not the person wearing it.

So, it had seemed as if quite a few ladies liked him. But *she* did not like him. She did not swoon when he was nearby. She did not blush. She did not pretend she thought him very clever. She did not fan herself. No, what she did was ignore most of his advice, bristle at his warnings, and blatantly mock his watchman.

George glanced at his aunt as Miss Yardley came near the end of the sonata. As he had expected, Lady Heathway appeared transported to heaven.

Whatever Miss Yardley was or was not, whoever she liked or did not, she had provided his aunt with a memory she would treasure always. And probably talk about forever, too.

Still, who *did* Miss Yardley like? He could not tell. Vance, perhaps? Lady Heathway would not particularly favor the match, but George would not be surprised by it. Vance was a genial fellow who seemed particularly good at entertaining ladies. Vance had probably never lectured her and had certainly never put a watchman outside her doors.

Vance was all wrong, though. That was the central problem—they were *all*, to a man, completely wrong.

Perhaps Miss Yardley would leave the season with no engagement. Certainly, if she did so, his aunt would bring her back for a second round. She might like him better then. She would have been *seasoned by last season* and her mother would be in better health and he would have no cause to lecture or hire a watchman.

They might come together on different footing. Of course, that was right.

Right as it might be, there was the difficulty of warding off all these men who fanned themselves round her. It was not just the rogues, like Jacobs and Skeffington, it was all of them! Bertridge, Vance, Blackwood, Ryland—none of them would be put off by Jacobs' story. Not when she walked into a ballroom and they looked at her.

My God, just now every man in the room seemed to be rapt by her playing. But it was not her playing, as good as it was. It was her!

But what would he do if he succeeded in keeping these men away? Was he thinking seriously of a future with Miss Yardley?

There was no need to consider that just now. Let her come back next year and they would just see how it unfolded. Perhaps his aunt might even invite Miss Yardley to a country party over the summer. And then the Christmas holidays. That way, there would not be all of *them* circling round.

Certainly that was the right course. Though, if he were to be successful in keeping her unspoken for, he would need his aunt's help. And, he thought he knew just how to get it.

⤜⤜⤜⤜

JACOBS PACED HIS library, having drunk far too much brandy and yet not enough to soothe him. His post, which had always been stacks of invitations, had dwindled to almost nothing.

Oh, he was still invited here and there, but not to any event of significance. He would dine with Lord Cahill on the morrow, but that would be what it always was—a collection of old bachelors and widowers who found him amusing.

Certain people had begun avoiding him at White's, as if he were a sinking ship and they did not want to be dragged under with him. They would not cut him outright, but it was obvious enough. Gresham practically fled through the other door out of the pool room when he'd entered it. Grubbs and Lester had begun attending parties *without* him. Grubbs said he'd brought it on himself for trying to sound like Brummel. Lester had responded that he did not think their voices similar. Grubbs had tried to explain he meant similar in their habit of composing insults, not the sound of their voices. Lester had been entirely lost and wandered off to Lady Caroline's card party.

Of course, Gresham and his ridiculous aunt must be at the heart of it somehow. His bon mot about Miss Yardley had somehow set them off. But the lady had been hanging onto a drainpipe! Anybody would have repeated the story for amusement.

He was not amused at the moment.

Ryland's mystery ball was in a few days and he'd been told not to come. He'd not answered though, and he planned to go and claim he'd never received the note. He'd claim it if he were even asked, which he doubted he would be.

Let society see that he could not be driven out by *Lady Naysay* and they would disregard whatever directive she'd put out in the world. He was amusing, she was irritating. It seemed an easy choice.

The lady was about to discover that rank was not everything.

CHAPTER TEN

A s the carriage had carried them home from Lady Redfield's musical evening, Lady Heathway had crowed in every possible manner. What had been the look on Lady Easton's face upon witnessing Grace's skill. Lady Featherstone had even fanned herself. Lady Redfield had used her handkerchief extensively, so moved was she. The duchess had taken to nodding vigorously in approval. And Lady Mendleton? She had been rather red in the face, as her own protégé had never yet been seen anywhere in the vicinity of a pianoforte that hadn't been roped shut.

Grace smiled and nodded. She was very much gratified. Not because of what the other ladies might have thought of her playing, but because she had very much wished to see Lady Heathway pleased. She had caused so much trouble, but this was one thing she could do to assuage some of that.

She had very purposefully chosen that particular sonata, as it had an importance and gravitas that a simpler air could not approach. It was structured and did not go willy-nilly all over the place. She thought it would suit and it seemed that it had.

Upon arrival to the house, Grace waved to the bushes, in case the watchman was still crouching amongst them.

When they entered the hall, they found Ranston on the alert, but happy to report that he had not heard any suspicious sounds out of doors.

Lady Heathway seemed approving of this calmer approach to the family's absence, but Grace rather thought it was a few good doses of brandy that had done it. At least, that looked to be the case, as he seemed rather red-eyed and unsteady.

A letter from the late post lay on the salver on the side table. Both Grace and Lady Heathway spotted it at the same time, and both recognized the handwriting well enough. It was from her mother.

"Now Grace," Lady Heathway said, "allow me to read the letter first. If Lady Barlow has written of all her complaints again, I do not want you to be upset by it. Because certainly, we would not wish that you..."

Lady Heathway did not finish her sentence, though Grace understood her well enough. She nodded, as she could see the lady was determined to understand its contents.

Lady Heathway tore open the letter and scanned it.

Grace had expected she would seem angry or irritated, but she only nodded and handed the letter over.

"She complains as much as ever, but in a far more encouraging manner. I believe she gets on very well. You will see what I mean."

Grace looked down at the letter in her hands and read it.

My darling daughter,

I pray you are being entertained in London. I, of course, am not so entertained. The nurse is the same terror she has been since she arrived. However, I remembered that I am a viscountess and have a certain bearing and dignity to fall back on. I have chosen to teach the old harridan a thing or two. When I am forced to walk, I speed up so that she is always behind me. When I wake, I open the window before she can get to it—it is my decision and my purview, and I can see very well it infuriates her. How is she to justify her pay if I am doing everything myself, I wonder. At meals, I do not give her the chance of urging more on me, as I take seconds before she can even suggest it.

She and I have been circling one another in battle and I

have been the clear victor.

I keep my spirits up by remembering that it will be very soon that you will marry well and we will leave this place for good. Each day that I wait for the post, I wonder if I will read the welcome news that I am to come for a wedding breakfast. I will lock Nurse Maddington in a closet before I set off.

All my love,
Your mother

"I am astounded," Grace said. "I have never heard her so...forceful."

"Quite right," Lady Heathway said, nodding. "She gets her health back and she can stride ahead of the nurse all day long if she likes it. Now, my dear, it was a pleasing evening all the way round and we can retire very satisfied with ourselves."

GRACE RE-READ THE letter a number of times. It really was quite marvelous. The only detail contained in it she was not entirely comfortable with was the idea that Grace should be married soon. She really was not anywhere near it and she feared her mother was pinning all her hopes on a speedy engagement.

Grace stared at herself in the looking glass as Betsy brushed out her hair. What was she doing, anyway? Her mother was quite right in expecting to hear of an engagement. It was her primary reason for coming. Somehow, she had been doing everything *but* getting engaged.

She must put all of her childish notions aside. Her mother was counting on her. For that matter, she ought to be counting on herself! Her entire future was at stake. She was here on serious business and there was no point in mooning after a gentleman who did not hold her in the slightest regard. Her inclination toward Lord Gresham had blinded her to any other possibility. She must open her eyes and be rational!

She was determined not to let her mother down.

Grace suddenly noticed that Betsy had been chattering on

without her.

Betsy ended the tale with, "So you see, the footmen were able to convince Mr. Ranston that a good dose of brandy would sharpen his hearing. As he intended it to be very sharp to be able to hear a criminal approaching, he had more than a few glasses. The end of it was he was remarkable calm and didn't hear any kind of sound out of doors that must be shot at. Good thinking from those two boys, I thought. Though mind, I did spy Jenny helping herself to the marquess' bottle too. She is positively wicked."

Grace smiled. She might well be amused at Lady Heathway's household. It seemed everything was a bit lighter on her shoulders, now that her own household in Kent got on so well.

And after all, what were her feelings for Lord Gresham? It was bound to be only a girlish infatuation. She was certain she'd look back upon those feelings someday and shake her head and laugh at them.

It was time to grow up and go forward. She must put all of her attention on doing her own part for her household and secure her and her mother's future. She must marry.

◆

LADY HEATHWAY HAD been up at dawn. Who could sleep when such a triumph was currently tucked into one's reticule? One must naturally have a great wish to pull the triumph out and wave it around for all to regard. Grace had been decisively the most skilled on the pianoforte the evening before. As her name gave a charming forewarning of, she was all grace at the instrument. It was just as Penelope had envisioned in her imagination so often over the years. Her girl had positively prevailed.

Though she would certainly never say it aloud, *her* girl had crushed the aspirations of those other young musical hopefuls under her delicate slipper. And so amiably too.

She'd since fired off notes to all the other ladies, congratulating them on the success of their project at last evening's soiree. Everyone attending was well aware that Miss Yardley was sponsored by their esteemed society, and so it must be considered a victory for all.

Naturally, in her note to Louisa, she may have offhandedly remarked that they all still looked forward to hearing Lady Langley play. If Louisa's own pianoforte ever did get repaired. Which to Penelope's mind was looking less and less likely, though she was too pleased with her circumstances at the moment to say so.

Certainly, last evening had squashed any unfortunate talk about Grace. Nobody could have witnessed her proper bearing and listened to how well trained she was and imagine she would find herself hanging on the side of a house by way of a drainpipe. Even if she *had* been hanging off the side of a house on a drainpipe.

The notes had been sent flying out of the house and Penelope was just dressed when she was told her nephew awaited her downstairs. He was finishing his breakfast in the breakfast room and would repair to the drawing room. It was not so entirely rare that George would take advantage of her board. He was just down the street and usually ate at his club, but on occasion he strolled into her house, especially for breakfast. He never ate that meal at his own house, thinking it was a waste to have his own cook provide a spread when it was him alone. What *was* so rare was that he wished to see her. When he did come, he so very often slipped in and then out again.

Surely, he wished to convey his congratulations over her triumph at Lady Redfield's musical evening. It was very kind of him to think of it!

"Tell my nephew I shall be down forthwith," she said to her maid.

GRACE HAD COME downstairs at seven, long before her usual time. She'd slept restlessly and had finally given up on it. She'd dressed herself in a simple muslin gown with not too many buttons and got her hair in some semblance of order, leaving Betsy to her bed. She'd become expert at the operation during those long months in the dower house and she saw no reason to rouse Betsy at such an hour.

She'd slipped into the drawing room and retreated to what she thought of as the *cozy corner* with a rather lurid novel in hand that she'd found on Lady Heathway's shelves. Apparently, every old house in the remote countryside of England was haunted, or seemed haunted, or someone attempted to make it seem haunted, and the house's hapless visitor was always an innocent young lady who'd landed herself in a haunted house through very improbable circumstances.

The alcove housed a soft bench with a padded back, all covered in cream velvet. There was not a pretty view out the window, as it overlooked a narrow alleyway and faced the brick of the house next door. However, it had the advantage of being out of sight of the rest of the room. At this early hour, a housemaid was bound to come in to straighten up and finding Grace there would only discompose the girl. As she knew from Betsy, servants liked to do their work without being stared at and there were times a family really ought to get themselves out of the way.

Grace heard the door open and stayed quiet as a church mouse so as not to irritate whichever maid had come in.

To her surprise, it was Lady Heathway's voice she heard. She almost rose to join her, but then she heard Lord Gresham's voice too.

What did he do here so early? At the same time she wondered about that, she also thought what a lovely timbre there was to his voice. It was deep, as many men's voices were, but it had a particular richness and tone that was all its own. And then, at the same time she thought about *that*, she reminded herself of her vow the night before. The time for being an impractical fool was over.

"I know why you wished to see me so early in the day, George," Lady Heathway said cheerfully.

"You do?"

"Naturally. You wish to congratulate me, and Miss Yardley of course, on our triumph of last evening. We, or rather she, was spectacular. Nobody could deny it. I defy them to do it."

Grace was flattered by the sentiment, but now what? Should she show herself after she'd managed to overhear a compliment? It seemed rather awkward.

"I am sure you are very proud, Aunt. I did have another thing in mind, though."

There was a long pause and Grace presumed Lady Heathway waited expectantly.

"Is Miss Yardley likely to come downstairs soon?" Lord Gresham asked.

"I doubt it, she generally would descend an hour from now. Did you wish to see her?"

"No, no," Lord Gresham said hurriedly. "I wished to have a confidential conversation about her and would not wish for her to walk in on it."

Grace was frozen. She could not reveal herself now, but to fail to do so… But why should he wish to have a secret conversation about her? Had he heard some new rumor?

"Gracious," Lady Heathway said, "you do look serious. You'd better just come out with it. Though, if it is to do with that Jacobs fellow, I'm likely to call the carriage, arrive at his house, and hit him over the head."

"No, nothing to do with that. It is just…I know what pleasure you have taken, having brought Miss Yardley under your wing, and I say nothing against it."

Grace could feel her heart pounding. It was clear enough he was about to say what he *was* against, in regard to Miss Yardley.

"And, I know you would consider it a feather in your cap were she to make a good match."

"The final and most glorious feather, if you must know it," Lady Heathway said.

"Yes, of course it would be a feather in your cap. But perhaps that feather ought to be delayed. I do not think Miss Yardley is yet ready for such a serious step. She is too young and far too naïve."

Grace felt her cheeks flame, while Lady Heathway laughed at the notion. "My dear nephew, every lady who marries at a sensible age is young and naïve. If anybody was ever old enough to rationally consider what marriage is, they'd never do it."

"That is a startling notion," Lord Gresham said. "But I was thinking, Aunt, what if it were better to allow Miss Yardley a second season? In between, she might come to you in the country, and perhaps even for Christmas. It would seem to me that would not only be to the advantage of Miss Yardley, but for you too. I think you would rather enjoy a second season with your protégé."

"Well, of course I would," Lady Heathway said softly. "It would be a delight."

"You see? That is what I say. Simply don't encourage her toward anybody and let her know that a second season is anticipated."

"But George, what if she is to get a good offer? Lord Ryland seems to admire her. He is a marquess. If he were to go forward, I really do not—"

"Ryland is not right for Miss Yardley," Lord Gresham said, interrupting his aunt. "He, well he is not, he is too worldly, I think."

"Do you really think so?" Lady Heathway asked.

"I really do."

Grace was dumbfounded. Why on earth would Lord Gresham wish to upset her plans in such a manner? Of course, he did not approve of her in general, but this idea! That he would absolutely attempt to prevent her from her future? Did he despise her? She had not thought so, but perhaps he did.

Perhaps he was so offended by the talk she'd caused that he wished to punish her in some manner?

And then, was Lord Ryland really interested in her? She had not looked at him in that light. But then, she'd stupidly stopped herself from looking at anyone in that light. Perhaps she needed to look again? Her mother would be mightily pleased with a marquess and he did seem a sensible and well-regarded sort of gentleman. Since she would not be one of those ladies who had the good luck to marry for love, would not a sensible and well-placed gentleman be enough?

Whatever she thought of Lord Ryland, or anybody else, she really could not fathom why Lord Gresham would wish to ruin her chances. A second season guaranteed nothing, as he well knew! To disregard an offer now would be foolhardy, as it might be the only offer that arrived. Especially in her circumstance. She did not come with a large dowry and there were rumors that she'd slid down a drainpipe.

"I even think, Aunt, that perhaps Ryland's mystery ball ought to be skipped."

"That is out of the question," Lady Heathway said. "Lord Ryland quite depends upon me."

"Does he?" Lord Gresham asked, the skepticism in his voice evident.

The door to the drawing room fairly crashed open.

"Goodness, Ranston," Lady Heathway said. "What is the matter?"

"Oh. The matter," Mr. Ranston said.

"Yes, why do you look round the room so wild-eyed?"

"I thought Miss Yardley might be in here."

"She is still above stairs, what do you want her for?" Lady Heathway asked, the puzzlement in her voice clear enough.

Grace was herself puzzled. She could hardly keep up with

everything she was hearing.

Ranston let out a long and sad sigh. "Her lady's maid says she's not there, and she's not in the breakfast room or the library and now she's not here..."

"Not there...not here...do you mean to say she is not anywhere...but you don't think...she would not have...there would be no reason..." Lady Heathway said, as if her thoughts would not compose themselves into some sort of reasonable order.

"Blast it! She's run off again!" Lord Gresham said loudly.

There was silence in the room as everyone except for Grace considered the idea that she'd run off again. What was she to do? Reveal herself now, after hearing everything that had been said?

"I'll go to the stables and discover if she's been there," Lord Gresham said. "If she has, I'll set off after her."

"Yes, do, very good thinking. I'll interview her lady's maid and discover what she knows. A lady's maid always knows everything," Lady Heathway said.

"And I will..." Ranston had trailed off.

Lady Heathway said, "Go have a lie-down, Ranston. We'll do what can be done."

Grace sat stock still, the horror of the situation covering her like a heavy blanket. She had not run off to Kent, but she could not reveal where she was.

The three left the drawing room and she heard the door close behind them.

Her thoughts raced, thinking about the layout of the house. Where could she have been that was not this alcove?

Her eyes settled on the window.

She leapt up and undid the latch with shaking fingers. She lifted it up and climbed out, dropping to the alleyway between the two houses. As she did so, she heard the clatter of Lord Gresham's horse galloping down the road.

Grace picked up her skirts, ran to the back garden wall and found a foothold. It was not a high wall and was meant for decoration rather than keeping anything in or out. She was over it and on the gravel path in a trice.

A housemaid came around a corner and Grace thanked the heavens the girl had not come a moment sooner. The girl was petite and her view had been blocked by Lady Heathway's shrubbery. The maid looked at her as if she'd seen a ghost and hurried to the opposite side of the garden.

Grace's heart pounded as if she'd run a mile and she willed it to slow.

She dashed to some early daffodils and broke the stems close to the ground to account for her being there.

Then she waited to be found.

GEORGE KICKED AT the carpet in his library. What a completely ridiculous morning. He'd gone to his aunt's house to apprise her of the plan he wished her to adopt and then discovered Miss Yardley missing. He'd raced out of the house to find out what the watchman had seen, ready to throttle the fellow if he'd noted Miss Yardley's departure without raising the alarm.

He'd found the fellow curled up under a bush, fast asleep.

After he'd fired Melberry, he'd mounted his horse and gone galloping to the stables to interrogate the stablemaster about whether *he'd* seen Miss Yardley. The fellow had looked at him as if he'd gone mad. She'd evidently not ordered either a horse or Lady Heathway's carriage.

His next thought was that she'd hired a carriage and he raced back to the house to interrogate the footmen. They'd not seen hide nor hair of her. His aunt reported that Miss Yardley's lady's maid had not attended her, as she had not been rung for.

He'd been at his wit's end. Where had she gone? *How* had she gone? Where was that mad, lovely girl?

Just as he had resolved to get back on his horse and ride for Kent, as surely that was where she was headed, Mrs. Redwiggin had marched in and said, "She's in the back garden. I just spied her through a window, she's picking daffodils."

Picking daffodils. He was at once relieved and ready to throttle her. What had she been thinking, to be out picking daffodils while they were searching for her?

He and his aunt had run to the back doors to confirm the truth of the report. There she was, strolling around with a fistful of flowers.

It was all very odd. For one, it was very early to be walking the garden. For another, she'd not even brought a cutting instrument with her—the stems were ragged as she'd evidently just wrestled them from the ground.

Still, it could not be denied that she'd been out picking daffodils and not racing off to her mother's side. She really was very confounding. Just when he was sure she would go one way, he discovered her going the other way.

He supposed he could not be dissatisfied with everything that had happened. Miss Yardley had not run off, he was not just now galloping to Kent to catch her, and he was confident that he'd convinced his aunt to fall in with his plan. Miss Yardley was to have a second season.

Now, all he'd have to do was drive Ryland and the rest of them away to a safe distance. Especially Ryland, as Lady Heathway thought so highly of him and he was a marquess. Every mama in Town thought him a good catch and it would be very difficult for his aunt to wish him away if he made any decided approaches.

Ryland's mystery ball was on the morrow. As it seemed that his aunt would not stay away, he would need to be prepared to charge in as the vanguard, pushing back any and all unwanted suitors.

CHAPTER ELEVEN

G RACE HAD CREDITABLY got through her discovery in the garden. Her heart pounded for quite a long time afterward, but she did not think anybody suspected she'd been anywhere *but* the back garden.

Lord Gresham had taken himself off shortly after she'd been discovered there, and as well he should. What a vengeful creature he was! What a situation she found herself in.

The one man she felt pulled toward not only had no interest in her but was now bent on ruining her chances. She had finally straightened out her thoughts and got serious about her prospects and her duty to her mother. *That* had seemed the hurdle. Now, a new hurdle had sprung up by way of Lord Gresham. She had of course realized that he was most unhappy about the talk she'd caused regarding her adventure on the drainpipe. It irked him to have his family connected to such gossip. Though, she supposed she had not realized precisely how much he had been affected.

It seemed he wished her away from his society so that London might forget there ever was a Grace Yardley. She was all but certain that once she'd been sent home to Kent, he would work on his aunt to drop her project of a girl. Lady Heathway might think a second season was in the offing *now*, but over time he would convince the lady that it was too much trouble.

What else could be his purpose? If he wished her ill, as it seemed he did, he would not wish her back next year. No, this current proposal was meant only to get Lady Heathway started on the path to his preferred destination.

She was both hurt and angry. She was both furious and dejected.

She wanted to both cry into her pillow and push his face into horse manure.

She would do neither of those things, of course.

Grace took in a long and slow breath, that being her father's recommended strategy when one found composure had placed itself on a rather distant horizon.

What did Lady Heathway think? Did the lady really believe her nephew's motivations? She had not seemed very moved regarding Grace's supposed naivete.

If the lord were to be successful in his machinations, Grace might find herself and her mother living forever in the dower house. Then, she would find that her only chance had slipped through her fingers. She would have let down her mother, and she would have let down herself.

Grace stabbed at the embroidery work in her hands. She really ought to stop working on it—it was a lovely piece and she was ruining it with her current impatience.

She must find her composure. Grace Yardley had a future to plan and she would not be defeated by anybody's spiteful nephew. Lord Gresham may have made every effort to keep her locked in the house, but he had so far been unsuccessful.

Lady Heathway had just left the drawing room, but not before she had told Grace all about Lord Ryland's mystery ball and listed which dresses she might consider wearing to it. It was definite—they would attend.

Understanding better what was involved, Grace realized it was less a mystery ball and more a mystery supper. The ball itself would be quite usual, but when they went in for supper, they would find a written-out mystery tucked under their plates. Whoever solved the thing first would be given some sort of prize.

Lady Heathway had sighed and said that whoever won, it

would not be Lady Featherstone. That lady would be convinced she would come away the victor, as she always was. And then, she would be embarrassingly dejected when she was not the victor, as she never was. It was Lady Heathway's opinion that Lady Featherstone believed she had the mind of a crack investigator, but really had a mind that was like a bird flitting from tree to tree. Lady Heathway and the duchess were quite agreed on that point.

Out of curiosity, Grace had asked who had solved the mystery the year before. This produced a surprisingly irritated sniff and the information that it had been Lady Langley when she had only been Miss Wilcox. It had seemed further irritating that the prize had been tea with the queen.

Lady Heathway had then mollified herself by reasoning that a person might well be skilled at solving a mystery when that person had so much time on their hands from never playing the pianoforte.

Grace did not know whether Lady Langley could play the pianoforte or not and did not much care. She liked the lady and was rather impressed that she'd prevailed and then had tea with Queen Charlotte.

The most important thing, though, is that she and Lady Heathway would be there for this latest mystery of Lord Ryland's. Grace would use the opportunity to see what she really thought about the lord. And any other gentleman she encountered. She would not allow Lord Gresham to dictate the terms of the rest of her life through his petty vindictiveness.

RANSTON LAID DOWN on his bed and stared up at the spot on the ceiling that always made him feel calm. He felt he was holding up rather well these days, considering the trying circumstances. There was pressure from every side!

First, there was the confounded Miss Yardley. How could one young lady be so vexatious? If she was not found clinging to the side of the house, she was positively missing! Then, as if she were some sort of sorceress, she turns up in the back garden. How did she get there? A housemaid had been out there cutting flowers for Lady Heathway's bedchamber and claimed Miss Yardley had appeared on the path as suddenly as an apparition on All Hallows Eve. Then, having mysteriously appeared, Miss Yardley had run to a patch of daffodils and set upon them as if she held a personal grudge against them. All the while, Lord Heathway's valet had been polishing the lord's boots on the bench next to the door leading to the garden since six-thirty in the morning and *he'd* not seen her go out. Had she flown out of her bedchamber window?

He supposed he should not be surprised if she had, as it would not be the first time she'd left the house via that particular aperture.

Then there was Miss Yardley's lady's maid, Betsy, who almost made him feel as if he was irrational for thinking there was anything strange about her mistress. According to Betsy, everything Miss Yardley did made perfect sense and was perfectly right. Miss Yardley was the daughter of a viscount and was absolutely incapable of doing or thinking anything at all wrong. If Miss Yardley deemed it necessary to climb down a drainpipe, then it had been necessary.

Ranston did not know if the blood of a viscount conveyed any particular wisdom, but if it did it seemed to have skipped a generation!

As if Miss Yardley and her infernal maid were not enough to contend with, there was Jenny. Why were kitchen maids always such a thorn in his side? It seemed as if all the diabolical females in the world had secretly met at midnight in some lonely location and said, "Let's be kitchen maids."

He'd just got rid of the last one for her cheeky responses to any and all questions. *That* one had the footmen in a constant state of near-rage and cook had once thrown a pot at the girl.

Now he'd got one who he was certain was making off with household provisions and selling them somewhere. She had also had the audacity to help herself to Lord Heathway's brandy.

Did the girl not see that it was one thing for a butler who was responsible for defending the house to gird himself with a judicious amount of brandy and quite another for a lowly kitchen maid to do it?

A lesser man could not have held up against this sort of turmoil.

Fortunately, he was not a lesser man. After his lie-down, he would have tea and a fortifying biscuit. Then he would bravely soldier on.

GRACE HAD DRESSED with particular care for Lord Ryland's ball. One of Lady Heathway's designs had been a light rose silk gown with subtle rosettes of the same color decorating the hem. As was Lady Heathway's preference and had become Grace's too, the waist, though high, was eased and not pinched in. Nor was the bodice gathered. This resulted in an elegant drape, rather than the straight drop from the bodice that caused a lady to look like a column ready to hold up a portico. The sleeves were capped, as Lady Heathway could not abide puffed—she thought they made a lady appear as if she were sprouting wings and planning to fly off somewhere.

Lady Heathway had approved her choice of dress, as it had been one of her suggestions to begin with, and she had lent Grace a delicate necklace to go with it. It was an intricate and graceful pattern of thin and winding silverwork made to look as stems and leaves, with gems of rose quartz set as the flowers. It was not too large, and it was not overdone. It was very much Lady Heathway's taste and Grace found she had become a great admirer of the lady's discernment.

She must look her best. She did not know how many chances she would have to secure her future and so she must take advantage of every one of them.

Lady Heathway had talked all the way to Lord Ryland's house, discussing the various mysteries presented by the lord in past years. All of them had to do with murder and so Grace supposed this one would too. It was an idea that did give her pause. It was all well and good to attend the ball and do one's best with the mystery presented, but could she really be contented being married to a gentleman who seemed to dedicate his life to examining the dark and dangerous? And what of Lady Barlow? Grace was fairly confident that one tale of murder would scare the wits out of her. More than one would be her undoing.

Still, Lord Ryland might turn out to be her only chance to rescue her mother from the dower house. She must remain open to the idea that she might one day be the mistress of bookshelves filled with criminal histories and gruesome ends.

Since she had determined to attempt to divine Lord Ryland's interest, and divine her own interest as well, she felt herself fluttery as they entered the house. It seemed somehow embarrassing, as if all those around her could read her thoughts.

Lord Ryland was at the door to greet them, and he was as he had been on prior occasions. He was a forceful sort of personality, though proper in every way. Grace did not get the slightest hint that she might be singled out in his affections. If there was anything different about him she could not say, though she was beginning to think him a bit odd. After he had greeted her, he said he was delighted to see her walking so well.

Had he ever seen her not walk well? What a strange thing to say.

Just as they'd moved on and were headed toward the ballroom, Grace heard something disturbing behind her.

"Jacobs, old fellow, what do you do here?"

Grace froze, as did Lady Heathway.

"Well good to see you too!"

The voice was unmistakably Mr. Jacobs. It was clear enough that Lord Ryland had chosen to accommodate Lady Heathway's and the duchess' request that Mr. Jacobs not appear anywhere they were to attend. It was equally clear that Mr. Jacobs had not paid heed to it.

What was to be the end of it? Was he to be admitted? Grace could not bear his sly smile and joking manner, even if she had been the cause of it.

"I did ask you to excuse yourself from this evening," Lord Ryland said.

Grace could practically feel Lord Ryland's eyes drifting toward her.

"What on earth are you talking about, Ryland?" Jacobs asked, his voice full of false jocularity.

"You know perfectly well what I'm talking about," Lord Ryland said. "Out you go, and we'll say no more about it."

"I see," Jacobs said, in a tone far more threatening than it had been. "Everybody is to rally round *her* and pretend she did not climb out a window, though you all know she did. Nobody seems the least curious as to why, though there must have been a gentleman involved. No, *I* am made the villain, though I did nothing!"

Lady Heathway took Grace by the arm and hurried her away.

As they approached the ballroom, Lady Heathway said softly, "Lord Ryland will deal with that scoundrel. Do not allow it to discompose you."

"I was afraid he would be exceedingly angry, and he is," Grace said. She did not add that Lord Gresham had thought the letters that had gone out were extremely ill-advised and would only compound the problem. As much as she did not care to believe Lord Gresham right in any matter, he was right about *that.*

"He is cooking his own goose," Lady Heathway said. "Lord Ryland may have pushed him off for this evening to please me, but it is unlikely that he would have carried on forevermore. I suspect now, he will."

"It is frightening, though," Grace said, "that he would have come despite Lord Ryland's request."

Lady Heathway stopped Grace and cupped her face. "He tried it once, but his failure will mean he will not try a second time. You will not see him again. Furthermore, you are to know that I can be a veritable Visigoth if someone under my wing is threatened. These wings of mine are big enough to protect you."

Grace was touched by Lady Heathway's words. Though she had sometimes thought of her as a Viking, her styling herself as a Visigoth was equally suitable.

The lady was so different from her mother! She was so bold and strong. Lady Barlow was affectionate in her own way, but she did not have the strength or fortitude to shield anybody from anything.

"Chin up, my dear," Lady Heathway said encouragingly.

Grace nodded. "Yes, thank you," she said, regaining her composure. "I know I have nothing to fear with you to protect me and I will not dwell on what has just occurred."

"That's my girl," Lady Heathway said. "And just in time too, as the gentlemen approach." With almost a sigh she said, "I see Mr. Vance is in the lead."

Grace was determined to follow Lady Heathway's directive and not allow Mr. Jacobs to discompose her. She was also rather cheered to see Mr. Vance, as he was a very genial gentleman. And, of course, she was resolved to view every gentleman she encountered with new, more open and realistic, eyes.

Mr. Vance bowed and said, "Lady Heathway, Miss Yardley, you both look exceedingly charming this evening."

"Am I to be charmed by supposedly looking charming, Mr. Vance?" Lady Heathway asked with an eyebrow raised.

"I certainly hope so, as I am determined to secure Miss Yardley for supper. I am all confidence that she is exceedingly clever and will solve the mystery speedily."

Grace was delighted with the idea; she was sure that Mr.

Vance would be diverting. However, she remembered Lady Heathway's lack of enthusiasm for the gentleman's pedigree and so she glanced at her. Lady Heathway only shrugged before her attention was pulled by the duchess, who had come sailing over in her usual brocade. Grace took that as acquiescence and presumed she was being indulged because Lady Heathway wished to keep her spirits up. She handed over her card.

As Mr. Vance wrote down his name, he said, "I am delighted, Miss Yardley. Of course, I understand you will want to sit out the dance *before* supper, on account of your ankle. I pray both you and Lady Heathway are amenable to our going into the card room. We might play piquet."

"My ankle?" Grace asked, having not the first idea of what he was talking about.

Now, Mr. Vance looked confused. "Indeed," he said. "Not a moment ago, Lord Gresham told me you had violently twisted your ankle in the garden this morning and would not prefer to dance."

Grace glanced at Lady Heathway, but she was whispering rapidly to the duchess on her other side, no doubt telling her of the arrival and departure of Mr. Jacobs.

Lady Heathway had not heard this unusual story and Grace hardly knew what to think of it.

Until suddenly she did.

It seemed far too outrageous to contemplate, but it appeared Lord Gresham was attempting to discourage dance partners by telling all and sundry she'd injured herself. *That* was why Lord Ryland had commented on her walking. Of all the highhandedness!

Grace willed herself to remain composed. She said, "My ankle is perfectly recovered, Mr. Vance."

GEORGE HAD CONSIDERED his plan well thought out. The gentlemen most likely to pursue Miss Yardley must just be turned from it. That would leave behind all the popinjays, fat widowers, and striplings just out of the schoolroom. Miss Yardley would be in no danger with that selection of jesters on her card.

How did one do that at a ball? Well, simply judiciously put it about that the lady was not inclined to dance. She was injured. Not seriously, just enough to take dancing off the table.

Was not a turning of an ankle a particularly common complaint in females? How many times had he been walking by the side of a lady when quite out of the blue she turned an ankle and then needed his arm to reach her destination? Really, it seemed to happen near constantly.

As to what he might say to these turned away gentlemen when it became all too apparent that Miss Yardley was perfectly capable of dancing? And that he himself had put his name down on her card though it was he that said she could not dance?

A sudden recovery. That was also terribly common. He'd noticed that, when he'd got an injured lady to her destination, she was often able to walk unassisted again. As if nothing at all had occurred.

But what was happening now? He'd warned Vance off and yet Vance had flown to her side before George had even seen her come into the ballroom. Now, there were others—Blackwood, Bertridge, even Ryland had left the door to go to her, and a few others he did not deem suitable for this moment in Miss Yardley's history.

It was as if he'd not said anything at all!

George hurried across the floor, practically knocking over Lady Easton as he went. He muscled Blackwood out of the way.

"Miss Yardley," he said, working not to sound breathless from his sprint. He held out his hand for her card.

She regarded him silently for a moment. George almost got the idea that she would not hand it over. He also got a sinking feeling that one of these scoundrels had mentioned that *he* had mentioned she could not dance.

She finally did hand it over and George was perturbed to see that supper, and the first, had already been taken. What was Vance thinking of, taking Miss Yardley into supper? Why had his aunt even allowed it? Lady Heathway did not entirely approve of Mr. Vance.

George wrote his name down for the third, all the while conscious of her stare. It was not a friendly stare.

She was all composure, but decidedly unfriendly.

He bowed and walked off. At least, he hoped he walked off—he rather felt as if he might have slinked off.

He would need time to think. Did she know? Or was she staring for some other reason? If she did know, what should he say about it?

George knew well enough he could not say the truth. That he was not ready to declare himself but did not want anybody else declaring while he was thinking about it. That was what the second season was for. It was an excellent plan, if only everybody would cooperate with it!

GRACE HAD HESITATED when Lord Gresham had approached her for a dance. What did he mean by it? Had not his aim been to see her sitting out, ignored because she had supposedly hurt her ankle?

She had never twisted her ankle in her life and very much doubted it was a thing easily done. Fortunately, there had been enough pleasant gentlemen who dared find out if she was indeed too injured to dance.

She had almost refused to hand over her card to Lord Gresham. But then, he had looked so uncomfortable under her stare. Which she found she enjoyed. She decided he might have a taste of Yardley medicine—she would be all composure.

The first set had been taken by Lord Blackwood and his conversation proved more entertaining than it had been in her prior experience. He usually spoke of his horses, which was not all that interesting. But he'd recently got a Danish boarhound puppy who was running roughshod over his household. The naughty thing growled at the servants as if he were seeing them for the first time every time, he had a penchant for destroying shoes and boots, he invaded the kitchens and growled at the counters because he could not reach what was on them, and he insisted on sleeping in the lord's bed. Lord Blackwood did not know what he was to do when the thing grew full size and he was very much afraid he would be forced to give over his bedchamber to the beast. Apollo, and Grace nearly laughed at hearing such a name for such a ridiculous creature, only took directions from his butler. Lord Blackwood could not yet divine how Mr. Sindu did it. For all that, he was rather besotted with the creature.

They went on to have a lively conversation about childhood dogs and Grace told him the story of Petal—a bulldog who used to push stools and chairs near one another to form a ladder to whatever she was intent on getting to. She was always exhausted when she reached her destination, and then depressed if there were nothing of interest. Her father used to say it was the only exercise she got so they'd better allow her to get on with it.

Lord Bertridge had taken her second set, and he was pleasant, as he always was. Of the more interesting things he communicated was that he had been at the table when Lady Langley, then Miss Wilcox, had solved the mystery the year before. He still could not account for how she did it, as he had been entirely convinced the guilty party had been somebody else.

Finally, and it did feel like finally as Grace experienced some trepidation over it, Lord Gresham came to collect her.

She really wished he did not look quite as handsome as he did. Always, he made her heart speed up, and that she could not help.

How odd, to like someone and not like them at the same

time. To feel what seemed like a deep attraction or affection or something for a person, but also a near-rage at them.

She must disregard her feelings though. She must remember that Lord Gresham worked against her. Twenty years from now it would not matter in the least how attracted she'd ever been to him now. She'd either be living comfortably, watching her children make their way in the world, or she'd be alone in the dower house or possibly not even welcome to live *there*, cursing herself for a fool.

"I'd best take your arm, Lord Gresham," she said serenely, "my violently twisted ankle, you know."

CHAPTER TWELVE

G RACE HAD FOUND herself satisfied to see Lord Gresham blanch over mention of her violently twisted ankle.

As they took their places for the dance, he said, "I did think you had a small limp when you came in from the garden this morning?"

"Indeed, I did not," she said.

"I did think so, though, and thought it would not be wise to put too much strain on it. Perhaps it was just a misperception, then?"

"It was of course very considerate to report my injury to other parties. My *violent* injury, to be more specific."

The music struck up and they took their turn first. Grace was satisfied that he did not appear to have an answer. Perhaps she had embarrassed him enough to turn him from his ridiculous efforts. He did not seem one who would be prone to being petty and vindictive, at least she had not thought so. Perhaps he would think better of it going forward. It really was not worthy of him, no matter how put out he'd been that she'd brought gossip down around the ears of the family.

He certainly was pleasant to dance with, that she could not deny.

"I suppose I was mistaken," Lord Gresham said.

"Very mistaken," Grace said. She kept her tone neutral and her expression just as vague. It was everything her father had taught her about composure.

"I noticed Mr. Vance takes you into supper?" Lord Gresham said. "I was surprised by it, naturally. I don't think my aunt would quite approve."

"Oh, but she did," Grace said, smiling.

"She did," Lord Gresham repeated, as if he needed to hear it again to be sure it was true.

"I quite like Mr. Vance," Grace went on. "He seems such a genuine and kind person. I imagine he is not the sort who might hold a grudge or engage in anything that might be considered vindictive."

Lord Gresham seemed mightily confused by that assessment and Grace thought he had certainly not unraveled the hint about himself.

They had returned to their places. After thinking for a few minutes—minutes Grace was perfectly happy to allow to go by in silence, he said, "I do hope you are not thinking anything serious regarding Mr. Vance."

He was outrageous. If he could not turn Mr. Vance away from her, he would try to turn her away from Mr. Vance? Did he really not perceive that his efforts were not up to the standards of a gentleman? She did not know if she would leave the season with a husband, or if she did who that husband would be. But if it were some gentleman present this evening, including Mr. Vance, it was none of Lord Gresham's affair.

"Any thoughts I have on that particular subject I will very sensibly keep to myself," Grace said.

"I only say, well that is, what I mean, you see, Vance is all well and good in his own way."

"I agree."

"Yes, well as I said, good in his own way, but…"

"Oh yes, he is *very* good in his own way," Grace said.

She was surprised to see Lord Gresham go rather red in the face. What in the world was he trying to accomplish? Was he really determined to turn her from anyone who might express an interest? It was bordering on nonsensical. After all, if she did marry Mr. Vance, she would no longer be connected to his own family—was that not what he wished for?

Whatever it was he meant to accomplish, he did not say anything further to her that was outside of the realms of weather and other commonplaces. He did act so odd though. He'd mentioned he thought it would rain on the morrow three times.

MR. VANCE HAD been as entertaining as she expected. He was quick to tell Grace that he was absolutely hopeless at solving Lord Ryland's mysteries. For one thing, he could never quite believe that anybody in the story was an actual murderer. For another, reading and eating supper at the same time was inconvenient. And for another, he always got a little bored with the whole operation. There had been some years when the mystery had been solved speedily, which had been a delight. But there had been other years when it just dragged on and on.

Grace had laughed and promised she'd do her best to solve it speedily so he would not find himself yawning.

Now, they had entered Lord Ryland's dining room. For all she'd been told of the mystery supper, nobody had mentioned the unusual aspects of the room and its set-up. It was the largest dining room she'd ever seen, or that she suspected existed in all of England. Perhaps only the palaces might claim one larger, though she could not know if that were true or not. There was not one table but many, all arranged to seat four people. Lastly, it appeared their places were assigned, though Grace could not work out what the formula was for who sat where. It was certainly not by rank, as the duchess was seated with Mr. Grubb, the eldest son of a baron and one of Mr. Jacobs' unfortunate friends. The duchess did not look at all enthusiastic about it.

Grace and Mr. Vance were led to a table with Lord Mullhill and Lady Featherstone. Grace had met the lord at Lady Easton's musical evening and found him a genial gentleman, and of course Lady Featherstone was always pleasant. Mr. Vance was equally acquainted with their tablemates, and it seemed as if it would be a jolly party.

As they were talking of this or that, Lord Gresham appeared from nowhere and broke into their conversation.

"Lady Featherstone," he said, "I wondered if you would not rather switch places with me? I am at a table with the duke, and I know you to be old friends."

The duke in question was the only duke present, the Duke of Stanbury, the duchess' husband. Grace stared at Lord Gresham in some amazement. Why was he trying to rearrange things? Was he intending to move in to try to put Mr. Vance off?

He could not possibly be…well, it would verge on diabolical. Certainly, he would not go so far?

Lady Featherstone laughed and said, "I adore the duke, of course, but you could not drag me from this table, Gresham." She glanced at Grace and Mr. Vance. "I have two bright young minds at my disposal and I shall require them! I am determined to prevail this year."

Lord Gresham had nodded and wandered away. Had Grace been left to her own devices, she might have mulled over the mystery of Lord Gresham's character for the next few hours, rather than any mystery Lord Ryland might present. As it was, her attention was captured elsewhere. Lord Ryland had dinged his glass to gain the crowd's attention.

"Welcome, my esteemed guests," he said, his powerful voice having no trouble being heard across the vast expanse of his dining room. "As my repeat visitors are all too aware, there is a little mystery tucked underneath your plate. As always, the prize will not be revealed until a solution has been found. I will only say that if you do not win it, you will be sorry you did not win it. Enjoy!"

Grace lifted her plate and pulled out the folded paper. Lady Featherstone had already applied a lorgnette to her eye and was scanning her own copy. Lord Mullhill nodded at her indulgently. They appeared to be longstanding acquaintances and he would no doubt understand Lady Featherstone's deep desire to come out victorious.

Mr. Vance pretended to suppress a yawn for Grace's amusement. "Speedily, Miss Yardley," he said laughing. "You did promise speedily."

Grace unfolded her paper and read the mystery.

On December 26 of this year, Mr. Robert Fortque, age 46, unmarried, was found dead in his office, with a half glass of wine at his elbow and a suicide note left on the desk. The wine was later discovered to contain massive doses of both arsenic and laudanum. The cause of death was initially ruled a suicide, but later changed to murder. Why did the investigators change their minds? Who killed Mr. Fortque? And why?

Mr. Fortque and Mr. Bernard Leslie, age 42, were longtime business partners in F & L Fine Goods, a venture that sold precious metal candlesticks, tea chests, and other household goods. The business has always been known for its quality of items, is located on Gracechurch Street, and is housed in a large building with other business tenants. Their company slogan is "The finest materials made to last."

The two neighboring offices that shared walls with F & L were occupied by:

Mr. Charles Remel, age 32, clerk for Hasbron Accounting Service

Mrs. Ophelia Welk, age 55, married to the owner of Welk Housekeeping and Cleaning

F & L's office was searched extensively with no relevant evidence coming to the fore. There were minimal paper records, the majority being held at the accounting service next door. Those accounting records were obtained and showed no inconsistencies or hints of mismanagement. Most of the items in the F & L office were boxes of products for sale. Despite the business' claim of using only the finest materials, many of the items were cheaply plated.

The two neighbors, Mr. Remel and Mrs. Welk were interviewed extensively, as the walls between offices were thin and they did occasionally overhear voices at F & L. Mrs. Welk was interviewed multiple times on-site, while Mr. Remel was interviewed once on-site and subsequently interviewed in Devon, where he has since retired.

Both occupants of the adjacent offices tell a set of consistent facts. Neither had ever had a conversation with either partner of F & L. Mrs. Welk had no business with him and Mr. Remel had only been employed a month prior. Both often saw Mr. Leslie coming and going and he was perceived to be the manager of the operation. They saw Mr. Fortque very seldom, but they heard him through the walls often, as when he was there, he was very loud and often distressed. Mr. Fortque was by turns angry, despairing, hysterical, and inconsolable. During these events, the neighbors could not hear Mr. Leslie's replies as he was apparently much more soft-spoken.

Mr. Fortque claimed he would commit suicide on at least two prior occasions, and it seemed his unhappiness was related to a lady he had asked to marry him, but who had declined. The last threat both neighbors heard was on the day of his death, when Mr. Fortque was heard to cry, "A lady has broken Robert Fortque's heart and there is nothing left for me. I will end it all as a mercy to myself." That was overheard early in the day, at approximately ten o'clock. Later, Mrs. Welk spied both gentlemen walking together to their office and presumed they had been out to lunch. At that time, Mr. Fortque did not appear distressed.

Neither of the neighbors overheard anything through the walls on that fateful late afternoon, though Mrs. Welk did see Mr. Leslie leave the premises near four o'clock. She did not see Mr. Fortque leave.

The investigators delved into Mr. Fortque's personal life to determine if he had any enemies.

The lady in question, who allegedly broke Mr. Fortque's heart, was never located and Mr. Leslie said he'd only been told her name was Miss Umbrell and that she was thirty-two.

Mr. Fortque was in an ongoing dispute with a Mayfair neighbor over a cockatoo who Mr. Fortque claimed was loud and disturbed his peace. According to the owner of the bird, Mr. Fortque had once threatened to strangle it, though at this time the bird remains living.

A nephew lived in Mr. Fortque's house and is generally regarded as a ne'er-do-well. He has no income, does not work, and seems exceedingly fond of brandy. The nephew has not benefited from the will, though he appeared shocked to discover it. Mr. Fortque's sister has inherited his very substantial estate, while Mr. Leslie will continue on as proprietor of the concern. Mr. Fortque's sister, a Mrs. Clampion, and her husband were found living in Hertfordshire and claimed surprise at the inheritance, as Mr. Fortque and Mr. Clampion despised one another. The couple has since relocated to Mr. Fortque's house in Mayfair and ousted Mr. Fortque's nephew, who is their son. The son's current whereabouts are unknown. Mrs. Clampion knew nothing of the mysterious Miss Umbrell, though she did believe that lady, or any other, would decline Mr. Fortque, as he had run to fat in recent years.

Who killed Mr. Fortque? Could it have been Mr. Leslie? Or perhaps it was the ne'er-do-well nephew who thought he'd inherit? Or maybe Mr. and Mrs. Clampion had known of the will after all? Or is it possible that the occupants of the neighboring offices, Mrs. Welk and Mr. Remel, colluded together for some reason? Or was there an unknown assailant with mysterious motives? Why does nobody know anything about Miss Umbrell?

Although the investigators concluded that this was a case of murder, it was not until they unraveled one particular thread that they were able to solve the case.

Unravel it too, if you can.

Lady Featherstone laid down her lorgnette decisively. "I really believe this is to be my year, indeed I do. I have already narrowed it down to two primary suspects. Do you wish to hear my theories?"

Lord Mullhill nodded, seeming to know that he would hear

them whether he wished to or not.

"I am on tenterhooks, Lady Featherstone," Mr. Vance said.

Grace gave him a scolding look and said, "Do tell us, Lady Featherstone."

Lady Featherstone looked enormously pleased to have developed her theories so quickly. She said, "I simply used my own investigative skills, honed and sharpened by my attendance at Lord Ryland's criminal society meetings, to narrow it down. First, it may seem that the date of the murder is just one date out of three hundred and sixty-five—it is December twenty-sixth, keep that in mind, as it is significant. Then, a lady hears of the death of a suitor and just disappears into the shadows? Highly unlikely. So, I conclude the first suspect is the mysterious Miss Umbrell. What happened? Well, I think that's clear enough. Mr. Fortque gave the lady a rather substandard Christmas gift and she was enraged. Now, I think to myself, what sort of gift would be that affecting? Paste jewelry would do it. Or even, he gave her one of his own products that he had laying around the office. They were cheaply plated, if you will recall. Goodness, I remember one year that my lord got me something or other, I think it was a set of books. I was very let down over it. I did not go so far as to kill him, but people do have differing temperaments, you know."

Grace forced herself to keep her composure and she did not dare even look at Mr. Vance. Lady Featherstone was a delight. And, she was also certain, very wrong.

"Now," Lady Featherstone continued, "you will wonder who my second suspect is. You may be surprised to know it is none other than the neighbor with the cockatoo. My reasoning for thinking so will make it suddenly clear to you. Mr. Fortque threatened to *strangle* that beloved pet. When I think what I might feel if someone were to threaten my pug Tulip! Well, I might not strangle them, but I might very well throttle them! Or insist my lord throttle them. Or perhaps my butler would throttle them. It's hard to say how it would unfold, but I would be very vexed! So, the neighbor, to save the life of his adored cockatoo, gets rid of the threat. He is very clever, you see. He murders Mr. Fortque in his office rather than his house, as that would be too close to home."

Grace fought to push down the bubbling laughter that threatened to overtake her. She was no longer in any wonderment as to why poor Lady Featherstone came away disappointed, year after year.

"That is exceedingly clever, Lady Featherstone," Grace said. "I can hardly keep up."

"You'll get the hang of it, Miss Yardley," Lady Featherstone said. "It only takes practice. Now, I must get to discovering which of these two is the real villain and how they managed it."

Lady Featherstone had picked up her lorgnette in determination and scanned her clues once more. Out of the corner of her eye, Grace noted that Lord Mullhill and Mr. Vance had quite given up on the effort and had taken to speaking quietly about a bet currently open at their club.

Feeling as if she must help the lady in some fashion, and help Mr. Vance too as it was looking like this might go on for some time, Grace studied her paper once more.

As she read of all these different people, it struck her that the two suspects that Lady Featherstone had selected had nothing to gain by Mr. Fortque's demise. Except saving a cockatoo from a throttling, she supposed, though that did not seem a strong enough motive for murder. So who *did* gain at Mr. Fortque's death?

Mr. Leslie, as the now sole proprietor. The nephew who thought he would inherit something. The sister and her husband who *did* inherit, though they claimed surprise.

Those were the people who had something to gain. But the sister was not even in Town at the time? And, how did the nephew get into the office if it were he?

Only Mr. Leslie had access to the office, as far as she knew. But why would he do it? He was the one person who knew Mr. Fortque was suicidal. If he wanted to be rid of him, why not just wait until Mr. Fortque took the fateful step? Why risk hanging when it seemed the desired outcome was a near surety?

"Oh dear!" Lady Featherstone said. "I wished to narrow it down to one and now I've got it up to three! I find Mr. Remel very suspicious. He left Town, you know. Does that not point to a man who does not want to be questioned?"

Grace nodded, hoping that she looked thoughtful, though she considered the notion of a clerk in the next office murdering Mr. Fortque rather absurd. If there had been a problem with the accounting, then perhaps it might be supposed that Mr. Remel had been stealing, but that had not been the case. Further, Mr. Remel *had* been questioned in Devon, so he had not exactly disappeared. He had only retired.

Grace paused and went back to the beginning of the paper. Yes, as she had thought she remembered. Mr. Remel was a thirty-two-year-old clerk. How had a clerk of that age afforded to retire? Further, he'd just been hired. Why accept a position if he intended to retire so soon?

Had there been some underhanded accounting and Mr. Remel had been caught out by Mr. Fortque?

No, that could not be right. Any clerk who stole money would have a clean set of books to show and they certainly would not leave their position. Leaving was a very good way to get caught, as the next clerk would eventually uncover the deed. It was especially not a good time to leave after there had been a murder next door and all eyes were upon one. In any case, Mr. Remel hardly had time to steal, so short had been his employment.

So where did Mr. Remel get the money? An inheritance? Or, perhaps he blackmailed the real murderer. Being just next door, he might have heard something.

And that brought her back to Mr. Leslie. Though she still could not work out why a man would kill another man who was already suicidal. That was the real sticking point.

"And now I find I cannot rule out Mrs. Welk either!" Lady

Featherstone cried. "She tells the same precise story as Mr. Remel. Is that not suspicious?"

Grace nodded, though it did not seem particularly suspicious to her. She supposed they told of hearing the same thing because they *had* heard the same thing. Mr. Fortque was in despair.

Grace glanced up and saw Lord Gresham heading toward their table again. What on earth was he doing?

"Did you call me over, Lady Featherstone?" he asked.

"Dear me, no," Lady Featherstone said, appearing rather flustered in keeping all her suspects in order.

"I could have sworn…" Lord Gresham trailed off.

Grace could not work out what end he worked toward.

Mr. Vance said, "Good God, Gresham, you're imagining quite a lot these days, eh? First Miss Yardley's ankle and now voices are calling to you?"

Lord Gresham turned on his heel and stalked off. Grace watched him return to his table. He practically threw himself into his chair. Neither Miss Huntskill nor Lady Mary appeared particularly amused. Miss Huntskill had just rolled her eyes and Lady Mary very decidedly turned to the duke.

Whatever Lord Gresham was doing, and Grace thought it was beginning to seem wildly childish, he was not proving himself a pleasant dinner partner to those two ladies.

"I am feeling very defeated," Lady Featherstone said. "I cannot work it out. Another year is slipping through my fingers. Perhaps my investigative skills are not as sharp as I had thought."

Poor Lady Featherstone. She really did look defeated.

"Certainly you are mistaken," Grace said. "Why, I have no suspects at all and you already have three."

"Four," Lady Featherstone said dejectedly.

Mr. Vance and Lord Mullhill had entirely thrown over the mystery and were now on to considering the various horses who would likely turn up for the two-thousand guinea stakes at Newmarket. Grace really wished they would take pity and help the lady.

She supposed it was up to her, if there was any help she could offer. She did feel Mr. Leslie was the most likely culprit, if only she could divine why he would risk his neck when there was no need.

But perhaps that was it. Perhaps there was a need. Mr. Leslie was the only one who knew Mr. Fortque was suicidal.

What if he wasn't? What if the voice the neighbors heard was not Mr. Fortque at all?

The neighbors had never heard two voices in the office, only one. They presumed Mr. Leslie was too soft-spoken and they presumed they heard Mr. Fortque because that gentleman identified himself by name. *A lady has broken Mr. Fortque's heart.* Who spoke of themselves like that outside of the king and queen?

The pieces began to come together quickly. Now, Grace must just get Lady Featherstone to see it.

"My lady," Grace said softly, "do have a look at this, and this also."

She directed Lady Featherstone's attention to the salient facts. Then she said, "I wonder if it were ever Mr. Fortque's voice at all. And I wonder how a clerk retires at thirty-two."

As if the clouds parted and shined the rays of the sun down upon Lady Featherstone, she saw what Grace had seen. She turned over the paper and grabbed a stick of lead. "Hold my lorgnette against my eyes, my dear, while I write out the solution."

CHAPTER THIRTEEN

G RACE HELD LADY Featherstone's lorgnette so she could see what she was putting down. She also read along as the lady wrote, making sure she kept heading in the right direction. Lady Featherstone finished with a flourish and raced to Lord Ryland, waving the paper over her head.

Mr. Vance and Lord Mullhill looked on with incredulity.

Grace laughed and said, "You did say speedily, Mr. Vance?"

Lord Ryland dinged his glass to gain the attention of the room. "Ladies, gentlemen, it is my honor to tell you that Lady Featherstone has solved what has been the most complicated mystery I have ever put forth."

There was a rather enthusiastic round of applause, as it seemed most in the room understood how much Lady Featherstone strived every year, only to be denied.

Lord Ryland continued. "The solution hangs on one particular deduction and that was, it was never Mr. Fortque ranting and raving about being disappointed in love. It was Mr. Leslie all along, working to set up his partner's character as suicidal so he might murder him and gain control of the business. He had been substituting what had been fine goods with cheap plate to widen his profit margin and pocket the difference. Mr. Fortque was on the verge of discovering it.

Grace smiled as there were various murmurings along the lines of *naturally, that is what I was thinking.*

"He was caught out and blackmailed by Mr. Remel, the newly-hired clerk next door, when Mr. Remel encountered Mr. Leslie in the corridor and asked him a question about the accounts. Mr. Remel instantly recognized the voice as the one he'd heard as Mr. Fortque. The investigators began to unravel the whole thing when the clerk could not account for his newfound money, which he had been paid by Mr. Leslie to keep him quiet. Mr. Leslie will hang in two weeks' time."

"Brava, Lady Featherstone!" the duke called out.

Lady Featherstone beamed and Grace could not be more delighted for her. To Grace, the mystery had meant nothing. She had her own mystery to think about by way of Lord Gresham's bizarre behavior. But to Lady Featherstone, this was a pinnacle of her investigative career.

Lord Ryland had bade Lady Featherstone wait where she was as he strode to meet a footman at the doors. The footman carried a cream velvet pillow, and upon it was a rather spectacular broach containing a large emerald surrounded by diamonds.

Lord Ryland presented it to Lady Featherstone and said, "This broach was designed by Louis David Duval for Catherine, Empress of Russia, to add to her emerald collection. The emerald itself was mined at special request by Mr. Duval, and many that were sent to him for inspection were rejected, until this one was selected for its color and clarity. It can be supposed that the empress favored emeralds as they are thought to sharpen the wits. Our Lady Featherstone has shown us that she has no need of *that* sort of help, but I hope she will enjoy the decoration all the same."

As the broach was pinned to her dress, Grace almost feared Lady Featherstone would faint. She did not quite hit the floor, though she did need assistance to a chair and a vinaigrette was procured to bring her back to her senses.

THE REST OF the evening had gone on jolly. Mr. Vance and Lord Mullhill may have ignored the mystery, but they fully understood their duty at this important moment in Lady Featherstone's career. The supper was one of congratulations and wondering how she did it.

Lady Featherstone regaled them with all of her thoughts about the neighbor, about the nephew, about the clerks, and about the mysterious lady, as if she had interrogated them all personally. Suddenly, the neighbor was found to be a nervous creature incapable of taking any decisive action on behalf of his bird, Mrs. Welk was discovered a motherly figure who would not injure a fly, the mysterious lady was just now married to somebody else, and the unfortunate nephew was dead from drink. That none of those ideas had been contained in the mystery seemed of no account.

As she observed the rather astonished faces gazing at her, Lady Featherstone merely patted her broach and murmured, "It's all in the training, you see. Do not be dejected that you did not win this year. You were up against far more experienced investigators."

Grace was rather tickled that the lady seemed to be inventing her own memories.

Now, as the carriage approached the house, Lady Heathway sighed and said, "I'm surprised she worked it out. She never works it out."

"Lady Featherstone was very clever about it," Grace said.

"So it seems. Of course, I am delighted for Anne. I only fear we'll never hear the end of it. She'll wear that broach everywhere, hoping to be asked about it. Will she even wait to be asked? Probably not. I suppose next year's dresses will be ordered to complement it."

Grace did not answer, but she thought Lady Heathway's fears on that front were well-warranted. Lady Featherstone's mind would be consumed with her victory and Grace found it rather charming and delightful.

The carriage rolled to a stop and Gregory ran down the steps to open the door. He helped Lady Heathway to the street as would be usual, though Grace could not help noticing he appeared rather wild-eyed. She hoped Mr. Ranston had not been waving around his gun in the garden again.

As they made their way up the steps, Grace began to wonder if Mr. Ranston was indeed out of doors waving his gun around, as he was not at the door. Benny was there, looking as if he'd seen a ghost.

Lady Heathway looked around and said, "Where is Ranston? Has he taken to his bed again?"

The two footmen stood silent and looked terrified, as if they were two rabbits staring down the barrel of a farmer's gun.

"Gracious, one of you had better say something," Lady Heathway said sternly.

Gregory cleared his throat and said, "Mr. Ranston is asleep. In the drawing room."

Lady Heathway's brows shot up rather high on her forehead. Grace supposed that, for all the latitude she afforded her butler, she did not approve of him napping in the drawing room as if he were the master of the house.

Lady Heathway strode toward the doors. Benny ran ahead of her to get them open.

Grace hurried behind Lady Heathway.

The scene that met them next was not one Grace would likely forget in her lifetime.

Mr. Ranston was sprawled face down on the floor, his hair askew and one shoe come off.

"My God," Lady Heathway said softly, "is he dead?"

"No, not dead, my lady," Gregory said, as if this was the one bit of positive news he could relate.

"But, what has happened to him?" Lady Heathway asked. "Why does he lie there like that? How did he get there?"

Benny nudged Gregory, as if to say—*you'd better tell it.*

Gregory, seeing he was nominated as the spokesperson, took a deep breath and said, "What happened, my lady, is that you might remember that Mr. Ranston found that a small amount of brandy did calm his nerves whenever he was awaiting an attack on the house."

Gregory's eyes drifted to the side table where the brandy was kept. Grace's eyes went there too. The decanter was tipped over and drained dry.

"So, I think his theory might have been that if a little helped a little, a lot would help a lot," Gregory said. "At least, that's my reckoning."

Seeing Lady Heathway's shock at realizing her butler was drunk on her drawing room floor, Gregory hurried on. "He weren't wrong, at first. He got ever so cheerful and even sang some songs. But then, he sat down in a chair and started weeping about some fella he met in the war. Then he stood and cried, "Wilbert Ranston will not retreat from danger!" Then he fell where he stood. Right there. We checked, he ain't dead."

"I see," Lady Heathway said gravely. "And did you not think to move him to his quarters?"

"We tried!" Benny said. "He's like a sack of lead, he's that's heavy. So then we were hoping maybe he'd just wake up before you came back."

Lady Heathway folded her arms and surveyed the circumstances. "Gregory, find the key to the drawing room doors. We will lock them. I do not wish Lord Heathway to come home and trip over him in the dark. If Mr. Ranston rises before morning, he will be able to unlock the doors from the inside. Benny, find a pillow and blanket and arrange Mr. Ranston as comfortable as you can. Then we'll say no more about it."

Lady Heathway took Grace's arm, and they left the footmen to their work.

They passed out the doors and Grace heard Benny say quietly, "He won't like the situation when he wakes up."

"It'll be all right," Gregory said. "He'll take to his bed for a few days and then be back to his old self."

What was said between them next Grace did not hear, though she was ever surprised at how sympathetic the two footmen were to their rather eccentric superior.

As she and Lady Heathway mounted the stairs, Grace whispered, "Will Mr. Ranston be dismissed?"

Lady Heathway looked at her in some surprise. "Goodness, no. Who would hire him?"

Grace was rather delighted with the response. It seemed that once a person was under Lady Heathway's wing, they were there forevermore. She supposed she should have realized that after her drainpipe adventure—another lady would have sent her packing.

At her door, Lady Heathway said, "It was a long and trying evening, so do sleep in on the morrow."

Grace thought that was very good advice. It had been a long, sometimes interesting and sometimes vexing, evening. She was exhausted.

>>>><<<<

GEORGE RODE SLOWLY by his aunt's house on the way to his own. The lights were still on and he wondered if he might stop in.

Then he cursed himself for a lunatic. Nobody stopped in at three o'clock in the morning.

Of course, he realized he had not just become a lunatic at this moment. No, indeed. He'd acted the lunatic all evening.

What had he been thinking, telling gentlemen that Miss Yardley had twisted an ankle? *Violently* twisted, he'd said. Nobody had believed a word of it, but one of them had been kind enough to inform Miss Yardley of the ruse.

Vance, probably.

Oh, that fellow had moved right in. He'd had the nerve to put himself down for supper! It was outrageous.

George was not so stupid as to believe his own internal ranting. It was not Vance who had been outrageous. It was himself.

Miss Yardley had not appreciated his little gambit, that much had been clear. She'd managed to let him know that fact, while still remaining exceedingly composed. He had not liked to find himself on the receiving end of her polite punishment, but he could not help but to admire it at the same time.

She really was such a lady. Yes, it was true that she'd climbed down a drainpipe. But that had been in service to her mother. Was that not what a real lady was? As graceful as a princess, and yet as strong-willed as a warrior queen?

But what had happened to his wits this evening? The story of the twisted ankle had been extremely ill-advised. Did he stop there? No! Then he tried to talk Lady Featherstone into changing places so that he might keep an eye on Vance. When that didn't work, he'd went so far as to pretend he'd thought Lady Featherstone had called him over. It had been stupid, he knew. And yet he could not stop himself. Who knew if Vance would suddenly decide to declare himself?

Vance knew, he supposed. The devil had been moving in with all his entertaining talk and jolly spirits. Vance really was too jolly for anybody's comfort. Certainly, Miss Yardley saw that. Did she really wished to be entertained her whole life? Would that not be exhausting? She was probably already finding him tiresome. Or would do soon. Hopefully.

Of course, Vance was not the only gentleman at supper who was found tiresome. Neither Lady Mary nor Miss Huntskill had been at all impressed by his performance. Miss Yardley had not been either, he could hazard a guess.

He reached his house, dismounted, and handed his horse over to a footman.

He had to get hold of himself. Miss Yardley was driving him insane.

JACOBS MAY HAVE been barred from Ryland's ball, but he had not immediately left the neighborhood. He'd lurked outside for some hours, seething that Ryland had not admitted him.

As he imagined what went on inside, his anger grew like a ball of fire in his belly. Who was this little chit from the countryside? How was it that she could be so outrageous as to climb down the side of a house, and somehow it was he who was at fault? It was he who must be punished?

He must get back into society. He must have invitations flowing once more. He could not bear to sit home alone as the world drank champagne without him. And what would his father say? He knew well enough his father would hear of it eventually. If there was one thing that could be counted on from the *ton*, it was that they never stopped talking. This one would tell that one who would tell another one. He'd used that precise knowledge to send his bon mots and jokes flying round the town.

Oh, he'd always known it was a dangerous sport. However, it had given him some welcome status and the fact was, he could not help it. It had always been so. There was something about poking at a person's weak point or making a joke about an embarrassing interlude that delighted him. His father called it a character flaw, but then the old man had not the sharp wit that he had.

Now, letters would be written to that dour fellow. Hints would be dropped. *My dear baron, your eldest son has managed to become persona non grata.*

By what mechanism had it occurred though? It must have been through Lady Heathway and her cabal of matrons. It certainly wasn't done by Miss Yardley. She did not have that kind of power.

How to undo it? There were only two directions to go. One, he could throw himself on the mercy of Lady Heathway and her friends and ask for forgiveness. Even if he could bear to do it, which he had his doubts, he did not believe it would work. Or, he chose not to believe it could work because he'd rather spit in their faces than say anything conciliatory. The other direction was to prove Miss Yardley had climbed out a window and that she was likely to do the same again. He must prove his moniker was all too apt. Miss Yardley was indeed *The Sprinter*. He just needed to figure out how to accomplish it. If he could do it, though, she'd be through and he'd be back into prominent houses.

As he watched guests eventually leave Lord Ryland's house, including Lady Featherstone who appeared to be celebrated from all sides, an idea began to form. An idea *before* an idea, actually.

He did not have enough information to form any kind of effective plan or strategy and so that was what he would seek—information.

And who better to supply information than a servant? There was always a servant or two who would do just about anything for the right price. The senior footman on his father's estate had always procured him anything he liked for a price—he'd been drinking brandy since he was eleven. On the rare occasion a bottle was noticed missing, a low-ranking servant was blamed and dismissed. Certainly, there was a person of that ilk working in Lady Heathway's house.

Jacobs smiled. He had one very important advantage in that sort of effort. He was very rich and he could pay very well.

⟫⟫⟩✳⟨⟨⟨

GRACE HAD TAKEN Lady Heathway's advice and stayed abed until late morning. Betsy had brought her a tray so that she might breakfast in her room.

While she did so, Betsy regaled her what had gone on in the house the night before.

"It all started out regular as anything," Betsy said. "Regular for *this* house anyway. We all had our wood clubs by our side in case of a break-in, and Mr. Ranston was prowling the house. Then, he starts taking nips of brandy here and there. And by the way, I think Jenny was doing it too, she really is a daring sort of kitchen maid. Then, as will be no surprise to anybody, the brandy made Mr. Ranston feel very heroic and he told us all sorts of stories of his derring-do in the war and how he even dragged one soldier out of a linen closet in a seminary and gave him a good talking to so as to restore the man's spirits and get him out into the fight."

"Oh, dear, the poor man was so terrified that he was hiding in a linen closet?" Grace asked.

"'Parently so, though Mr. Ranston fixed him up by explaining his patriotic duty and how the king was counting on him. Then," Betsy went on, "he sang us a few songs and that's when I really started to wonder if he hadn't drunk enough of Lord Heathway's brandy. Then he ran out of the room crying and so I thought I better see where he was going as I still remember him shooting at you."

Grace certainly did remember that too and was not likely to ever forget it.

"So I follows him to the main hall, and Gregory and Benny came too. Mr. Ranston walks right into the drawing room and sits himself down as if he owns the place and then starts crying about the fellow in the linen closet which just an hour before he'd been so cheerful about. Then he stands up and shouts something about not hiding from danger and falls over like a pile of bricks on the carpet."

"Lady Heathway says he's not to be dismissed, which I thought rather kind," Grace said.

"Or loony, if you ask me," Betsy said. "He's stayin' abed today and Mrs. Redwiggin is feeding him tea and toast, on Lady Heathway's orders. The lady has also moved the brandy to a locked cabinet and gave Lord Heathway the key, so don't ask me how Mr. Ranston will fortify himself the next time he's guarding the house."

Grace was rather bemused by what had gone on in the house, and sympathetic to how Betsy viewed it. When she attempted to imagine Manfred getting drunk and falling over in one of the drawing rooms of Barlow Hall, she really could not picture it. Or imagine what would have been the aftermath. Though, she was fairly certain a day of rest with tea and toast would not have been on the list of possibilities.

Betsy left her to her own tea and toast and Grace leaned back and allowed all the memories of last evening to flood over her. Mr. Ranston lying unconscious on the drawing room floor had really been the least of it.

How far would Lord Gresham take this spiteful little game he played? Must she always be looking over her shoulder to determine what he would do next?

It was upsetting enough to have encountered Mr. Jacobs and seen how angry he really was over being excluded. But now it seemed she had a second enemy.

But it made no sense! He was Lady Heathway's nephew, and she was being shielded by Lady Heathway. Why should he wish to cause more trouble?

Was she in some way misreading the situation?

She did not see how she could be.

Grace wiped away a tear that had somehow had the audacity to present itself. It was so unfair that she should be drawn to him and also punished by him. She should find it easy to thoroughly dislike him. And she did. But then she didn't.

Her mind disliked him because her mind was a very sensible creature. Her heart, though, was unruly and nonsensical.

She did not know what she was to do about it, other than be rational. Everything she did from now on must be rational.

Mr. Vance seemed to have some small interest in her. Was there something there?

There was not something romantic there, of that she was sure. But had not couples got on very well, simply as friends? He would be a rather marvelous friend, she was certain.

She would have time to think it over, as the next two days would be very quiet. She and Lady Heathway would make some calls, of course. But the evening entertainments would only be tomorrow evening when the duchess and her duke would come for whist with Lord and Lady Heathway. It was a longstanding engagement between the couples during the season—once a fortnight they would play one another and then have a buffet supper. Grace's only duty was to spend some time softly playing at the pianoforte while they played their games. She was at once hopeful that it would be a peaceful evening, and fearful that it might not. Lady Heathway and the duchess were so competitive with one another that Grace could only imagine the less than cheerful spirits of the lady who lost.

After that evening, they would attend Lady Tredwell's masque ball. Lady Heathway had met with Madame LeGrange to have something made for Grace to wear to it, though she did not yet know what it was. All she did know was that it would throw Miss Wilcox's dress of last year into shadow and that dress had been a ridiculous collection of petals meant to appear as a rose. So, Grace supposed she would not turn up as a rose of any sort.

The masque would be her next venture out into the wider world and Grace was determined to make some decisions. Did anybody prefer her to other ladies? Did she prefer anyone, excepting the diabolical Lord Gresham, of course? And if she did not prefer someone who seemed to prefer her, what could she live with? Might it be Lord Ryland and his odd interest in murder? Or Mr. Vance, who was always so jolly but for whom there was not a spark at all? Or even Lord Bertridge, though he was rather straitlaced. Or maybe Lord Blackwood? After all, Lord Blackwood had just got a rather charming puppy—might that not be pleasant?

If any of those gentlemen asked, she would accept. She would say yes. Because Grace Yardley was not an idiot who would end a spinster on account of her ungovernable heart.

THE TWO DAYS had passed by peacefully, just as Grace had supposed they would. Reading and sewing and occasionally playing the pianoforte had been good for her. Especially reading, as it could take her mind well away from her own thoughts and plunk them into another world. In that world, a heroine might face all sorts of danger, but Grace could close the book and be satisfied that it was not herself chased by a ghost or finding oneself in the clutches of greedy and dangerous relations or looking everywhere for a missing fiancé. Though, she supposed after all she *was* looking everywhere for the missing fiancé.

Mr. Ranston had recovered from his adventure with Lord Heathway's brandy, though whenever he entered the drawing room he glanced at where the decanter had once stood as if it were a constant scold against him.

Betsy said he'd regained his dignity below stairs by claiming he was not drunk at all, but merely experienced a fainting seizure. Which ran in his family. If he were to suddenly crash to the floor in future, they were to immediately apply a vinaigrette.

Betsy could not say if anybody believed this story, only that she certainly did not. Nor did the kitchen maid, she supposed. When Mr. Ranston wasn't looking, Jenny had taken to falling to the floor behind the kitchen counter, which seemed to entertain her more than it did anybody else. Mrs. Redwiggin had even threatened to dismiss her, but the cheeky girl only laughed at the idea.

Grace had donned a simple but exceedingly well-cut muslin gown and gone down to the drawing room to await the duke and duchess for their game of whist.

She did not wait long, as that couple arrived promptly at eight o'clock. The duchess told her she looked charming, and the duke was kind enough to hope that they did not bore her too terribly much by staying in.

Grace assured him she would not be bored in the least. The truth was, she would be delighted to find herself bored for once. It felt as if her nerves had been in a constant high pitch these past weeks. It was of course, all her own fault. It had begun with her believing her mother did poorly, but since then Lady Barlow had written of her various triumphs over her nurse and it seemed she did well. Grace had been the author of her own trouble, but that was over. From now on, she would be the author of her own rationality and success.

She sat herself at the pianoforte as the couples began their game. Grace had been certain that the couples would play against one another, but that was not the case. It was the duchess and Lady Heathway ranged against their husbands. This might either end exceedingly pleasant or exceedingly awful. Were the two ladies to win, they would happily crow about it and congratulate one another. Grace did not think either of the gentlemen would be too devastated if they lost the game. However, if the ladies found themselves the losers, then there would be *two* very unhappy ladies rather than just one.

Grace chose a pleasant little group of Haydn's sonatas that stayed away from the lower octaves. She could play them softly and they would have a soothing quality, which might be needed, depending on how events unfolded at the card table.

Mr. Ranston came in and Grace did not at first see that he led someone in behind him.

CHAPTER FOURTEEN

M R. RANSTON HAD led Lord Gresham into the drawing room.

Grace's hands froze over the keys. Why was he here? He was not a part of their game. He should not be here.

"George," Lady Heathway said, "what do you do here, I had not expected you."

Lord Gresham bowed and said, "Aunt, duchess, duke." He paused, then said, "Miss Yardley."

Grace merely nodded. She flipped through sheet music to seem as if she were doing something, though she did not have any particular need for the sheets.

"I simply found myself at loose ends this evening and thought I would stop in. I quite forgot you had an engagement."

"You are very welcome of course," Lady Heathway said. "Perhaps Grace will indulge you with a game of piquet?"

"Oh no, Lady Heathway," Grace said hurriedly, "I'd much rather play for you. I do not favor the game and am quite bad at it."

Lady Heathway nodded, though Lord Gresham appeared perplexed.

"Remind me another day, Grace, and I will give you some pointers on the game," Lady Heathway said. "Well, George, you might take up a book?"

Lord Gresham had nodded at the suggestion, but rather than

go to the bookshelf, he came to the pianoforte. "I suppose I could turn the sheets?"

"I don't actually need the sheets," Grace said firmly.

"But you were just looking through them," Lord Gresham said.

"I was only curious to see what was here. That is all."

"I see," Lord Gresham said.

Grace had hoped he would then go find himself a book. His standing so nearby made her…what? Nervous? No, unsettled.

The card game across the room had begun and Grace began to play. Lord Gresham did not go anywhere. Rather, he leaned himself against the instrument and regarded her.

"I suspect you are put out about my comments regarding the suitability of Mr. Vance," Lord Gresham said. "I have nothing against the man, but he is only to be a baron. I imagine my aunt would wish you to shoot higher than that."

Grace reminded herself to remain composed, but it really was getting difficult to do so.

"I suppose Lady Barlow, too," Lord Gresham went on. "Would she not wish you to shoot higher? Well, she probably wishes you to take your time, a second season even, and *then* shoot higher."

Now he was supposing he understood her mother's wishes too?

As Grace's fingers lightly flew across the keys, she said, "I believe it is my purview to *shoot*, as you term it, as high or low as I like."

"Yes," Lord Gresham said slowly, "but a lady as young and inexperienced as yourself must also wish to take the advice of older and wiser people."

"I am twenty, my lord. I have hardly just broken out of the schoolroom."

"I am twenty-six."

"Congratulations."

There was a long pause after that particular statement. Grace was not surprised by it, as it had been the sort of thing she ought to have thought, rather than said.

"I only say," Lord Gresham plowed on, "that older and wiser people may know what would be best for you."

Though Grace's composure was generally so reliable, it had never been tested to such a degree. Who did he think he was? Why did he think he was so clever? Did he really imagine she did not see through his ruse? He wished to ruin her chances and mask that effort by pretending it was only concern for her future. Because he was twenty-six?

Her composure, as long a rope as it might be, had an end as all ropes did. She'd finally come to it.

"Lord Gresham, you should know that I am a sensible person who is all too cognizant of her duty to a widowed mother. If a gentleman asks for my hand, I will very sensibly accept. Immediately. And that includes Mr. Vance. I intend on marrying and making provisions for my mother at the very first opportunity. I would appreciate it if you would cease your meddling, as it is none of your affair."

Grace bent over the keys and concentrated on her playing, lest she tip over and hit the carpet like a pile of bricks, just as Ranston had done two days earlier. She'd never given anybody such a dressing-down in her life. She suspected her father would not be approving of precisely how discomposed she'd become.

Lord Gresham did not answer her salvo, but rather marched to the bookshelf, took a book and threw himself into a chair.

Her fingers trembled and she willed them to stop, but in the meantime, she chose a much slower piece of music so she could keep control of where her hands were going.

Fortunately, the duchess and Lady Heathway provided some distraction. First, they'd had a thorough discussion about the shock of Lady Featherstone figuring out Lord Ryland's mystery and their trepidation over how many lectures would be foisted upon them regarding how she'd done it. They were in total agreement that they were already tired of her staring down at the emerald broach and it would probably be with them like an unwanted extra person for the rest of their days.

Then, they were in total agreement that their lords were not playing very well and that it was nearly a forgone conclusion that they would come out the victors.

Then the duchess commented that there was a certain nobility in the composition of Lady Heathway's furniture. While Grace was well aware that Lady Heathway thought the duchess threw round the word *noble* excessively, she seemed to take that particular application in cheerful stride.

Finally, they had an in-depth discussion about Lord and Lady Wunderman. Grace did not know them, nor had she even heard of them. But it appeared as if Lord Wunderman was irate that his lady had redecorated their entire house while he was on the continent attending to some government business. Lady Wunderman, for her part, felt it was a suitable answer to her lord's seemingly unending and embarrassingly schoolboy appreciation for Lady Calhoun's wit. If Lady Wunderman could not be as witty as that irritating lady, she would at least have new drapes, carpets, bedding, and sofas.

Lady Heathway and the duchess appeared to find great amusement in the idea, though when Grace glanced over it did not seem as if the two lords were equally diverted. Perhaps they wondered what would happen to their own houses should they find another lady too witty for their wives' comfort.

In the end, Lady Heathway and the duchess prevailed at whist over their husbands. It seemed an outcome that was very usual and Grace wondered if the lords did not find it more convenient to come out the losers as it kept their ladies in such good spirits.

Grace was relieved that supper had been announced as her fingers were quite worn out. She would have stopped playing ages ago, but what was she to do? Sit across from Lord Gresham as he pretended to read? She was certain he was not reading as she did not think he had at all turned a page.

She had thought about claiming an illness and retiring, but she was starving and did not think she could manage until morning with only the biscuits in the tin in her room. She could also do with a glass of wine.

At least now he would go, and she could have her glass of wine in peace. She might even ask for madeira. Truthfully, if it would not have shocked, she'd ask for Lord Heathway's brandy.

"Do you stay for supper, George?" Lady Heathway asked. "It will be no trouble at all. We have a buffet on these nights so it is quite casual."

"Delighted, Aunt."

Delighted? Why should he be delighted? He had sat an entire evening pretending to read a book. One would think he'd be ready to get out of the house and go to his club. Or go home. Or jump off a bridge if that would be more convenient.

"Come, Grace," Lady Heathway said kindly, "I fear you have quite worn yourself out providing us with music for so long a time. I ought to have told you to rest ages ago, but it was so very pleasant."

"Miss Yardley plays beautifully," the duchess said. "Of course, we all did wonder when we'd hear Miss Wilcox play."

The duchess and Lady Heathway gave each other meaningful frowns and Grace supposed they were of one mind regarding Lady Langley's as yet undiscovered musical ability.

THE SUPPER WAS indeed a buffet and whatever Ranston's nerves might be, he certainly could rally the staff to produce quite a good dinner. There were cold dishes of meats, salads, jellies, and pickled vegetables, as well as hot dishes of a ham, a chicken, a roasted beef, and a dish of fish in a sauce, along with broiled onions and stewed cabbage. At the end of the board, there was a selection of cakes, candied fruits, and stewed pears.

Grace attempted to be delicate in her selections, but really she felt as if she could eat a mountain of food. Her appetite always grew when she was out of sorts. She had eaten all the day long when her father had died. There were some who wasted away from upset, her mother was such a person, but Grace only piled her plate ever higher.

The addition of Lord Gresham seemed to only increase her appetite. She had been placed next to the duke, who was on Lady Heathway's right. That left Lord Gresham across the table, seated next to the duchess.

She really wished he would have gone home. She had decided, firmly, to go forward with practicality at the forefront of her mind. It might be difficult to pledge herself to someone she did not love. She really did not appreciate Lord Gresham making it even more difficult. He must just go away and allow her to get on with it!

"Now, Penelope," the duchess said, "what do you do for Lady Tredwell's masque? I, myself, will go as Minerva. There is something noble in her, I always thought."

Grace saw a flicker of irritation cross Lady Heathway's expression. It seemed it was perfectly fine for her furniture placement to be noble, but that was where it ended.

"I have chosen Boudicca," Lady Heathway said. "I feel it will send the right message."

"Ah, the lady warrior," the duke said.

"Just so."

"And what does Miss Yardley come as?" the duchess asked.

"That is to be kept a surprise, even from you, Theodosia. But rest assured, it will reflect well on Grace, and our society at large."

The duchess nodded. "I am intrigued, Penelope. I look eagerly forward to see what you have designed. Of course, I will at some point be taking my own girl to this sort of thing and I probably ought to be thinking of ideas now."

"I highly advise it," Lady Heathway said. "One cannot plan too much. Preparation is the key to everything and cannot be done too thoroughly."

"Though I wonder," Lord Gresham said, "is Lady Tredwell's

masque really suitable to a young lady just out?"

Grace nearly dropped her fork. What now? Was this an attempt to convince Lady Heathway to leave her at home? Though she nearly *dropped* her fork, she had a great wish to use it as a trident and hurl it across the table.

"Goodness, Gresham," the duchess said laughing, "you are becoming rather a stickler in your old age. One might think you've been spending too much time with Bertridge."

Lord Heathway and the duke both laughed heartily over the idea, as Lord Bertridge was very well-liked, but he *was* a terrible stickler. He could at times make his aunt, Lady Easton, seem positively carefree, so strict were his ideas of what was right.

Though the two older gentlemen laughed, Lord Gresham did not seem as amused.

"I would not say there is anything of the stickler in the opinion," he said. "I only wonder if anybody had considered that there will be so many there who are disguised as to their real identity. So many men in disguise."

"My dear nephew, if you are afraid that some lothario will carry Grace off, put those fears aside. The lady warrior Boudicca will be by her side."

Lord Gresham did not seem to have an answer to Boudicca and only stabbed at his chicken.

Much to Grace's relief, the conversation turned and the matter appeared to be settled. She was rather admiring of Lady Heathway, and not for the first time. It seemed no matter what sort of machinations Lord Gresham attempted to launch to hinder her progress, Lady Heathway was there to bar the door against them.

GEORGE STORMED DOWN the road. He had not brought his horse, as his aunt lived so nearby. He had not even been sure he would go in until he was positively at her door. He was perfectly aware that it was his aunt's and uncle's evening to play cards with the duke and duchess. How could he not be? They'd had the same appointment once a fortnight during the season for above ten years.

He'd assumed Miss Yardley would remain in with them, and probably be left to read or sew or play some music.

That was about all he'd got right on this blasted night.

First, he was informed that she wished to marry immediately.

Immediately, she said. And she would be delighted to accept anybody who was not the butler. Vance included!

What happened to the idea of a second season? What happened to her taking her time?

And then, to accuse him of meddling? What had he really done but provide her with some hints that would be to her benefit? And perhaps mention to certain individuals that she had hurt her ankle...

Well, once he had been apprised of her wish to throw herself at the nearest gentleman, then of course he'd had to take steps.

He really thought that once he pointed out the dangers of the masque, because of all the men in masks, his aunt would perceive the threat instantly. But no! They'd all laughed at him and compared him to Bertridge. They'd called him a stickler.

He was not a stickler. Certainly, he was not.

Now what, though? Miss Yardley might be asked for her hand by anyone at any time. There would be no days of her thinking about it when he might step forward himself. No, she would accept on the spot!

"I won't have it," he said loudly as he bounded up his steps. "I will not brook this nonsense."

A footman had flung the door open at his approach and looked at him in near terror. George strode past him and into the library to find his brandy.

"Tell Pemmington that if my brandy decanter is not filled, I want it filled," he shouted over his shoulder.

If that little miss thought she was going to wed herself to the likes of Harry Vance, she had another thing coming!

>>>×<<<

JACOBS HAD NO trouble at all discerning who in Lady Heathway's household might be prevailed upon to be bribed to do his bidding. There were some officious-looking lady's maids and an even more officious-looking housekeeper. The butler looked as they always did—as if they found the world a very dreary place. The two footmen gave themselves away by always looking to the butler for his opinion, so they would never be disloyal and throw in with an outsider.

He had almost given up on watching the comings and goings from the house. But just before he did, he found Jenny.

She was precisely what looked for and he'd known it in a moment. She'd walked by him and given him a daring and saucy smile. He'd followed her and struck up a conversation. She'd looked his clothes over and said he seemed like a rich swell. He mentioned he was very rich and might share some of his riches for certain information.

For a mere ten pounds, he'd already been informed of why Miss Yardley had been climbing down a drainpipe—she had got the idea of flying to Kent to rescue her malingering mother. Now, apparently, the mother had made improvements and was no longer a concern.

He also discovered the mechanism for the abuse heaped upon his head. Lady Heathway and the Duchess of Stanbury had sent out letters asking that he never be invited anywhere they chose to bring Miss Yardley.

It had taken all his self-control not to shout to the wind when he'd heard that. He did control himself though. Because Jenny had given him a rather ingenious idea that would put a period to the end of Miss Yardley's sentence, thereby restoring himself to society's good graces. He had an idea of how to make the sprinter sprint again. Publicly, this time.

He'd promised Jenny twenty pounds if she could deliver what he required. He needed the latest letter written by Lady Barlow.

Jenny seemed a brazen thing, so he had every confidence in the world that she would breeze right into Miss Yardley's room and breeze back out with it. How a kitchen maid was to explain being above stairs was her own problem. There was no risk to himself if she were caught—he'd told her his name was Mr. Smythe.

In the meantime, he'd take a little trip to Kent. There was nothing further he need know about Lady Barlow, but he did need to know a few things about her neighbors.

DESPITE THE UPSET of the past few weeks, Grace found herself looking forward to Lady Tredwell's masque. She'd never attended one before and it seemed rather delightful to disguise oneself in some manner. While she could hardly imagine the costumes she would encounter, on her own behalf Lady Heathway had outdone herself.

Grace was to be a butterfly and the gown was positively lovely. Done in a deep blue satin with subtle purple stripes and thin yellow swirls, it caught the candlelight and shimmered. A voluminous cape was sewn onto the back of the dress and then attached to her wrists in purple ribbon so that when she raised her arms she would have the wings of a butterfly. It would look divine on the ballroom floor.

Dyed deep purple gloves and a delicate mask of blue and purple iridescent sequins that Betsy had since secured to her hair completed the ensemble.

Lady Heathway was magnificent as Boudicca. She wore a pleated white silk dress gathered at the bodice with ropes of gold braid. The pièce de résistance, however, was the war-like helmet fashioned in gold. The lady's hair was swept up beneath it and it had a clever gold mesh mask dropping down from the rim.

Grace was confident they should make a good impression. As least she thought so, as Benny and Gregory had seemed slack-jawed upon viewing them and Ranston claimed there could be nobody as well-turned out as the house of Heathway. Grace appreciated the sentiment, though she could not help noticing that Ranston's eyes were darting around the foyer as if he were already ginning himself up to guard the house. Grace just hoped there would not be any actual gin involved since he'd been barred from the lord's brandy.

The carriage had come, which was entirely ridiculous, as Lady Tredwell lived on Berkeley Square just as Lady Heathway did. They would embark, ride from the west side of the square to the east, and then disembark. There would hardly be time to sit down.

Grace was so filled with energy that she felt she could have kicked off her slippers and run across the park and around the plane trees to Lady Tredwell's doors.

She must give her lady's maid the credit for her high spirits. Betsy had given her quite the lift-up as she did her hair. Whether or not Grace should have been confiding in her maid about a particular lord was beside the point. Betsy was the only person who knew her well enough and would be on her side no matter what. Lady Heathway was a stalwart ally, but she would hardly side against her own nephew. Betsy, however, would land firmly in Grace's court even if the other party were the King of England.

She'd told Betsy of Lord Gresham's various machinations, the latest being the suggestion that she should not attend the masque.

Betsy's outrage had been positively inspired. Betsy's father had never counseled composure and so she let loose with such a string of insults that Grace was nearly crying with laughter. She was also blushing, as even a sailor would, over the various expletives Betsy peppered amongst her insults, some of which

Grace had never even heard of and did not dare to ask the meaning of.

It had been a good dose of commonsense. Betsy had pointed out that Lord Gresham was only one gentleman among hundreds and yes, he was handsome as a devil, but that would not last and was half due to his valet anyway. What would Grace think of him when his jowls drooped and all that was left of him was his less than genial manner? Who would swoon over the fellow when his middle paunched out and he had hair growing from his ears and his most charming quality was attempting to stop people from going to masque balls? He would not seem so prepossessing *then*.

Grace had not felt so lighthearted in ages. Dear Betsy had known just what to say. She'd finished by attaching Grace's mask securely to her hair with a myriad of hairpins and saying, "Fellas like that are a pence to a pound. The mighty Lord G might be better dressed than most, but he's only one grain of salt in the cellar."

Now they were on their way to the masque, though not for long. They descended from the carriage after their exceedingly short journey. "You could not look more charming, my dear," Lady Heathway said. "I congratulate myself, if I may be so bold."

CHAPTER FIFTEEN

L ADY TREDWELL'S BALLROOM was a swirl of color and unusual sights. There was a Persian potentate, a dairy maid, a Robin Hood, a country vicar, a pirate, a soldier, and more ominous-looking dominoes than Grace could count. The duchess was, Grace knew, Minerva. Though, she would not have guessed it if she had not known. The lady was dressed in her usual brocade, with perhaps the only hints being the gold color of the dress and the gold crown she wore on her head. Grace suppressed a smile as she imagined what Lady Heathway would have to say about the crown. Fortunately, she had not yet noticed it as she was too caught up in talking to Lady Mendleton, who had come as the Egyptian goddess Nut. As that particular goddess was responsible for swallowing the sun in the evening and birthing it again at dawn, Grace presumed this was a tipped hat to her new role as mother-in-law.

Lord Bertridge was a jester, which Grace found enormously amusing, as there was little of the jesting about Lord Bertridge. He was kind enough to take her first though, and she reminded herself that from now on she only looked at the world through practical eyes. The lord might not be wildly entertaining, but he was both practical and eligible and not at all unpleasant to look at.

Lord Blackwood had dressed himself as…she was not alto-gether certain. Was it a wolf? Or a long-ago warrior? He wore an enormous grey fur-like cape around his shoulders which might very well be a rug he'd taken from his house. He took one of her dances, but her supper was still open. As he'd not taken the opportunity, perhaps he was not interested in her in any particular manner. Her consideration of whether or not his puppy might be a pleasant companion might have been for naught.

This was the first ball Grace had attended that had a master of ceremonies available to make introductions. In fact, there appeared to be several. This was a very sensible idea as it was already a bit confusing when one could not see faces clearly. One of those helpful gentlemen had just arrived with an unknown person in tow.

At least, she presumed he was unknown. He wore a full mask of a goblin of some sort, his hair was covered in a hood, and he was caped from head to toe.

"Miss Grace Yardley, daughter of the late Viscount Barlow, may I present the Earl of Glendower."

Grace curtsied and waited for the gentleman to speak, but he did not. He seemed very mysterious and merely reached for her card. He quickly wrote in his name, bowed and moved off. How odd. He'd taken her supper without a word. Well, she supposed he'd have to speak *then*.

Lady Heathway turned back to Grace as Lady Mendleton moved off. "She has styled herself as the mother god of Egypt," Lady Heathway said. "She has convinced herself that she's somehow become the greatest mother in England, but I don't see it."

Grace could not help that a small giggle escaped her.

Lady Heathway scanned the crowd. "And the duchess wears a crown, do I dare express surprise? How is your card coming along, my dear?"

"It is nearly filled," Grace said. "Some of the gentlemen I already know, but some are new to me."

She handed the card to Lady Heathway for examination.

"Ah, Lord Glendower," Lady Heathway said, "He has finally come back from Scotland! It's been a few years, I believe. How fortunate, he's an earl and very unmarried." Lady Heathway ran her finger down the rest of the list of names. "Good, good," she murmured.

She handed Grace back her card. "Excellent. One may hope that Mr. Vance does not suddenly appear to take the last spot. Though if he does, I am certain we will see him coming dressed as a tradesman just to vex me."

Grace would not at all mind if Mr. Vance, dressed as his gunmaker grandfather, were to make a sudden appearance. However, she had not seen him so far. What she did see at this moment, which nearly sent her into fits of laughter, was Lady Featherstone bearing down upon them.

The lady appeared to be dressed as Catherine, Empress of Russia. She wore an elaborate dress identical to the one in the empress's coronation portrait, including the sash and the medals and even the scepter. The emerald broach had not been a part of the copy of the portrait Grace had viewed in some periodical or other and did not really complement the blue and silver of the gown, but it took pride of place on her heaving bosom.

"Good Lord," Lady Heathway muttered.

Grace would have been delighted to hear what would be said between them, but another of the masters of ceremonies had arrived with a gentleman.

The gentleman was tall but a little paunchy and had dressed himself as a bishop.

"Miss Grace Yardley, daughter of the late Viscount Barlow, may I present the Earl of Lymington, eldest son of the Duke of Hastings."

Grace curtsied. Lord Lymington said, "Miss Yardley, charmed. Just got to Town, and all that. Horses, you know."

Grace of course did not know and could not imagine how his horses had kept him from getting to Town, as horses were generally known to assist in that operation. She smiled by way of vague response.

He took her card and studied it for a moment. She was not

certain what he was looking for as there was only one spot left open.

"Aha!" he said, and penciled his name in.

Out of the corner of her eye, Grace saw Lord Gresham approach. She had thought he'd be one of those gentlemen who couldn't be bothered to think of a costume and would just rent a domino, or in the case of Lord Blackwood look around for a handy rug to fling over one's shoulders. However, it seemed Lord Gresham *had* made an effort, though she was not entirely clear what the effort was. Some sort of Greek soldier perhaps? A white tunic and red cape, topped with a rather large and ornate metal helmet.

As seemed to be always the case, she wished he did not come. Even as ridiculously attired as he was at this moment, her heart skipped a beat upon noting him.

This was not a very good time for that! Everything was going quite according to plan. Her card was filled, and there were even gentlemen she had previously not met put down on it. Any one of them might prove to be a future husband.

She was in such good spirits, she did not wish for Lord Gresham to put her out of them.

"Miss Yardley," he said, bowing and edging Lord Lymington out of the way.

As he bowed, the visor of his helmet slipped over his eyes and Grace could not be sorry to witness his consternation over it.

He pushed it back up on his forehead and glared at Lord Lymington as if he would say something about it.

The lord only handed back her card and hurried away.

"May I?" Lord Gresham asked.

Why? Why would he wish to put himself down on her card? Was there another lecture he felt driven to communicate? Perhaps he would attempt to sprain her ankle *for* her so she could not dance? Or perhaps he wished to remind her that she was naïve and he was twenty-six?

Fortunately, he would not have the opportunity to do any of

those things. Her card was full.

"I am entirely engaged, Lord Gresham," she said cheerfully.

"Entirely?" he said, practically snatching the card from her hands. As he examined the list, his frown grew ever deeper. "Lymington? Get ready to hear about his horses, and then his horses again. Blackwood and that stupid dog. Glendower? He's meant to be in Scotland. What's he doing *here* taking anybody into supper?"

Grace did not think there was a required answer to any of those remarks and merely stood waiting to be returned her card.

To her left, Lady Featherstone had sailed back into the crowd, her rather long train trailing behind her and tripping up footmen.

Lady Heathway turned back to them. "Ah, there you are, George. Smashing costume. By the by, Lady Featherstone is convinced she can feel the Empress of Russia's spirit through the emerald. I believe we may expect further lunatic ideas in our future."

⤜⤜⤜⤜

JACOBS WAS WELL-SATISFIED with his plan. Jenny had done her part and delivered him what he'd asked for. He'd gone to Kent to gather certain needed information—who lived in the neighborhood, and what sort of liveries did they employ. The details needed to be right to lend the necessary verisimilitude to the plan and he had got all he needed.

He had come in a costume that covered him head to toe and had passed himself off as Lord Glendower. It had been the perfect choice. Glendower had not been in Town for two seasons so who would even remember what his voice sounded like? They'd remember his accent though, that long O that Jacobs recalled when he'd drunk brandy with Glendower at the club all those years ago. He'd since called in a stable hand who hailed from

Edinburgh and spent hours talking with the lad to pick up the pronunciation and cadence. He thought if he said little and moved off quickly he could pass it off, and he had done. He'd got past Lady Tredwell with alacrity, claiming a sudden stomach complaint. Whatever she'd thought of *that*, she hadn't dared hold him up on his way to relieving himself.

But most importantly, he'd secured Miss Yardley's supper. That had been the lynchpin of the entire operation. Only he could give her the long lead time necessary before raising the alarm.

Now, he must only do two things: first, he must take himself out to the balcony and find some quiet little corner so he was not observed or engaged in conversation. If word went round that Glendower was back in Town there might be no end of people who wished to renew the acquaintance. Second, and he had not considered it until just now, he had to keep his eye on Gresham, who seemed to be keeping a close eye on Miss Yardley. He could not allow Gresham to interfere until the plan was well underway. Then, the fellow could do what he liked.

In a day or two, the invitations would begin to flow again and he could take back his rightful place. As for Miss Yardley, she could spend the rest of her days hanging off drainpipes for all he cared.

⟫⟫⟪⟪

As soon as Lady Heathway and Miss Yardley had left the house, Ranston had felt his blood bubbling around like it did when he was in a state of nerves. On other nights, a few drops of brandy had worked wonderfully to settle him. That was, until that recent night when *too* many drops had worked a bit *too* wonderfully and he'd woken in the morning on Lady Heathway's drawing room floor. There had been no hope that particular misstep had gone unnoticed, as he'd been covered in a blanket and had a pillow under his head. It had taken a full day of tea and buttered toast to get back on his feet again.

Lady Heathway had since locked the brandy decanter in a cabinet, though it did not appear that she'd told Lord Heathway why he was to need a key to get at his own brandy. It seemed the lord was under the impression that it might be one of the maids who'd developed an unfortunate habit.

Well, he supposed he could not be entirely opposed to the lock and key, as it at least stopped the diabolical Jenny from helping herself to it. He would have to do something about her soon. He hated having to do things about people! Why could they not just go away when they were not wanted?

He did not know what the girl had stolen from the house and sold off, but she suddenly seemed to have quite a lot of money about her person. She had even gone so far as to buy herself an alarming purple bonnet sprouting a criminal number of silk daisies that she put on for any and all reasons. It was like she was taunting him with it. He was also perfectly well aware that she periodically fell behind the counter as some kind of joke against him. He'd explained to the staff that he'd ended up asleep on the drawing room floor because he had a fainting seizure. Was she mocking seizures?

Now, he'd been left to guard the house again. He'd wondered what he could do to soothe his frazzled nerves now that the brandy had fled. He realized he would have to think of *something* when Gregory had come up behind him, silent as a cat, and scared the wits from him. He'd clutched at his heart to start it beating again and very much wished to go for a lie-down, but he could not! It was his duty to lead the battle against any invaders, should there be invaders and an ensuing battle.

Then it came to him. He remembered that he had a draught stored away that had given him a calm and fuzzy feeling the last time he'd been in bed with a cold.

He'd dug it out of his medicine case and drained the bottle, as he felt he must stay very calm. Now he was feeling a good deal better, other than finding it a bit of a challenge to keep his eyes open.

He paused in the drawing room to listen for unusual sounds. As he assessed the regular household noises, he widened his eyes in an attempt to keep his eyelids up where they were supposed to be. He noticed that the fireplace seemed to be gently swaying to and fro, which seemed a very un-fireplace-like thing to do. The chandelier was just now sliding sideways along the ceiling. Then, interestingly, the carpet decided to race toward his face at a surprising speed. He felt it crash into him rather violently and he wondered what the carpet was doing, flying around like that. It seemed rather funny.

Very faintly, as if from a long distance away, he heard Gregory say, "He's down again. We'd better get a blanket and pillow."

GEORGE CURSED HIS costume. He would have been much better off in a domino. He could have pulled his hood low and nobody would know which direction he was looking. He needed to be looking at Miss Yardley at all times, as he did not know if some fellow might decide the masque would be the right time to declare himself. If he saw even a hint of it, he'd have to launch himself between them and declare first.

Oh yes, he was very decided on that. After drinking his way through half a decanter of brandy the night before, he'd resolved to do it. He'd thought he'd need another season to absolutely decide, but that was before she'd told him she would accept the first offer thrown at her. Once that bit of information had sunk in, he'd realized he had no time to waste. He'd realized he could not bear for Miss Yardley to marry another.

The very thought of Vance prevailing with the lady enraged him!

He had, perhaps, been a bit *too* enraged the night before, after a certain ill-advised number of glasses of brandy. Fortunately, the scathing letter he'd written to Vance, daring him to turn up at dawn with pistols by the pump house in the park had never left the house. He had ordered Pemmington to have it delivered immediately, but his butler had very sensibly put it in his pocket and returned it to him on the following day. It was well he did, as dawn had seen him in no shape to duel a newborn kitten.

He'd been rather pleased to see that Vance had failed to get on Miss Yardley's dance card and had since heard the fellow had gone to Cornwall to attend the bedside of a dying uncle. While George did not wish anybody actually dead, except perhaps Vance himself, it was convenient that he'd been called out of Town. That was at least one problem dealt with.

But now there were others. Lymington had turned up as great a fool as he'd ever been, but what matter? Miss Yardley was prepared to accept absolutely anybody and he would be a duke, after all. And Glendower too. Why had he come *now*? He hadn't been seen in years, why did he not make himself scarce one more year?

George was supposed to be on her card for supper. That was the plan. He was going to declare himself at supper. He was determined to do it.

He would have done it too, if not for his tyrannical valet. Mason had taken receipt of the costume that had been hastily ordered and delivered. First, it was supposed to be a Roman soldier, but it appeared to be some combination of Roman senator and soldier. Second, Mason deemed it not at all ready to don. The scoundrel had insisted on a washing, bluing of the white tunic, and careful ironing.

What Mason had apparently not taken into consideration was the necessary drying. It had been a damp and overcast day with no wind whatsoever and no amount of hours would accomplish it. Mason had finally resorted to dressing the footmen in the garments and having them run around the drawing room, with the clothes flapping around them, in front of a roaring fire. Even after that, they'd only achieved damp and he was already verging on late. Then, the iron had come out.

By the time he had finally wrestled the costume away from his valet he was exceedingly late. He'd had hopes that his aunt and Miss Yardley would be late too, but they had not been. He'd known it as he passed the house and looked through the open curtains of the drawing room. He'd almost stopped and gone in, as he was certain he'd seen Ranston fall to the floor, but he would not be diverted from his purpose. If Ranston had managed to trip himself, his footmen could very well help him up.

And so, he had arrived late, but exceedingly determined. His determination had not fled him, but since Miss Yardley's supper was not to be his, he must think of a new idea.

The only thing that still lurked in his mind, that shook his determination just the smallest bit, was that she had said she would accept absolutely anybody. That meant him too, he supposed. But what would that be like, exactly? Did she dislike him but would marry him for her mother's sake? Or would she say she liked him, but he could never be sure? Or would she dislike him and grow to like him?

He did not know. The only thing he did know was that she could not be permitted to chain herself to one of the fools on her card. Or Glendower, who he knew well enough was not a fool.

GRACE HAD WONDERED about the newly acquainted gentlemen on her card. Of course, she had also wondered about the gentlemen who were not on her card. Where was Mr. Vance? Where was Lord Ryland?

As for those who *were* on her card, she did not wish to admit it, but Lord Gresham had been accurate in his assessment of Lord Lymington. It seemed horses *was* his only mode of conversation, his only interest, and his only information. Even that appeared limited in scope. She had found it rather trying to hear the story of a mare who'd gone colicky. And then hear the story again when he realized he'd not told her she was a chestnut. How that had led to another full recitation of events, she could not fathom.

As much as she was determined to be sensible and consider every gentleman, she thought Lord Lymington must be taken out of consideration. She could easily envision ten years hence throwing herself out a window to get away from yet another horse story. She must be sensible, but there was no need to be perverse.

Lord Blackwood, on the other hand, had proved diverting. It seemed his puppy had taken to shredding his neckcloths. His valet had thrown down the gauntlet and declared it was either him or the dog, so he was looking for another valet.

Now, Grace thought she came to a more interesting part of the evening. The mysterious Lord Glendower was to take her into supper.

He had proved a competent dancer, though he had been still very reticent and speaking little. Grace heard well enough his Scottish accent, which was rather heavy, and wondered if it made him feel an outsider in London. For all she knew, he might be very voluble in Edinburgh. She was determined to draw him out.

She would also not mind seeing what he looked like, and she supposed she would. He'd have to remove his mask for supper.

It all felt deliciously mysterious.

Lady Heathway and her friends were all being led into the dining room by equally high-placed gentlemen, and the crowd had parted to allow them through. Grace was delighted to see Lady Featherstone nodding graciously to those she passed by, as if she were the empress of Russia herself.

"Miss Yardley!"

Grace turned to find a young footman, entirely out of breath. It was not one of Lady Heathway's footmen. Oddly, she was near certain that the livery was Lady Marilyn's, a close neighbor in Kent. The garb was unmistakable, it had odd yellow cuffs and a ruffed yellow collar and Grace had never seen another outside of

Lady Marilyn's household sporting such a bold uniform.

"Is Lady Marilyn here?" Grace asked in some confusion.

"No, miss," the footman said, "but I have been sent by my lady with an urgent message."

The boy handed her a tightly folded paper. Grace hurriedly opened it, terrified that Lady Marilyn would have written to her—and then to send it in such a manner! Certainly it spoke of something dire.

Chapter Sixteen

Lady Marilyn's footman had handed her what turned out to be two separate letters folded together. Grace scanned the first.

My Dear Miss Yardley,

I am afraid I must bring you some very unwelcome news. Your mother does not do at all well and it seems there have been some underhanded doings regarding her care. I blame myself for not visiting the dower house sooner, else this would not have gone on for so long.

Rest assured that the neighborhood has banded together and driven Nurse Maddington back to wherever she came from. Manfred and his wife, née Mrs. Bellevue, have taken over Lady Barlow's care. So, my dear, while the prognosis does not appear hopeful we are making her as comfortable as possible.

I have sent my own carriage so that you might return to your mother immediately. Do not allow anything to delay you!

Marilyn Cobbs

Grace's hands shook as she turned to the second page and recognized her mother's handwriting.

Dear Darling,

I have finally been rescued from the clutches of that nurse. She convinced Sir Henry he need not come more, barred the door to

Doctor Gregory, dismissed Cook and Maggie, and has been selling off my jewelry. I had hoped you would realize that the letters that claimed I did so well could not have been true. She forced me to write them. Lady Marilyn finally discovered all when she would not be put off at the door.

I do very poorly, worse every day, and now Doctor Gregory says I can only be made comfortable.

Please come to me as soon as you can.

Your mother.

Grace stared at the footman. "I must inform Lady Heathway immediately!"

"Lady Marilyn said you ought to get in the carriage straight-away," the footman said hurriedly, "else anybody tried to convince you to delay until morning. She says Lady Barlow may not have until morning."

Grace turned to Lord Glendower, though she did not know what he could offer to the situation.

"If the woman that born ya is ready to depart the world, you'd best get to the bedside, lass."

Grace nodded, of course the lord was right. She would like to inform Lady Heathway of what had happened, but she knew all too well that the lady might be skeptical. She would almost certainly insist on waiting until morning. Grace herself might have been skeptical of her mother's letter, as it did seem fantastical. But she did not question Lady Marilyn.

Further, she had indeed been surprised by her mother's last letters. They had sounded forceful and energetic and not at all like her.

The truth of what had happened settled over Grace like a shroud. While her mother needed her, she'd been in Town going to parties. Now the lady might only have hours left on earth. Nothing would stop Grace from reaching her.

"The carriage is ready?" Grace asked the footman.

He nodded and said, "The horses have already been changed,

miss. Please hurry."

"Let us go, quickly!" Grace said. She strode across the floor and toward the front doors.

>>>><<<<

JACOBS GLANCED AROUND at the crowd still filing into the dining room. His little ruse could hardly have gone better. His footman, dressed as one of Lady Marilyn's own, had been positively inspired. He would have to give the fellow a bonus for it. He casually strolled to the back of the crowd and out onto the balcony.

As he stood on the darkened patio, looking in at the revelers, all he had to do now was wait. Once he was certain enough time had passed, he would make his next, and his final, move.

>>>><<<<

WHERE WAS MISS Yardley? George scanned the long table and the people still streaming in the doors. She was nowhere to be found. Neither was Glendower for that matter.

Blast it, had he pulled her into a quiet corner for some private conversation? He'd just met her!

But then, she was so striking and why had Glendower come down from Scotland anyway? The fellow hated London, he'd always said so.

George got a sinking feeling as to why Glendower had come. He was a decisive sort of gentleman and did not go flying about the country without reason. If he'd come to a place he did not like and dressed himself in costume which he also would not like, he had a purpose. He'd come to get a wife.

Of course he had! He was nearing thirty, he could delay no longer. In typical Glendower fashion, he'd set his purpose and moved toward it with alacrity.

Those two could not be left alone together! *Glendower* had come to accomplish his business as quickly as possible and then return to his beloved Scottish estate with his bride. *She* was prepared to accept the first offer that came her way. It was disastrous.

He must find them and break up whatever conversation they were having.

He realized Lady Gentian had been talking to him. He merely nodded at her and jumped out of his chair. He would find them and drag them in here!

⟫⟫⟫✳⟪⟪⟪

GRACE HAD FLED past Lady Tredwell's butler and ignored his query of whether she required assistance. She would never forgive herself if she did not reach her mother in time.

Lady Marilyn's carriage stood waiting for her. It was not the carriage she remembered, but then the lady had not been to visit since she and her mother had moved to Barlow House. Lady Marilyn had issued plenty of invitations to attend her in her own house, but Grace had always thought she was too embarrassed to come to the dower house and witness their own embarrassment at their reduced circumstances. She and Lady Barlow had always met on equal footing It was meant as a kindness that Lady Marilyn would avoid witnessing her friend's comedown in life.

"Is this new?" she asked the footman as he helped her in.

"Very," he said, "the coat of arms has not even been painted yet."

It certainly was more luxurious than Lady Marilyn's last coach, but more importantly it was sure to be better sprung. It was pulled by four sturdy-looking bays, if they changed horses at the halfway mark and got horses of equal quality, they might arrive in less than three hours. They would need to make all speed.

How had she been so stupid as to believe that last letter she'd received? How had she failed to recognize that it had not even sounded like her mother? Her own mother!

Betsy had named Lady Barlow a wilting flower needing extra water and that had been true all of Lady Barlow's life. Suddenly, she was to believe the lady was out walking, and eating with an appetite, when that had never been true. Here was her daughter, dressed as a ridiculous butterfly, while the poor lady had undergone such suffering!

As the carriage barreled out of London, Grace had a passing thought that Lady Heathway was sure to be vexed. She supposed Lord Glendower would explain the situation and after all it was not the least like the last time she had attempted to reach her mother. She was not shimmying down a drainpipe, she was safe in Lady Marilyn's carriage. She wished she had been successful at that last attempt though, as she might not have been fooled for so long. She might have been able to save her mother from a deal of pain and hardship.

No matter. She was going now. She must only get there in time.

⟫⟫⟫✦⟪⟪⟪

THE LAST OF the guests had filed into the dining room and Jacobs thought he might relax for a half-hour. At least, he *had* thought so, but Gresham had just come bounding out of it and was racing to alcoves and dark corners.

The devil was looking for Miss Yardley, probably convinced that Lord Glendower had stolen her away somewhere. And so he had, Jacobs supposed, but the lady was in a carriage, not a corner.

Were Gresham to raise the alarm it would ruin everything! It must be done as he planned it, with himself publicly vindicated.

He would have to act sooner than he'd thought.

He waited until Gresham made his way to the front hall and

then could wait no longer. It would not be a moment before he discovered she'd left in a carriage and he'd raise the alarm.

Jacobs gave the signal to a footman dressed as a domino who was in fact one of his own, then he slipped into the ballroom and sprinted across it. He would watch from a dark corner with a view into the room to see the effect of what was to be announced, and then Lord Glendower would slip away and be seen no more. Nobody would know who'd sent a carriage claiming to be one of Lady Marilyn's own and even if some guessed at it, they would not be able to work it out. The scheme was too elaborate for anybody to unwind it. It would not matter if they did—Miss Yardley had made a second sprint and her credibility, and that of the duchess and Lady Heathway too, would be in tatters. Poor Mr. Jacobs had been sat at home all the while, his reputation tarnished for no reason at all. He would comport himself graciously to those who had snubbed him.

His footman entered the dining room. Loudly, he called out, "I have just been informed that *The Sprinter* has sprinted once more."

He bowed and left the room's occupants to their amazement. Jacobs was delighted to see them all looking at one another, and then at Lady Heathway. *That* lady was scanning the table and failing to find her protégé.

She rose as Gresham ran back into the room.

"George," she said, "where is Grace?"

Her nephew motioned her to come out of the dining room.

"Where is she?" Lady Heathway cried.

Somebody somewhere said, "She's sprinted again," and there were titters up and down the table.

Somebody else said, "Perhaps it's to Gretna Green. Where is Glendower?"

Jacobs was deeply satisfied, but he also knew it was his time to fly. He did not need the party searching high and low for Glendower. Let them think the lord and Miss Yardley had flown off together to marry over the anvil. He had not planned that circumstance, but it was very convenient. Any search for her would travel in the wrong direction.

He adjusted his mask and set off out of the house while there was still time to do so.

Just as he reached the doors that would lead him to the front hall, he heard Gresham behind him.

"Glendower!" Lord Gresham called. "Hold up!"

He took off in a sprint.

⟫⟪

GEORGE HARDLY KNEW what to think. He'd been intent on discovering Miss Yardley and Lord Glendower and interrupting whatever tête-à-tête they were engaged in. Now he was informed that Miss Yardley had left and Glendower himself was at a run.

My God, had Glendower insulted the lady? Had she returned to Lady Heathway's house to escape him? What was going on?

He'd chased Glendower out the front doors and tackled him on the street. As they rolled on the cobblestones, George said, "What is the meaning of this, Glendower? What have you done to Miss Yardley?"

As George pinned the man facedown to the ground and used his forearm to put pressure on the back of his neck so he could not overturn himself, he thought it ominous that Glendower would not even speak. Was he so ashamed of whatever he'd done that he could not speak? Had he groped her in some way?

The thought of that sent a rage through his body and he leaned ever harder on Glendower's neck until the man was choking for breath.

He would make him speak. He would know all of what occurred.

George used his left hand to grab at Glendower's mask and pull it off.

Then he fell back. It was not Lord Glendower at all. It was

204

Jacobs.

A crowd had begun to form round them. Lady Heathway pushed her way through, followed by the duchess, her crown rather askew.

"Mr. Jacobs!" Lady Heathway cried. "But you...you are supposed to be Lord Glendower!"

"It was just a funny ruse," Jacobs said. "It was my costume, I came pretending to be Lord Glendower."

George grabbed Jacobs by his collar. "Where is Miss Yardley?"

"Put him upright, Lord Gresham," the duchess said imperiously. "Lady Heathway and I will get to the bottom of this. I can assure you, if he has harmed Miss Yardley, I will borrow Lady Featherstone's scepter and beat him to death in front of all!"

Lady Heathway nodded vigorously and seemed all too willing to help in the murder.

George eased off of Jacobs and hauled him to his feet.

"What have you done with her?" Lady Heathway said in a rather deadly tone.

"I did nothing," Jacobs said. "A messenger came and she said she was going to Kent in Lady Marilyn's carriage. At least, that's what she said. I only came to have some fun, I had nothing to do with her...sprint."

"Who is Lady Marilyn?" the duchess asked.

"I don't know," Jacobs said, "somebody who wanted to give her a lift."

"There is something wrong, I am certain of it," George said. "And equally certain this scoundrel is at the bottom of it. I will ride after her."

"Yes, do George. I don't like to think of a young girl alone in a carriage at this time of night!"

"Lymington," George said, "take charge of Jacobs and don't let him go anywhere. Tie him up and take him inside."

"Indeed," Lady Heathway said, "he is not to go anywhere. The duchess and I have quite a few questions."

Lord Lymington did not look particularly enthusiastic to have been assigned jailer, but he nodded and went off to get some rope.

Lady Heathway and the duchess peppered Jacobs with questions while they waited. They did not get much out of him, though. Miss Yardley had received a letter by messenger and had got into a carriage owned by a Lady Marilyn. That was all he knew. Or so he said.

Meanwhile, George could already hear the whispers around him. Was it true Miss Yardley had sprinted? Did that mean she'd done it the first time? Had she really gone alone, or was there someone with her?

Lymington finally came back with a rope. George handed Jacobs over to him, though the fellow was now loudly complaining that he was being abused yet again because of Miss Yardley.

George ignored his complaints and sprinted across the green to his house. He would need Mercury—he was both swift and had endurance and they might just be able to overtake Miss Yardley's carriage. He would keep him at a canter and change horses at Eltham. God willing, he could change to a horse just as swift as his own, and God willing, Miss Yardley had not met with danger. He did not know what the truth of this scheme was, but he did not believe Lady Barlow was dying. If that was not true, then there was a plot afoot and that mad, lovely girl had fallen right into it.

GRACE WAS AT once encouraged that they seemed to make good time, anxious that they did not make good time enough, and terrified at the manner with which the coachman drove the carriage. The turns were especially frightening and she'd already been thrown clear across the compartment twice. The coachman would not drive so recklessly if her mother was not running out of time.

She was grateful though, that the horses had been changed speedily and they had been on their way in short order. They were coming very near the turnoff that led to the lane to her father's estate. Please God let her mother still be with the world. She would never forgive herself if she came too late.

Now, they were on the lane! Almost there. Just ahead, the circular drive of Barlow House.

She could see the house! The downstairs still had lights burning, but above stairs was dark. What did it mean? Was her mother sleeping, or was she…

The coachman pulled up to the doors and the footman barely had time to help her down as she fairly leapt to the gravel.

Grace raced to the front door and threw it open.

Her heart nearly stopped beating when she saw her. The nurse. Nurse Maddington, who had been driven out. Why was she there? How had she got back in?

The lady had been sleeping in a chair by the fire, her lacy nightcap askew. She was a short and plump individual with fat cheeks and deep-etched lines running from either side of her nose to the corners of her mouth. She'd started at the sound of the door crashing open, rubbed her eyes, and looked about her.

"You!" Grace cried, pointing at her.

"Who are you?" the nurse said, sounding fearful. "Why have you crashed in here uninvited?"

"Who am I?" Grace asked with incredulity. "I am Lady Barlow's daughter!"

"Well, goodness, this is a surprise," the woman said, clutching at her nightcap to right it.

"I am certain it is a surprise. Where is she? What have you done to her? Where is Manfred and why has he let you back in?"

Nurse Maddington appeared stupefied in the face of these questions. Grace did not wait for an answer but instead swept up a candle, picked up her skirts, and raced up the stairs.

Her mother's bedchamber was dark. She used her candle to

light one on the dressing table and the room came into view.

Lady Barlow's bed was made and quite empty. She was too late. Her mother was gone from the world.

Grace felt a shroud settle over her. She'd failed her own mother. Her poor father looking down from heaven must weep with disappointment over his stupid daughter.

It was the first thing she'd ever done in her life that could not be somehow fixed.

She must see her! But where had they taken her? Why was the nurse here in an empty house?

Grace flew back down the stairs. She was determined to be by her mother's side, even though it would do Lady Barlow little good now.

As she reached the bottom of the stairs, she saw the nurse cowering in the chair she had left her in, staring at the staircase as if it were a goblin. A very sleepy-looking Maggie stumbled out of the servants' quarters.

"Miss Yardley," Maggie said. "We did not expect you!"

"Maggie," Grace said, choking back sobs, "I am too late!"

Maggie scratched her nightcap and said, "Well, it is late, I suppose. But then I also suppose it's never too late for a daughter to visit her ma."

Grace could not make heads or tails of Maggie's answer. "Where is she?" she said. "I demand to know where my mother has been taken."

"Why, she's been taken to the Munsons'," Maggie said, beginning to look worried over Grace's state of mind.

"The Munsons'? Why would she have been taken there?"

"'Cause they was the ones having the card party," Maggie said.

"A card party?" Grace repeated. "But why...but then, do you say my mother is not dead?"

"Dead?" Maggie said laughing. "Now that's a joke, as I never did see Lady Barlow more alive than she's been these weeks past. Nurse Maddington here has got your ma back on her feet again."

"I don't understand," Grace said, her thoughts spinning in tight circles of relief and confusion. "Lady Marilyn sent a carriage for me and I received a letter from that lady as well as from my mother."

"A carriage?" Maggie said. "I wonder how she could do it? She only has the one and it was here to take your mother to the Munsons'. How does it get all the way to London and back since then?"

"Then, she did not get a new carriage?" Grace said. "And my mother isn't dying? And I suppose the nurse did not drive you and Cook from the house?"

"Nurse Maddington drive us from the house?" Maggie said laughing. "We've been gettin' on like wool on sheep, we have."

Grace sank down on a chair. Nothing she had believed for the past few hours was true. Her mother was alive! But who would wish to make her believe she was dying?

The nurse approached her warily. "There dove, I think your nerves have got the better of you. Like mother like daughter, I expect. Maggie, perhaps a bit of sherry from my special bottle?"

"Well, I thought...that is, I was told...that you'd done something to my mother."

The nurse laughed, rich and deep. "Oh, I done something to her all right. I got her up, I got her some fresh air, and I got her some good food. She hardly needs me now, I don't think, but she says I must stay. She rather enjoys speeding ahead of me on our walks and tells me she would miss it."

Grace did not know how she came to be in a carriage that was not Lady Marilyn's, racing to her apparently not dying mother late at night. But it seemed that was what happened.

What had also happened was that she had run from the masque without a word to Lady Heathway. She had been tricked, she had run off again for no reason, and she'd most probably embarrassed Lady Heathway and all her family. Again.

Mr. Jacobs must have planned it. Grace did not think there was anybody else capable of it or wishing her such ill-will. Lord

Gresham did not wish her a happy future, but he would never be so outrageous as to embarrass Lady Heathway in such a manner. Though, if it *was* Mr. Jacobs, she could not fathom how he'd done it. The letter from her mother had been in her own handwriting! At least, she'd thought so.

She must be grateful that the letter had not been from Lady Barlow after all. What mattered most was that her mother still lived. And thrived, apparently. Lady Barlow had not been out to an evening entertainment since the viscount died.

Of course, it also mattered that she'd fallen for the trick.

But who drove the carriage? She might be able to pry some information out of that footman who had apparently lied so smoothly.

Grace raced to the door and flung it open.

The moonlight showed the drive empty. The carriage was gone. It must have gone so stealthily, at a slow walk, to get away without her hearing it.

Whoever those devils were, they had disappeared into the night.

Grace stood very still. In the distance she could faintly hear the pounding hooves of a horse. It sounded like a lone horse, though. It could not be the carriage, that was long gone.

She could never go back to London. As kind as Lady Heathway was, Grace was all but certain she would not be wanted back after this disaster.

She would never see *him* again. She would never lay eyes on Lord Gresham again.

What was wrong with her? That was the least of her problems! She was supposed to be practical and steely-eyed and devoid of silly emotion. She was supposed to be rescuing her mother out of this wretched cottage.

Instead, she was pining over a gentleman who had no interest in her, other than making sure she did not embarrass his family again. Which she had just handily done. It was a disaster! No matter who she married, if she ever had a chance to marry anybody, she would always think of him. She would compare and be dissatisfied—dissatisfied with whatever poor man she'd married and dissatisfied with herself for being dissatisfied. And especially dissatisfied that she'd been such an idiot!

What a fool Grace Yardley was, to have ruined her own chances. She turned and shut the door against the empty moonlit drive.

The nurse had brought her a glass of sherry, a rather large glass she thought. Grace took it gratefully—she would need courage to face down the next few hours. Her mother would return from her card party and Grace would have to inform her that their chances of escape from Barlow House were ruined. She would like to have been able to say that they were ruined through no fault of her own, but that was not the truth. She had been rash and impulsive and ill-considered. Twice. She had not depended upon the wisdom of Lady Heathway, though that lady had proved her worth time and time again.

Nurse Maddington had guided her to a chair and sat her down as if she had become a patient, along with her mother.

At this moment, she must just keep the one piece of good news at the forefront of her mind. Lady Barlow lived and found herself well enough to attend a card party. Whatever was to happen next, she still had her mother.

A sudden clatter of hoofbeats and a pounding on the door caused Grace to almost drop her glass.

CHAPTER SEVENTEEN

THE POUNDING ON the door had caused them all to stare at it.

"What on earth?" the nurse said, glancing at Maggie.

Maggie whispered, "We'd best not answer it. It sounds dangerous, it could be thieves or rogues who've spied on the house and know we're unprotected."

Grace did not know if that was the case, but thought an encounter with thieves or rogues would certainly top off what was looking like the worst night of her life.

"Lady Barlow," the voice shouted through the door, "I am searching for your daughter, please open this door at once!"

Grace felt as if time had slowed down as the seconds ticked by. She knew that voice as well as her own. The nurse looked at her inquiringly. Maggie whispered, "That sounds like Lord Gresham if I remember rightly."

Grace nodded, the truth of what was occurring presenting itself. Lady Heathway had sent her nephew to accomplish two things: assure her that Grace had reached home safely and inform Miss Yardley that she was to *stay* home.

Maggie hurried to the door and opened it. Lord Gresham strode in, looking like there was fire in his eyes.

"You're here," he said.

Before he could begin whatever rage he seemed set on, Grace said, "I thought my mother was dying...but she's not dying."

"Of course she's not dying!" Lord Gresham said. "She's been

under the care of the most skilled physician in England and has an experienced nurse living in her very house! How could she possibly be dying?"

"It was in the letter, you see," Grace said softly, before taking a rather long sip of the sherry.

Lord Gresham threw up his hands. "Another letter? You climbed down a drainpipe because of the *first* letter! Did it not occur to you to come to me? Or if not me, then my aunt?"

"Yes, I did think of that, but then I thought you'd say no or that I ought to wait until morning."

Lord Gresham raked his hand through his hair. "That's exactly what I would have said."

"And so you see the problem," Grace said.

"I *do* see the problem. It's *you* who do not see the problem," Lord Gresham said. He paced the small floor of the cottage as Nurse Maddington and Maggie slowly backed out of the room and took refuge in the kitchen.

"You are the most impossible and unreasonable creature who ever set London ablaze!" he said. "You heed no advice and you make the most rash decisions!"

"Yes, well of course I see that now."

"Now?" Lord Gresham said incredulously. "Now does nobody any good. Your departure was announced at supper. *The Sprinter* has sprinted once more."

Grace shrank back. She had not imagined anything like that would have happened. She'd assumed she had caused some kind of talk, perhaps one person told another that they'd seen her leave precipitously and on down the line it would go. A public announcement to an entire tableful of people was rather more serious. And it was a tableful of people that included Lady Heathway and her friends.

"That is unfortunate, indeed," Grace said so softly she barely heard her own voice.

"Unfortunate," Lord Gresham said, as if she could not possibly have chosen a more ill-suited adjective for this debacle. "Do you understand the kind of gossip that will go round? Miss Yardley slipped away. Slipped away with who, they will wonder. I know well enough that Jacobs set this ruse up, but there is no direct evidence against him and he has denied it. The talk will be all about Lady Heathway's charge, Miss Yardley, disappearing from the masque in an unknown carriage!"

Grace was sure he was working up to the news that Lady Heathway did not want her back. She wished he would just say it. She also wished she did not think him so handsome in his high dudgeon with his hair mussed. His cravat had become completely undone and his coat was dusty from the road. He really was rather glorious in his déshabillé.

"It is a confounded mess," Lord Gresham said. He paused and spied her glass of sherry on the table, picked it up and drained it. He paced the small room, muttering to himself. Finally, he turned and said, "The only answer, as I see it, that is, the only way out, obviously must be...well, there's nothing for it...we'll have to marry."

Grace stared at him. What did he say? Was he really suggesting it? Was he really intending to give up his happiness to protect his aunt from gossip?

It was absurd. He would regret the notion in the cold light of day. And he would regret *her* forevermore if she allowed such a thing to go forward. No, regret was too kind a word, he would begin in dislike and end in hate. They would be one of those awful couples who were rarely in the same room and when they were, there was a noticeable chill. Mr. and Mrs. Rebrum from the neighborhood were such people—they managed to be painstakingly polite to one another while still giving the impression that they'd like to stab each other's eyes.

It was so lovely to hear him say those words, though. If only they were of his own volition and not forced from him in some mad effort to maintain his aunt's dignity.

"Certainly not," Grace said firmly. Whatever she was, she would not sacrifice a gentleman's happiness so entirely, simply for her own gain. At least, not his. Not one who she liked so much. Loved, even.

"Certainly not?" Lord Gresham said. "Not just not, but *certainly* not? You have said very clearly that you would marry absolutely anybody turning up, but I am to be dismissed as a certainly not?"

"You cannot marry me. You do not even like me," Grace said. "It is a very noble idea, but you would be miserable, you know you would."

"If you do not mind, I think I may be able to consider for myself if I will be miserable. And, as a matter of fact, I don't think I would be. You see, I seem too...well it appears that...very unexpectedly...I happen to be in love with you. I don't know how it happened, especially in light of your very rash nature, but there you have it. I know you do not return the feeling as you've made it clear enough that you'll marry absolutely anybody except myself who is a *certainly not*, but I wonder if, over time, you might..."

Grace jumped up from her chair, the empty glass beside her tumbling to the floor and rolling away on the carpet. "But that's *why* I was going to marry absolutely anybody. Because I love *you.*"

"Certainly not? Though...really?"

"Truly! I always have! I didn't always know it, because you did make it very hard with all your very terrible scoldings and unasked-for advice."

Lord Gresham took her in his arms, and his arms were very strong indeed. "Well," he said softly, "you are just impossible."

"Yes, I know," Grace said.

He gently kissed her and Grace sank into it, realizing that she had thought about it more than she might care to reflect on. She had not known if his lips would be soft, and now she did know. They were, delightfully so. Then he kissed her again. Grace began to lose a sense of time. It seemed they had always been there and would always be there, perfectly wrapped round one another.

How could she have even thought of marrying another? What a stupid idea...

Grace's hair was quite undone by the time the front door opened.

"I am back, Nurse," a cheerful voice said.

Grace froze and Lord Gresham slowly unentangled himself from her person.

"Goodness!" Lady Barlow said. "Grace, Lord Gresham, what do you do here? Grace, what on God's green earth has happened to your hair?"

Lord Gresham stared at the lady, speechless. Grace did her best to fix loose hairpins and said, "We are engaged, Mama."

Lady Barlow's surprise could hardly have been greater, though her attention was for a moment taken up with the nurse bustling to the scene to help her out of her coat. Nurse Maddington had rushed to Lady Barlow's side and was fussing over her and questioning her over whether she'd become chilled.

Grace whispered to the man standing by her side, "We are engaged, are we not?"

"Of course we are, who else would put up with such an impossible creature?" Lord Gresham whispered back.

Grace smiled. She supposed she *was* impossible, and she did not know how things had ended so wonderfully considering she'd done everything to work against it. He loved her! That scolding and irritated man loved her.

Lady Barlow had been divested of her coat and assured her nurse that she was not at all chilled. She turned back to Grace and Lord Gresham. "Engaged! I am delighted. How thoughtful of you to come personally to tell me the news," she said. "But gracious, it is so late and what are we to do with you in this tiny house, Lord Gresham?"

Grace glanced at him, as neither of them had considered that problem.

"I will go to a nearby inn," he said. "I'll return in the morning with a carriage back to London."

This seemed to suit Lady Barlow and Grace was grateful her mother did not appear disposed to inquiring any further about the state of her hair.

Grace walked Lord Gresham out to his horse, who had not even been tied such had been the lord's hurry. The creature was calmly eating the grass that lined the drive.

"I really do not understand," Grace said, "you did tell me quite clearly, when you took me into supper at that first ball, that I was not to presume anything by the attention."

Lord Gresham looked down at her and said, "I was not talking of myself, I was warning you against *them*."

"Who is them?" Grace asked.

"All of them—Bertridge, Ryland, Jacobs, Skeffington, and especially Vance. Oh yes, especially Vance."

"But Mr. Vance is a jolly sort of person."

Lord Gresham appeared very put out by this assessment. "You are never to consider Vance jolly again! I put my foot down about that."

Grace worked to hide her amusement. If this was the sort of thing Lord Gresham was determined to put his foot down about, she was sure she could live with it.

She nodded. "On further reflection, perhaps he is only amiable."

"I am not sure I even approve of amiable," Lord Gresham said.

"Then I had better stop you from thinking about it too much," Grace said, standing on tiptoes to kiss him. As she had noticed at Lady Redfield's when they'd sat so close together, he smelled wonderfully clean and of the woods.

He dropped his horse's rein and held her tightly. "Now, you mad, lovely girl, there are to be no more rash decisions. I am not to arrive on the morrow and hear you've changed your mind. I absolutely forbid it."

Grace began to laugh into his coat lapel. "You are a terrifying taskmaster, Lord Gresham."

"You had better call me George," he said.

Seconds ticked by, and then minutes, while Grace occupied herself with feeling the outlines of his arms and the broadness of his chest. She undid his neckcloth to better feel his skin, warm to the touch. George occupied himself with her hair, then her neck, and then her lips. There was so much to discover about his person, and he was doing a remarkably thorough job of discovering *her*.

Lady Barlow called from the front door. "Grace? Engaged or not, there are limits. Good night to you, Lord Gresham."

⋙✶⋘

GEORGE SET OFF on his horse, entirely satisfied with the evening. Of course, it had not unfolded the precise way he'd planned. He had been set on taking Miss Yardley, or Grace the future Lady Gresham and one day Countess of Clayton as he would think of her now, into supper. At an opportune time, he would deliver his carefully composed proposal. The only hurdle had been convincing himself that she might love him someday, though she'd only married him because she was set on marrying absolutely anybody.

He had definitely not foreseen discovering she'd sprinted again and then having to make a mad dash after her to Kent.

On the other hand, why had he expected any less from the lady? She was a rather stalwart daughter, after all.

In truth, it had all worked out rather marvelously. She'd wished to marry absolutely anybody because she loved *him* and thought he disliked *her*!

Why would she think he disliked her, that charming lady?

Well, it could have been some things he'd said...or did. He had perhaps not gone forward in the usual manner of a courtship. But no matter! She was in love with *him* and he had successfully reduced Vance to only amiable. In a year or so, he was convinced he could work Vance down to an absolute bore.

Of course, there were some new hurdles ahead. The talk around the town would have to be shut down. His first instinct was to throttle Jacobs into confessing, perhaps he might challenge him to a duel. He was a crack shot and everybody knew it. Jacobs might well take the easy way out and own his crimes.

Though, duels could be very unpredictable, even if one came in with the advantage. He did not think his future wife would be very pleased with him if he lost an arm or got shot through the heart.

Perhaps the best way to go forward was to confirm the lie. Grace had left in Lady Marilyn's carriage because she got word her mother was dying. A dutiful and courageous daughter, which indeed she was. Lady Barlow had since made a miraculous recovery. That, coupled with their engagement, ought to tamp down the rumors.

As he walked the horse down the lane, it suddenly occurred to him that he did not much care. So what if the *ton* talked all the day long about *The Sprinter*. She had sprinted herself into his arms and that was all that mattered.

He had a future to plan and society could jump off a bridge if they did not like it.

The only other hurdle was perhaps his aunt. His mother and father were not in Town and it would be some time before they heard anything via letter from one of their friends. He would send word to them by fast messenger with news of the engagement and the truth of the story and that would be that. At least, the truth of the story he'd settled upon. His parents would be delighted, as they had been hinting that he ought to marry for above two years.

George could not say how Lady Heathway would take the news, as she was never very predictable. She might be outraged or delighted. However she was, they would face her together on the morrow. She was bound to come around, in any case. She'd longed for a daughter, and now she was to at least have a niecein-law she already knew and liked. The idea that Lady Mendleton had not managed to outdo, her via Miss Wilcox would probably assuage any shaken feelings she might have.

He would send a messenger from the inn to assure his aunt of Miss Yardley's safety. The further news would be delivered in person on the morrow.

"It's all gone very well," George said to the darkness, "if I do say so myself."

GRACE HAD SLEPT in the bed with her mother, as Nurse Maddington had taken over her own bedchamber. Her happy thoughts had bounced between two ideas: she was engaged to Lord Gresham, and Lady Barlow was livelier than she'd ever seen her.

While they should have been sleeping, they talked for hours about the future. Grace did not know where they would live, but Lady Barlow would not live *here*. Nurse Maddington had once come into the room to scold them into sleeping but Lady Barlow had only laughed at her and said, "Go back to bed, you horrible old witch."

The nurse seemed satisfied enough with that response and closed the door on her.

Lady Barlow had whispered, "I tell her she's a horrible witch but I'm actually very fond of her."

They'd then talked at length about Lord Gresham, or George as was his given name. They'd examined him from every angle and Lady Barlow had finally said, "It is a very good match, my dear. I hope he makes you as happy as your father made me. He promised to treat me as a jewel in a velvet-lined case and he was as good as his word."

Grace had nodded, though she did not for a moment think she was to be handled so delicately. Nor did she wish to be. The treatment had not done her mother any good at all and Lady

Barlow was just now emerging from a lifetime of lassitude.

The next morning, after much talking at the door, Lady Barlow had sent them on their way.

To her delight, Grace was not handled so delicately in the carriage as they made their way toward London. George pulled the curtains closed on either side and...well... she was beginning to get the idea that marriage would suit her very nicely.

They had made a stop at Eltham to retrieve George's horse, the plan being he would ride Mercury alongside the carriage. However, when the time came they decided George really ought to stay in the carriage with the curtains closed and a fellow was hired to do the duty.

Now, the curtains were opened and her hair had been straightened and they approached Berkeley Square. They were to inform Lady Heathway of recent developments and Grace quaked at the thought of it. It was not at all unknown that a well-placed person would deign to assist a lady not as fortunate but be outraged if that lady thought to connect herself forevermore to the family. More than one ward had discovered the truth of it. Gratefulness was expected, but having the audacity to put oneself on equal footing might not be.

She must just remember she was a viscount's daughter. And remember her composure.

George squeezed her hand, and she realized her trepidation had been writ large on her features. "She is not a Viking bent on destruction, you know," he said.

"Of course she is not," Grace said, "she told me herself that she is a Visigoth."

The carriage came to a halt and seeing as there was no footman on the lookout, George opened the carriage door and helped Grace to the pavement. He took her arm and led her up the steps.

Gregory opened the doors just as George reached for the handle.

"Do tell my aunt we will see her in the drawing room at her earliest convenience," George said to the very surprised-looking

Benny.

"Lady Heathway is already in the drawing room, my lord," he said.

"Excellent."

Grace was pulled along toward the doors, though she would not have minded to pause in the great hall and...do what? Delay. She would like to delay.

"Lord Gresham and Miss Yardley, my lady," Benny said.

Lady Heathway appeared delighted, though Grace did not know if that attitude would hold.

"Grace, there you are, safe again. George, I was most relieved to get your note last night, else I would not have slept a wink. I knew you would bring her back."

"I did wonder, Lady Heathway," Grace said, "if you would want me back."

"Why ever would you think it" Lady Heathway asked. "Now, I will admit, you were very, very wrong to not come to me last evening and I am certain I could have saved you a world of trouble. But then, you were the victim of an elaborate scheme and you *are* a loyal and dutiful daughter. One cannot fault you for that."

"If only we could get Jacobs to admit to the whole thing," George said.

Lady Heathway laughed and said, "You do remember you left him in the clutches of myself and the duchess? Well, we had him hauled into Lady Tredwell's library and browbeat the truth out of him. Then, we made him write out a confession in case anybody wondered about the veracity of the tale. He is packing up and will be out of Town before the sun sets today. We have told him he will stay away for two years and then when he returns there is to be a more sober and dignified Mr. Jacobs or there is to be none at all."

"That is probably for the best," George said. "Hanging the idea in front of him that he might someday be able to redeem himself and rejoin society is probably the only thing that will keep him from making trouble. A man with nothing to lose can become dangerous."

"As we have seen, I'm afraid," Lady Heathway said. "In any case, how many seasons could the duchess and I keep writing those letters about him? Eventually, people would begin to let him back in. He *is* very rich and people *do* enjoy his wit, scathing as it may be."

Grace was rather stupefied, though she supposed she should not be. If anybody could overpower the likes Mr. Jacobs, she supposed it would be those two ladies.

Mr. Ranston had come in with a tea tray and almost stumbled on seeing her. He recovered himself and set the tray down with a clatter.

"Aunt," George said, "we are engaged."

"Who is engaged?" Lady Heathway asked quizzically.

"I, to Miss Yardley," George said.

Before Lady Heathway could express joy or rage, happiness or sadness, Mr. Ranston hit the carpet with a thud.

All three of them, and Gregory who had just come in, stared at the fainted butler.

"Gregory," Lady Heathway said with the faintest of sighs, "you'd best get a pillow and a blanket. I fear the last two days' events have been entirely too much for Mr. Ranston. Then, take the tea tray into the breakfast room."

Gregory had nodded and it seemed he did not have to go far for the requested blanket and pillow as he pulled them out of a cabinet. Grace began to wonder exactly how many times this particular operation had been performed. She also began to wonder how Lady Heathway would react to the news, as so far she could not tell what the lady's feelings were.

"Now, you two, come into the breakfast room and tell me all about it. I am surprised, I saw nothing developing between you! I had my eyes firmly staring in Lord Ryland's direction. And perhaps a sideways glance at Mr. Vance, though I hoped he'd go away."

Lord Gresham looked to his fiancée with raised eyebrows. "It seems we were all concerned about the amiable Mr. Vance."

Lady Heathway was tapping her chin with her forefinger, completely ignoring her nephew's thoughts on Mr. Vance. "It occurs to me that Louisa might finally stop crowing about her dear Miss Wilcox once she hears this! I am to have a daughter who *does* play the pianoforte."

They followed Lady Heathway out the door, stepping around Mr. Ranston. George leaned over and whispered, "I told you Lady Mendleton would come into it. Lady Langley's firm resolve to steer clear of a pianoforte has served us well."

It had gone smoother than Grace had dared hope. Lady Heathway was not outraged. She could finally breathe a sigh of relief. The alarms that had rung so loud in Grace's thoughts ever since they'd reached the outskirts of Town could quiet.

Once they were situated in the breakfast room and tea had been served, a new set of alarms began to ring.

Grace and George held on to their chairs as Lady Heathway laid out their future for them.

"Now, of course," she said, "My brother and the countess are fine people. You will find them very genial in-laws, Grace. But I and my lord must come first, we must be considered the *real* in-laws. One need not say so outright, at least not to them, but it is our rightful place. We must have you at Christmas and most of the summer too. You might even think of living with us in the country, you could have most of the east wing. Let's see what Lady Mendleton makes of that!"

George held up a hand. "Aunt, I do not know—"

"As for children," Lady Heathway barreled on, seemingly unconcerned with what her nephew did not know, "I plan to be highly involved! Particularly when it comes to granddaughters! I intend their accomplishments to be astounding and far exceeding anything Lady Mendleton might accomplish with her own grandchildren. Yes, they really must be considered *my* grandchildren, I do not care what your mothers have to say about that. I will not take no for an answer on that front!"

Grace did not think Lady Heathway had ever taken no for an answer on *any* front. She also did not think her nephew would agree to move in with her. For all the alarms she was just now setting off, though, Grace held an ever-growing affection for her Lady Visigoth.

CHAPTER EIGHTEEN

T HE WEDDING BREAKFAST had been a great success. It seemed everybody in Town longed for an invitation as Grace was celebrated as the daring daughter risking all for her dear mother. Lady Barlow found herself both confused and delighted, as she never did get the full story of drainpipes and mad dashes in unknown carriages and she certainly had no idea she'd ever been at the point of expiring.

Lady Barlow was to stay with Lord and Lady Heathway until Grace and George returned from their wedding trip. Nurse Maddington too, as Lady Barlow thought she could not do without her. Grace did not know how her gentle mother would get on with her Visigoth aunt-in-law, but she supposed Lady Barlow could always retire to her bedchamber and call for her nurse if she felt overwhelmed by the energy of the lady.

Italy was the destination for the wedding trip and George had planned it for two months, as he had a specific idea in mind for their return. *What* that idea was, he would not say. As they sampled wines and stayed abed most mornings and basked in the Italian sunshine, letters from his solicitor followed them on their travels. Grace thought he was being rather secretive about those missives, and so he was.

On their return, she'd thought they would go to the London house. They bypassed Town altogether and Grace began to see recognized landmarks in Kent.

"My dear George," she said snuggling against his person, "certainly we do not go to Barlow House? Have you forgotten that my mother is with your aunt in Berkeley Square?"

"I have not forgotten anything, you impossible girl," he said. "Have you not wondered about your wedding present?"

"Well, I thought you might get me a nice piece of jewelry on our return. Or perhaps I will have leave to redecorate the house we go to, though you have been very secretive on that front. And then, you did buy me ever so many exquisite pieces in Florence and Rome."

They made the turn to the lane that led to the house and the hall. Grace peered out the carriage window and they passed by the little dower house.

"I do not understand…" she said.

"As you know," George said, leaning back and looking very satisfied with himself, "the entail of Barlow Hall has run out and it was never the property granted with the patent to begin with, *that* piece is forested and was never cleared or built on. As you may *not* know, my aunt and I made the new viscount persona non grata in Town because of his treatment of you and your mother. It turns out the neighborhood does not like him either. My solicitor explained to him that it would be much more sensible to sell off the estate and return to York, where he still has friends. He remains the viscount, he still holds that section of forest should he ever wish to do something with it, and he has a deal more money than he had. He should be well-pleased with the arrangements."

Grace sat back. "But…you bought Barlow Hall?"

"I did," George said proudly. "My aunt and your mother are already there and Manfred and Mrs., well I suppose she's Mrs. Manfred now, have been reinstalled."

Grace threw her arms around her husband. "How glorious! My mother must be astounded. I am astounded. You are the best husband living."

"That is all too true," George said, nodding as if this were a universally known fact. "As well, Barlow Hall is very far away from the amiable Mr. Vance's neighborhood."

"And you are also impossible."

"As are you."

"We are well-matched, then."

"Perfectly so."

LADY BARLOW WAS indeed delighted to move back into Barlow Hall. She was given her old suite of rooms and she installed Nurse Maddington in one of them as she could not ever see her way clear to allowing the lady to leave. They got on very well together, walking every afternoon, with Lady Barlow surging ahead.

Lady Heathway had hoped she might convince her nephew and his bride to live with her, but when she was crossed on the idea she sent off a few strongly worded letters. Eventually, she admitted defeat and got on with it. She blew into Barlow Hall on a regular schedule, and she did come in like a blustery north wind. Lady Barlow was always worn out by the time she left again. Despite the exhaustion, they became fond of one another and discovered a shared love of faro, which they played with regularity. Nurse Maddington acted as the bank and money changed hands with rapidity.

When daughters eventually came, and they did come three times, Lady Heathway and Lady Barlow found themselves sometimes at odds. Lady Barlow was interested in dressing these divine little creatures, feeding them marzipan, and sewing them stuffed woodland creatures they might take to their beds. Lady Heathway was determined to form them into the most highly accomplished little misses in England. The lady had yet to hear Lady Langley, née Miss Wilcox, play on the pianoforte, she was pleased as punch about it, and she was intent on raising a whole new crop of musical prodigies to further make her point.

The girls did not mind much, as Barlow Hall was so full of secret passageways and twists and turns that when they wished to escape their tutors it was easily done. It was discovered quite by accident that the two eldest girls had commandeered a room of the hall that was part of the old barracks and had been quietly moving furniture in there for any number of years. Tucked away at the very end of the long corridor of dreary apartments, they had their own sanctuary that was the height of luxury. At least, it was luxurious by their youthful standards.

The attics had proved a treasure trove and Poppy and Ellie found the game of getting something from there to their secret room unobserved to be positively thrilling. They had stolen away with five rugs of various sizes and piled them one atop another, there were two purple velvet fainting couches that were very convenient to stretch out on, and there was even a stuffed squirrel they propped up on a side table and named The Admiral.

They might never have been discovered if they had not set a pair of recently acquired curtains on fire by way of a recently acquired candelabra.

There were no sons born and so Lord Gresham found himself surrounded by females. All of them apart from Lady Barlow, from his aunt to his wife to his daughters, were rash and headstrong and impossible. He grew rather close to Lady Barlow in those years, as she was an easygoing mother-in-law who had not the energy nor the interest to meddle in his affairs. He sometimes had tea with her in her sitting room, just to find some peace and quiet.

His eldest had been named Penelope in honor of Lady Heathway, though she would always be known as Poppy. She would inherit Barlow Hall and he had no doubt it would be in good hands. She was very like Lady Heathway—an arranger of other people's lives. She had already explained to her sisters Ellie and Jane that they were welcome to live at Barlow Hall forever and might even bring their husbands if they liked it. However, dinner was always to be served at seven and include a variety of desserts, and as the mistress of the house she would not be moved on that point.

Lord and Lady Gresham regularly attended the London season, especially early on as it was always of interest to see what the Society of Sponsoring Ladies would do next.

It turned out they had not long to wait. At the start of that very first summer of their marriage, as they settled themselves in Barlow Hall, they had a letter calling Lady Heathway to Brighton. Lady Easton had inexplicably brought the daughter of an obscure baron to that seaside town to launch her there.

This had seemed to be caused by Lord Easton suddenly taking it into his head to have ideas and opinions, which according to Lady Heathway, he'd never had before.

George and Grace could not make heads or tails of it, but they were delighted to hear that the duchess had named the girl "both naïve and bold."

Mr. Jacobs did eventually return to Town, and he took Lady Heathway's advice when he'd crept back into society's good graces. He returned more sober and dignified than when he'd left. This change in temperament was likely caused by a variety of factors. One, he'd spent two years in the company of his dour father and would pay any price to escape him. Two, Grubb and Lester had both married and were rarely in Town anymore. Jacobs made more sensible friends who guided him in a better direction.

But most of all, three—Miss Marigold Dunston had certain requirements of him. He was entirely besotted with the lady and so he worked very hard to be what she wished him to be, and she wished him to be good-natured and kind. As practice makes perfect, he did eventually become those things. There were even times he pulled aside some young fellow determined to make his mark as a wit and quietly explained the possibilities of a downfall.

Lord and Lady Gresham would never count Mr. Jacobs among their friends, but they became amenable to exchanging passing greetings at a ball or a rout. After all, but for Mr. Jacobs, how else would the proposal in the dower house have happened?

Grace also noticed, over the years, that Ranston had seemed to settle and have fewer nervous fits. Or fainting seizures. Or crying jags.

Ranston had found it a struggle to finally rid himself of the diabolical Jenny, but he finally did rid the house of her. He never did figure out what she'd stolen to buy the alarming purple bonnet, but she'd finally gone a step too far. She'd switched the sugar with the salt as a joke upon Cook. It had not gone to the dining room, as Cook had instantly perceived it, but Cook had threatened to quit in the strongest terms if Jenny were not removed from his sight forthwith.

This departure turned out to be very much to Ranston's benefit as the new kitchen maid had grown up in the country and had a wide and deep knowledge of herbal remedies. Peggy had observed him for a few days, one of those days involving a collapse over a scorched tablecloth that included rather copious weeping, and she'd given him some advice. He would not normally take the advice of a kitchen maid, but on the other hand he could not deny that his tablecloth breakdown had been a bit excessive. Even for him.

Peggy had recommended certain items to soothe his nerves, valerian being the foremost, and that had settled him for the most part. He began to think less often of rogues invading the house and he told fewer stories about the horrors of war he'd in fact not witnessed. He still had his moments occasionally, but he only took to his bed three or four times a year and had not since fainted in the drawing room.

As for Grace and her lord, they had learned a lesson in misunderstandings very early in their acquaintance. Going forward, whenever there was any little disagreement, Grace might say, "I feel I have misunderstood you, my dear out-of-sorts husband. Is that what you meant to say?"

Lord Gresham might answer, "Of course I meant it, my darling impossible wife."

Lady Gresham might, by way of response, tug him by his neckcloth into their bedchamber to better settle their differences.

It might be that Lord Gresham wished to know what happened to his favored chair and he did not see why a ripped cushion should prompt its departure. Or perhaps Lady Gresham was forced to explain why there were unknown people streaming in and out of the house and did she entirely forget to tell him they were hosting a ball? Or had the lord really woken the children in the middle of the night to view Jupiter in the night sky? And if so, why was his wife not woken too?

All of these knotty problems needed to be settled between them, and it turned out talking was not their most effective way of communicating.

Once the bedchamber door was closed, however, they understood each other perfectly. Both of them were delighted that it was so.

The End

About the Author

By the time I was eleven, my Irish Nana and I had formed a book club of sorts. On a timetable only known to herself, Nana would grab her blackthorn walking stick and steam down to the local Woolworth's. There, she would buy the latest Barbara Cartland romance, hurry home to read it accompanied by viciously strong wine, (Wild Irish Rose, if you're wondering) and then pass the book on to me. Though I was not particularly interested in real boys yet, I was *very* interested in the gentlemen in those stories— daring, bold, and often enraging and unaccountable. After my Barbara Cartland phase, I went on to Georgette Heyer, Jane Austen and so many other gifted authors blessed with the ability to bring the Georgian and Regency eras to life.

I would like nothing more than to time travel back to the Regency (and time travel back to my twenties as long as we're going somewhere) to take my chances at a ball. Who would take the first? Who would escort me into supper? What sort of meaningful looks would be exchanged? I would hope, having made the trip, to encounter a gentleman who would give me a very hard time. He ought to be vexatious in the extreme, and *worth* every vexation, to make the journey worthwhile.

I most likely won't be able to work out the time travel gambit, so I will content myself with writing stories of adventure and romance in my beloved time period. There are lives to be created, marvelous gowns to wear, jewels to don, instant attractions that inevitably come with a difficulty, and hearts to break before putting them back together again. In traditional Regency fashion, my stories are clean—the action happens in a drawing room, rather than a bedroom.

As I muse over what will happen next to my H and h, and

wish I were there with them, I will occasionally remind myself that it's also nice to have a microwave, Netflix, cheese popcorn, and steaming hot showers.

Come see me on Facebook! @KateArcherAuthor